What Pippa saw when she looked in the mirror pleased her immensely. The dress had been made by the most fashionable modiste in London. It fit Pippa to perfection. But even more perfect was the material that Pippa had chosen. More specifically, its color.

She was dressed from head to foot in scarlet, and she could just imagine the expression on the Viscount Allingham's face when he saw her. For scarlet was the very color he had forbidden her to wear, and tonight she would be wearing it on the arm of his oldest enemy, the dazzlingly debonair Baron Seagrave.

Vengeance would be sweet on the man who tried to rule her life.

If only she could rid herself of one nagging question.

Would it be as sweet as his kisses . . . ?

The Crimson Lady

by

Margaret Summerville

A SIGNET BOOK

SIGNET
Published by the Penguin Group
Penguin Books USA Inc., 375 Hudson Street,
New York, New York 10014, U.S.A.
Penguin Books Ltd, 27 Wrights Lane,
London W8 5TZ, England
Penguin Books Australia Ltd, Ringwood,
Victoria, Australia
Penguin Books Canada Ltd, 10 Alcorn Avenue,
Toronto, Ontario, Canada M4V 3B2
Penguin Books (N.Z.) Ltd, 182-190 Wairau Road,
Auckland 10, New Zealand

Penguin Books Ltd, Registered Offices:
Harmondsworth, Middlesex, England

First published by Signet, an imprint of Dutton Signet,
a division of Penguin Books USA Inc.

First Printing, December, 1995
10 9 8 7 6 5 4 3 2 1

1

Pippa Grey sat reading in the fashionable London drawing room, a huge black-and-white dog lying at her feet. She was so immersed in the pages of the book in her lap that she didn't notice when her mother entered the room.

"Pippa, there you are," said Mrs. Grey. Both Pippa and the dog glanced up in unison.

Closing her book rather reluctantly, she looked over at her mother. "Did you have a pleasant nap, Mama?"

Mrs. Grey sighed as she sat down next to her daughter. "No, I couldn't sleep. I kept worrying about that hat."

Pippa raised an eyebrow slightly. "You were worried about a *hat*, Mama?"

"Yes," replied her mother a trifle impatiently, "that hat. You know, the one I bought this morning at Madame Angelique's. I am not certain that it is quite the thing. Do you not think that the purple feathers are perhaps a trifle overdone?"

"Nonsense, Mama," said Pippa, who could not imagine spending a second's thought on such a silly matter as a hat, "it is splendid."

Since Phillipa's mother did not credit her daughter with much fashion sense, she looked rather doubtful. However, she turned her attention to the book in Pippa's lap. "I fear you are reading too much, my dear. You'll ruin your lovely eyes."

"Then I shall just get myself a pair of spectacles, Mama," said Pippa matter-of-factly.

"Pippa!" cried her mother, a horrified expression on her face. Her daughter merely laughed and leaned over to pet the dog at her feet.

Mrs. Grey shook her head. It was difficult having a daughter who constantly had her nose in a book. Certainly Pippa did not get her intellectual bent from her side of the family, she thought. Although she loved her daughter dearly, Mrs. Grey considered her too much of a bluestocking. And even worse, her strong-

minded Pippa was always voicing opinions on matters that most
ladies wisely left to gentlemen.

Fearing that Pippa's unconventional behavior would scare off
potential suitors, Mrs. Grey worried about her daughter's matri-
monial prospects. Indeed, she was already four-and-twenty, an
age that most would consider to be firmly on the shelf.

Of course, it was not that Pippa had not had her share of suitors. Back in Portsmouth, numerous gentlemen had made her of-
fers, but Pippa had refused them all. Being a very particular
young lady, she had informed her mother that they were all block-
heads, interested only in her fortune.

Although it was true that Pippa would bring considerable
wealth to the gentleman she married, she was quite mistaken if
she thought her fortune was the only magnet that attracted suitors
to her door. A very pretty young woman, Pippa received much
masculine admiration. While she was not beautiful in the accepted mode of the day, being too tall with features somewhat off
the mark of classical perfection, Pippa was really quite striking.
She had a voluptuous figure and auburn hair much envied by
ladies of her acquaintance. However, her best feature was a pair
of remarkably fine blue eyes. Indeed, one lovesick gentleman had
poetically rhapsodized that the lady's eyes had reminded him of a
cloudless summer sky.

The thought of her daughter's beautiful eyes behind a pair of
unattractive spectacles did not please Mrs. Grey at all. She looked
down at the book again. "And, pray, what are you reading now,
Pippa?"

Pippa, although somewhat uncertain of her mother's actual interest, picked up the volume and handed it to her. "It is called *A
Discourse on the Evils Inflicted Upon the Poor in London.*"

"Oh, dear," said her mother, eyeing the book with dismay.

"It is very shocking, Mama, to read how people are forced to
live and work in such horrible conditions here. Indeed, to think of
the small children toiling away in those wretched factories. . . . "

"Yes, yes, it is disturbing, my dear," said Mrs. Grey, "but it is
best not to think of such things. They just make one miserable."

Pippa's blue eyes flashed. "One has to think of such things,
Mama! One must do something about the wrongs in society!" In-
stantly sensing that her mistress was upset, the huge black-and-
white dog rose from the floor and rested her massive head in
Pippa's lap. The dog, who obviously had a substantial amount of
Newfoundland in her somewhat checkered ancestry, then gazed
up sadly at her mistress. Pippa smiled and fondly patted the giant

canine on her velvety head. "Do not worry, Patches, surely there must be some things that can be done to help."

Mrs. Grey sighed again, realizing that London had only increased her daughter's other passion—philanthropy. Ever since she was a little girl, Pippa had been engaged in worthy causes. There was never a stray animal or unfortunate child that had escaped her attention. Although she thought that her daughter's compassionate heart was quite admirable, Mrs. Grey found that it could sometimes interfere with the more serious business of finding a suitable husband.

Mrs. Grey frowned down at the book and for the first time noticed the author's name on the cover. "Josiah Kent?" she said aloud. "Is he not the fellow who was imprisoned for writing that scurrilous piece about the Prince Regent?"

Pippa nodded. "He is indeed. What a courageous man Mr. Josiah Kent is. How I should like to meet him!"

Her mother eyed her in some alarm. "Do not even suggest such a thing, Pippa! Oh dear, to have that thing lying about. What if a caller should happen to see such a . . . a seditious book here in our drawing room?"

"It is not sedition, Mama, to seek to bring attention to injustice and evil." She paused and smiled. "But, do not fear, if someone calls upon us, I shall quickly toss it out the window!"

Mrs. Grey did not find the situation amusing in the least. She was about to say something when the butler entered the room carrying a silver salver. "Why, Hawkins," said Pippa in surprise, "do we have a caller?"

The servant shook his head apologetically. "No, Miss Grey, I have just brought in the post."

He presented the salver to Mrs. Grey who eagerly snatched up the pile of letters. "Thank you, Hawkins," she said and the butler quickly left the room. Once he was gone, Mrs. Grey no longer concealed her excitement. "Oh, my heavens, look, Pippa! These must all be the replies to our dinner party invitations!" She looked at the envelope on top of the pile. "It is from the Marchioness of Rutherford!" she cried. Pippa watched in trepidation as her mother hastily opened the missive. Since they had not exactly been welcomed into London Society with open arms, she feared her mother was in for considerable disappointment.

Scanning the contents of the note, Mrs. Grey frowned. "The marchioness sends her regrets. She will not be attending our dinner party." She threw down the letter and took up another one. As she perused this reply, her face grew grimmer. She looked up at

Pippa. "Lady Seymour also sends her regrets." She handed the rest of the missives to her daughter. "You open the rest of them, Pippa," she said. "I cannot bear it."

Pippa took up the letters and quickly went through them all. " 'I very much regret,' " she intoned, reading one and casting it aside. " 'We will be unable to attend . . . ' " she continued, taking up another. " 'We must send our regrets . . . ' " When she had gotten through the stack, she glanced at her mother. "I am sorry, Mama, it appears they are all sending their regrets."

"Regrets," sniffed Mrs. Grey ironically, "they do not regret treating us so abominably at all. How dare they snub us?"

"But, Mama, it is hardly surprising. We have already been turned away from most of the fashionable addresses in the city. It seems they all view us as unworthy of their rarified company."

Mrs. Grey abruptly stood up and walked angrily toward the window. Looking out at the fashionable brick town houses, she shook her head. "I will not be humiliated in such an infamous manner! How dare they look down their noses at us!"

Pippa got up from the sofa and walked over to her mother, followed by the solicitous Patches. She gently put her hand on Mrs. Grey's shoulder. "Mama, who cares a fig for these people anyway? They are insufferable snobs! Indeed, why do we not go back to Portsmouth? We had good friends and pleasant company there. I cannot understand why you wish to stay here."

Mrs. Grey regarded her daughter with a serious expression. Of course, Pippa could not understand. She had little regard for their position in Society. Indeed, Mrs. Grey knew that her daughter was just as happy conversing with a scullery maid as with a duke. But Mrs. Grey, who cared very much for her position, felt the slight very keenly.

A still attractive woman of six-and-forty, Louisa Grey was intent upon seeing herself accepted in London society. Born into the Devonshire gentry, the lovely Louisa had been much sought after in her youth. Her family had been certain that she would make an excellent match and they had been devastated when she announced she wished to marry Peter Grey, a man engaged in the shipping business.

When her father had forbidden her from entering into such an unsuitable marriage, Louisa had eloped with Grey. Her family had never forgiven her for her scandalous behavior in marrying against their wishes. The fact that her enterprising husband had soon become one of the richest men in the kingdom had made no difference whatsoever.

Mrs. Grey had spent much of her life enduring the rejection of her family and snubs of her former friends. She was determined that one day she would show them all. Oh, it was true that they had many friends and acquaintances in Portsmouth. Indeed, they had had very busy social lives there.

But Portsmouth was scarcely the equal of London and Mrs. Grey longed to have a place among the glittering company of the great city. That was why she had convinced her husband to move to London where she felt certain that they would be accepted into the elite circles. After all, her husband was now a very important and wealthy man.

Mrs. Grey frowned again as she glanced back out the window at the elegant row of houses. She had had such high hopes when they had moved into the fashionable neighborhood three months ago. But thus far no one from the exclusive area had called upon them and they had not been received by any of their aristocratic neighbors. Why in the world had she been so foolish to think they would attend a dinner party?

Her unhappy reverie was broken by the appearance of a carriage in front of their house. "Why, it is your father, Pippa!"

Pippa looked out the window. "And it appears Bertie is with him. Oh, dear," she said eyeing her brother with disapproval, "whatever is Bertie wearing?" However, before Pippa could get a good look at her younger brother, he and her father disappeared into the house.

It did not take long for father and son to make their way to the drawing room. Mr. Grey, a handsome robust gentleman with sandy red hair was the first one to enter. "Ah, my two favorite females!" he exclaimed. Patches, who was almost as devoted to Mr. Grey as she was to Pippa, happily rushed up to him with a happy bark. Pippa's father leaned down and rubbed the dog behind her ears. "Sorry, Patches, old girl," he said with a grin, "I should have said my *three* favorite females."

Albert, Pippa's brother, entered on his father's heels. A tall, handsome man of one-and-twenty, Bertie's ambition was to become the perfect London dandy, as his current outfit attested. He was dressed in a coat of olive superfine with a waistcoat of purple- and mustard-colored stripes. His neckcloth was tied in an extravagant fashion that made it somewhat difficult for him to turn his neck while his red hair was curled in the popular Corinthian style. "Hello, Mama, Pippa," he said with somewhat practiced nonchalance.

Grey eyed his son with an indulgent expression. "I decided to

come home early today and what do I find but this young popinjay walking along the street."

"Oh, Papa," said Bertie, dropping into an elegant armchair.

"You look splendid, my dear," said Mrs. Grey, smiling fondly
at her son. "I daresay there is not a more handsome young man in
all of London."

Bertie grinned at his mother. "Such bosh, Mama."

"It is not at all bosh," returned Mrs. Grey. Then turning to her
husband, she frowned. "Oh, Peter, I'm so glad you are here. We
have just had the most wretched news."

Putting his arm around his wife, Grey led her to the sofa.
"Now, my sweet," said Grey, patting her arm, "whatever is the
matter?"

Mrs. Grey sighed somewhat melodramatically. "We have just
received the replies to our dinner party invitations." She paused.
"They have all refused to come!"

Bertie leaned forward, a disturbed expression on his face.
"Surely not all, Mama?"

His mother nodded.

"Well, I'm not surprised," said Grey. "Since moving here we
haven't exactly been deluged with company."

"It is too dreadful," said Mrs. Grey. "To be snubbed so!"

"Now, don't worry your pretty head about it, my dear," said
Grey. "I have been giving considerable thought to the matter. I've
decided that what is needed is someone influential to help you
gain entry into Society."

"Indeed, Papa," said Pippa, taking a chair beside her brother,
"but will the Prince Regent agree to do such a thing?"

Her father laughed. "Oh, I did not have that royal personage in
mind, Pippa. But I must say, the gentleman who I did have in
mind is almost as exalted. With his assistance you will have no
difficulty entering society."

"Why whoever do you mean?" asked Mrs. Grey.

Grey smiled over at his wife. "The Viscount Allingham."

Although this news provided little enlightenment to Pippa, both
her mother and brother appeared amazed. "The Viscount Allingham!" exclaimed Mrs. Grey. "My dear, you cannot be serious."

"Allingham!" cried Bertie, his eyes widening in astonishment.
"Allingham introduce us into society! That is a rare one, Papa!"

"Really, Papa," said Pippa, "who is this Viscount Allingham? I
have never heard of him."

"Never heard of the great Allingham?" said her brother, regarding her as if she were some sort of ninny. "Why he is a tulip of the *ton*! Everyone seeks his advice, even His Royal Highness."

"Indeed?" said Pippa. "And what type of advice do they seek from this tulip?"

"Why, advice on what to wear, of course," said Bertie. "He is the absolute arbiter of fashion, Pippa! His neckcloths are absolute perfection and his boots positively gleam."

"My goodness," said Pippa, casting her father an ironical smile. "He does sound like a paragon. But how would you know such a man, Papa?"

Her father grinned in reply. "Oh, I don't know the fellow."

Mrs. Grey regarded her husband in frustration. "But, Peter, if you don't know him, how could you believe he would help us?"

"Yes, Papa," said Bertie, taking out his snuffbox. "I cannot imagine how you would think that Allingham would help us. It is too ridiculous."

"I'm not so certain of that," replied Grey. "While I have yet to make the great man's acquaintance, I've found out some interesting things about him. It always pays to be informed, you know. My sources tell me that this Allingham is terribly in debt. He is a horribly extravagant fellow, it seems, one with an unfortunate passion for losing at cards as well. Although it is not well known in Society, Allingham is in serious financial trouble. In fact, his creditors are hounding him as if he were a poor fox trapped in a burrow. And unless Providence helps him, the poor fox will be packing his bushy tail off to the Continent."

A sudden light of understanding came to Pippa. "Do not tell me, Papa, that you are intending to act the part of Providence for this Allingham?"

"I certainly have a clever daughter," said Grey, slapping his knee. "You've guessed it, Pippa. I shall offer to pay off the fellow's debts if he agrees to help my family gain entrance to his elite circle. I daresay he will be able to give you some of that famous advice while he's at it, Bertie." Grey, looking extremely pleased with himself, turned toward his wife. "Well, my dear?"

Mrs. Grey appeared startled by her husband's plan. "You cannot be serious, Peter!"

"Indeed, Father," cried Bertie. "You cannot expect that Allingham would accept such . . . such an offer?"

"And why not?" asked Grey bluntly. "Unless, of course, as well as being the 'arbiter of fashion' this Allingham is an utter fool."

"Really, Peter, you are being ridiculous," said Mrs. Grey.

"Papa," said Bertie, "you cannot approach Allingham with this idea of yours! We should never be able to live down the humiliation!"

"I really do not think it would be wise, Papa," said Pippa, regarding her father with a serious expression in her blue eyes.

Grey stared from face to face. He did not understand his family's reluctance about his scheme. Although he himself was not at all interested in entering what he considered a society of peacocks and idlers, he knew it was his wife's most ardent wish. And fulfilling his wife's most ardent wish was also his.

A canny businessman who well understood the power of money, Grey had no doubt that Allingham would jump at his offer. He smiled. "Now, now, don't worry, my dears. Just leave everything to me. Now where is tea? I am deuced famished!" Grey jumped up to ring for a servant while Pippa, her mother, and brother all exchanged glances.

2

The butler entered the dining room, somberly walking along the long cherry table to where his master, John Edmund Montfort, the Seventh Viscount Allingham sat with his breakfast. "I beg your pardon, my lord," said the servant in an apologetic voice, "but that *person* is here again. He insists upon seeing your lordship."

The viscount, who was perusing the morning newspaper while drinking from a fine china teacup, did not even deign to look up. "And what person would that be, Morris?"

"He says his name is Mr. Nathaniel Boggs, my lord."

Glancing up from the newspaper, his lordship's handsome face showed a slight trace of annoyance. "Boggs?" he asked in a scornful tone. "Who the devil is this Boggs?"

The servant cleared his throat in some embarrassment. "He called here yesterday and the day before that, my lord. It seems he wishes to see your lordship concerning the matter of an, er . . . account you have that is, ahem, overdue."

This news did not seem to disturb the viscount at all. He picked up a knife and skillfully cut off the top of the hard-boiled egg that sat in a porcelain eggcup before him. "Really, Morris," he said in a bored voice, "must you disturb me with such trivialities? Tell this Boggs fellow that I will take care of the situation and then send him on his way."

"He is rather persistent, my lord."

"Then you be persistent, too, Morris." The viscount took a bite of the egg and opened up the newspaper to an inside page. When the servant hesitated, Allingham glanced back up at him. "Is there something else, Morris?"

The servant tried to look as emotionless as his master. "No, my lord." He started retreating quietly from the room when the viscount stopped him.

"Oh, and Morris . . ."

"Yes, my lord?"

"Do try to keep fellows like Boggs from hanging about the front door, would you? They detract from the architecture."

The butler nodded slightly. "Very good, my lord."

As the servant left the dining room, Morris's expressionless demeanor was replaced with a look of concern. It was easy for his lordship to tell him to keep the fellows from hanging about, but he was the one who had to confront them every day. And this Nathaniel Boggs person was a rather menacing-looking chap.

Morris frowned. For some weeks there had been a steady stream of creditors appearing at the viscount's fashionable London town house, demanding to see him. The worthy butler had managed to put all of them off, but it was becoming more and more difficult. The servant wondered just how much trouble his master was in. Of late, he had worried that his lofty position in the viscount's household might not be all that secure.

Shrugging his shoulders, Morris started toward the door to give Mr. Boggs the unhappy news. However, as he neared the entry hall, he decided it might be best to fetch Tom first. A footman in the viscount's employ, Tom was a hulking youth who could certainly toss out Boggs if the need arose. With somewhat more confidence, the butler hurried to the servants' quarters to find the young footman.

Although he had displayed an admirable coolness in hearing about another creditor at his door, Allingham was, in truth, discomfitted by it. While in the past he had counted on his illustrious name and position to ensure him credit, it had seemed that lately they were not enough.

Extremely bad luck at cards combined with careless extravagance had put the viscount in a very precarious financial state. His many creditors who had not been paid in months were fast losing patience. They were beginning to appear regularly, circling his house like vultures.

Of course, since Allingham was a gambler, he was always certain that his next card game would provide him with an escape from the whole damnable business. He would win enough to pay off some of the worst of the hounds dunning him for money. But somehow the viscount's luck never seemed to change. His losses at cards had put him only deeper into debt.

Buttering a slice of toast, the viscount frowned as he thought of his last disastrous game of faro. He did not even like to think of the amount of money he had wagered in the ill-fated game. And the worst of it was that he had lost to that blackguard Seagrave.

Allingham had known and despised the Baron Seagrave ever

since the two of them had been boys together at Eton. In the form above the viscount, Seagrave had been one of the worst bullies at school. He had delighted in tormenting Allingham and his friends. His lordship's frown deepened. And now the baron could take pleasure in tormenting him again over the money he owed him, thought Allingham.

"Damn his eyes!" muttered the viscount in an unusual display of feeling. Indeed, Allingham was well known in society for his dispassionate nature. He regarded the world with an aloof and superior expression.

While it might have been thought that such hauteur would have made the viscount unpopular, it had just the opposite effect. Hostesses clamored to have him grace their affairs and gentlemen were desperate to get even an approving nod from him. His tastes in clothes were widely imitated, although they never quite looked the same as on the viscount himself. The gentleman who faced Allingham's disapproval over the cut of his coat or the way he tied his neckcloth was utterly crushed.

Allingham was, then, a most influential and sought-after gentleman in the elite company of London society. He was considered to be the successor to the legendary Brummell, who was now living in ignominious exile in France. However, there was considerable danger that the viscount would also follow the unfortunate Beau's example in losing everything through his extravagance and addiction to gambling.

Allingham continued to ponder the sorry state of his affairs as he ate his breakfast. Taking up a piece of sausage with his fork, the viscount was somewhat irritated by the reappearance of his butler. "What is it now, Morris?" asked his lordship. "Didn't you get rid of that fellow? What the devil was his name?"

"Boggs, my lord. Yes, Mr. Boggs was persuaded to leave," said the butler with an impassive expression. He refrained from informing his lordship about the scuffle between Boggs and the footman, Tom, which resulted in the creditor departing the viscount's residence with a black eye.

"Don't tell me there is some other fellow who wants to see me?" asked Allingham, frowning as he imagined a long line of persons dunning him for money.

"Yes, my lord. No, my lord. Not some *fellow*. It is His Royal Highness and Colonel Crawford."

Allingham raised his dark eyebrows in surprise. "Prinny? Here at this hour? Very well, Morris, send them in."

The butler returned a short time later followed by the Prince

Regent and another gentleman. The viscount, who had stood up respectfully, smiled and bowed. "Your Royal Highness." He then nodded to the other gentleman whom he knew well as one of the prince's aides and constant companions. "Crawford."

The prince's aide nodded stiffly in reply.

Attired in a bright blue coat and buff-colored pantaloons, with his reddish brown hair stylishly curled around his chubby face, Royal George wasted little time in getting to the point of his unusual morning visit. "Ah, Allingham," he said. "Do forgive this intrusion, but I need your opinion about something."

"It is no intrusion, Your Royal Highness. Would you care for some breakfast?"

"Later, later, Allingham," said the Prince Regent a trifle impatiently. "I said I wanted your opinion." He posed somewhat stiffly in front of the viscount. "Well, what do you think of it, Allingham?"

"Of what, sir?"

"The coat, the coat, of course! Crawford says it is splendid, but I cannot rely on his judgment."

Allingham's expression implied that this was certainly true. He walked slowly around his prince, casting a critical eye upon the garment in question. "Well, well?" cried the Prince Regent eagerly.

"I fear that coat," began the viscount, giving the word "coat" a disagreeable intonation, "simply does not do justice to Your Royal Highness."

Royal George grew red in the face as he shouted, "I knew it, I knew it! Damn that tailor of mine. And I told Crawford the lapels were all wrong! He thought them excellent. You are an idiot, Crawford."

The colonel felt it best to make no reply. Well accustomed to taking abuse from Royal George, he directed a long-suffering look at the viscount.

"I'm afraid, sir," sniffed Allingham, "the lapels are the least of the crime."

"What?" cried the Prince. "What do you mean?"

The viscount approached the royal personage and pulled at the front of the coat. "The cut is all wrong. The shoulders are dreadful. And the color . . . "

"The color?" repeated the Prince Regent in surprise. "I picked it out, Allingham. It is called lapis lazuli!"

"Lapis lazuli," muttered the viscount, "good God."

The Prince Regent crossed his arms in front of his corpulent belly. "What is wrong with it, pray tell? I find it quiet dazzling."

"Blinding is more like it," replied Allingham. "You know I have always said true elegance is achieved through understatement, Your Royal Highness."

"Oh, dash it, I know what you've said, but understatement can be so deuced boring." He paused and looked down sadly at the coat. "I daresay you are right as always, Allingham."

"I would not argue with you on that, Your Royal Highness," said the viscount with a slight bow. The Prince Regent laughed and a slight smile appeared on Allingham's face.

The future heir to the throne suddenly eyed the viscount with considerable interest. "I say, Allingham, what a splendid-looking neckcloth."

"Thank you, sir. I call it 'The Cascade.' "

"The devil you say. You must show my man how to tie it." The Prince Regent was somewhat resentful as he noted the viscount's typically splendid appearance. Allingham was dressed in ivory-colored pantaloons with a superbly cut coat of dove gray superfine. His linen neckcloth was as white as snow and his hessian boots positively gleamed.

Of course, thought the Prince Regent glumly, the fellow was also damnably handsome. Tall with broad shoulders and muscular calves, the viscount would have looked good in rags. He had dark curly hair, a large, intelligent brow, a somewhat aquiline nose, and light gray eyes that could sometimes chill a person to the bone.

Allingham seemed unaware of his prince's scrutiny. He motioned toward the table. "Now that that matter is settled, sir, will you join me for some breakfast?"

"I can never refuse such an offer, Allingham, knowing what an excellent cook you have. Come, Crawford, we shall have some of Allingham's breakfast."

The viscount led the prince to the head of the table and the prince sat down. Colonel Crawford, who seemed pleased at the prospect of food, happily sat down as well. The butler rapidly hurried over to their royal guest, offering him one silver serving dish after the other.

After consuming a prodigious number of sausages and blueberry scones, the Prince Regent took his leave with the colonel following behind him. Relieved by the royal departure, Allingham made his way to his favorite haven, the library.

The viscount was justly proud of his fine library. It was an imposing room with tall wainscoted walls and oak shelves laden with books. An elegant Queen Anne desk sat near an impressive black marble fireplace. There was a family portrait above the fireplace and landscape paintings hung in the few bare areas that were not taken up by bookshelves.

One of Allingham's few passions was his book collection. His love of books had started in his childhood when his indulgent parents had showered him with illustrated editions of fairy tales and adventure stories. Over the years his eclectic tastes had resulted in a wide-ranging collection that included poetry, literature, travel, mathematics, astronomy, botany, and animal husbandry.

Going over to a shelf, the viscount pulled out a well-thumbed volume of poetry and returned to his desk. He had scarcely begun to read when a maid appeared in the room. The young girl quaked a little under Allingham's disapproving gaze. "I am sorry to disturb your lordship," she said, "but a messenger has brought this letter."

"And where is Morris?" asked the viscount somewhat sternly.

"Talking to another gentleman at the door, my lord, so he asked me to bring this to you."

Allingham took the letter from the girl. He eyed the envelope curiously for a moment and then opened it. The letter before him was in a broad, vigorous hand. It said, 'My Lord, It has lately come to my attention that you are experiencing some difficulties of a financial nature. I daresay you are wondering what business this is of mine, but I have an idea which would end your embarrassment in addition to being beneficial to myself. I would like to meet with you to discuss this matter at any time that would be convenient to your lordship. You may call upon me at the offices of Grey Shipping Ltd., number 19 Hamilton Street.' The letter was signed, 'Your servant, Peter Grey.'

The viscount was at first so startled by this missive that he read it over again. "Damn the fellow's impudence," he muttered.

"Excuse me, my lord?"

Allingham looked up and frowned to see the maid still standing before him. "You may go. . . . " He eyed her questioningly.

"Sarah, my lord." She hesitated. "The messenger was waiting for a reply, my lord."

The viscount regarded her with an icy expression. "Tell the messenger that I will not reply to such an impertinent letter."

The maid quickly backed out of the room. "Yes, my lord."

Allingham read the letter one more time and then cast it aside on his desk. Who the devil was this fellow Peter Grey anyway? How dare he write to him about his private financial affairs! Determined not to give the letter another thought, the viscount picked up his book and began to read.

However, he soon found it impossible to concentrate. Putting down the book, he rose from his desk and walked over to the large portrait hanging above the fireplace mantel. It was a family portrait of his parents and himself when he was a child. The painting always invoked a combined sense of nostalgia and melancholy in the viscount.

Painted at his family's ancestral estate, the picture showed the sixth viscount, a tall, distinguished-looking man who bore a striking resemblance to his son. The lovely fair-haired lady in the portrait, Allingham's mother, gazed out from the painting a bit wistfully. One of her hands rested upon her son's shoulder. The present viscount, a child of seven in the portrait, was looking out with a somewhat arrogant expression, his arm draped around his beloved pet, a large bullmastiff named Hannibal.

The painting always managed to bring back memories of what the viscount considered his golden childhood. An only child who was viewed as something of a miracle, Allingham was greatly indulged by his doting parents. In truth, many of the Montfort relatives thought he had been dreadfully spoiled. Some of them said it was no surprise that the viscount had become an extravagant, arrogant man.

Taking one last glance at the portrait, Allingham went back to his desk and took up his book once again. Some time later, the butler entered the library. The viscount threw his book down in a rare display of temper. "Good God, what is it now? Can I have no peace in my own home?"

"I am sorry, my lord. It is only that Sir Henry Lonsdale is here and . . ."

"Good God, Morris, why did you not say so in the first place?" asked Allingham. "Send Sir Henry in immediately."

The servant retreated and returned a moment later with a slight, blond gentleman who was as impeccably dressed as Allingham.

The viscount was very happy to finally have a welcome visitor, his best friend Sir Henry Lonsdale. Living on neighboring estates, the Montfort and Lonsdale families had been friends and allies for generations. Allingham had known Sir Henry ever since they were toddlers. Having been at Eton and Oxford together, the viscount and the baronet had remained on the most excellent of terms.

"Harry," said Allingham, shaking his friend's outstretched hand. "You don't know how glad I am to see you."

Sir Henry plopped down languidly in an armchair next to the viscount. "My dear Jack, how can you stay inside on such a glorious day? Come, I shall take you for a ride in my phaeton."

"Good lord, I'm not a fool, Harry. You drive like a madman."

Instead of taking offense, his friend laughed. "You are a coward, Jack. Come, you could use some excitement."

"Damn it, Harry, I think I've had enough excitement for one day. I had a visit from Prinny already."

"The devil! Prinny called upon you this morning? That is dashed odd."

Allingham nodded. "He wanted my opinion on an abominable coat he was wearing."

"Oh, dear. I suppose you exhibited your usual tact, my friend?"

Allingham smiled slightly, "Of course, Harry."

"And did HRH remain long?"

"No, thankfully, his visit was brief. But it has been a trying day."

"I fear I will only make it more trying for you, old fellow."

"What do you mean?"

"I saw Seagrave at the club last night. He was going about telling everyone about his victory over you in faro the other evening." He paused. "And that was not all, Jack," he said with a serious expression. "He was saying that you would be a long time in paying your debt to him."

The viscount frowned. "Dammit, Harry, I intend to pay him."

Sir Henry regarded his friend sympathetically. "I say, old man, you aren't in trouble, are you?"

Allingham smiled. "Don't be absurd, Harry." The viscount was reluctant to tell his best friend the true state of his affairs. He knew that Sir Henry would insist on giving him help, help his friend could little afford to give.

The viscount found himself thinking that he had better consider selling his cherished book collection. It would not do for Seagrave to be putting it about that he would not pay his debts. Yet the thought of parting with his beloved books depressed him. His glance fell upon the letter from Grey and he looked back at his friend. "Tell me, Harry, do you happen to know someone by the name of Peter Grey?"

His friend looked thoughtful. "Peter Grey? Why, yes, I have heard of him. If he is the man you mean, my sister-in-law just mentioned him. It seems his wife invited her to a dinner party. Of course, Catherine wanted no part of it. This Peter Grey is not the sort one would wish in one's dining room. He is in the shipping

business or some such thing. And frightfully rich, so they say."
Sir Henry noted that his friend was listening to him with considerable interest. "Why on earth do you want to know about this Grey?"

Allingham shrugged. "The name was mentioned to me. I was just curious."

"Well, I daresay you will not be likely to meet the fellow."

"I hardly wish to meet such a person," returned Allingham, a thoughtful expression on his face. So this Grey was a rich tradesman, he told himself. The viscount wondered at the man's effrontery in writing to him.

"Is something the matter, Jack?"

The viscount shook his head. "Nothing. On second thought, Harry, I think I will risk a ride with you after all."

"Capital!" cried Sir Henry, quickly getting up from his chair. Allingham followed his friend out of the room, eager for some diversion that would take his mind off of his monetary woes.

3

Three days after receiving the "impertinent" letter from Peter Grey, the Viscount Allingham lay in his large four-poster bed. Sunlight streamed in through a chink in the bedchamber curtains and there was a loud chatter of birds outside his window.

Awakening from a troubled slumber, Allingham moaned and put a hand to his brow. He had a horrible headache, no doubt due to his improvident consumption of brandy the night before.

It was unusual for the viscount to suffer the ill effects of alcohol, since he was well known in society for his moderate drinking. Rarely did he ever take more than a glass or two of wine at dinner and a small bit of port or brandy before bedtime. Unlike most of his noble friends, Allingham did not drink to excess. Indeed, the viscount's temperate behavior was the one thing that was not aped by his ardent followers.

However, feeling somewhat overwhelmed by his financial worries, the viscount had poured himself several large glasses of brandy the previous evening. His butler had been quite disturbed to see that the bottle had been practically empty when his lordship had finally retired for the night.

Allingham sat up and then, flinging aside his covers, got out of bed. After putting on a purple silk dressing gown, he walked over to the window. Pulling aside the curtains, he squinted out into the bright spring sunlight. Trees were blooming in bursts of white and pink along the fashionable street and every so often there were clumps of yellow daffodils. The cheerful sight did nothing to improve the viscount's mood. Muttering a curse, he closed the curtains.

Allingham still remembered the vivid dream he had just been having. In it, a group of people had burst into his drawing room and had proceeded to carry out all of the furniture and paintings. When he had protested, his enemy Seagrave had appeared, towering above him. "I've always wanted this house, Allingham," he had sneered in the dream. "And now I've got it! Get out, you con-

temptible worm!" Seagrave had then put back his head and roared
with laughter.

Fearing that this dream might be a premonition, the viscount
frowned and once more put his hand to his forehead. In hopes of
replenishing his stores, he had, over the past few days, tried to
win some money at the card table. His efforts had met with dis-
mal failure, for he had had very ill luck indeed.

At that moment, Allingham's valet entered the room, and his
lordship was temporarily distracted by the ever important ritual of
getting dressed. Some time later, displaying his usual sartorial
splendor, the viscount made his way to the dining room. However, since he was not very hungry, he merely fortified himself
with a cup of tea, which he carried off to the library.

Allingham sat down at his desk in the library and stared glumly
at the pile of bills in front of him. He had not even bothered to
open his mail from the previous day, which lay in a separate stack
next to the bills. Picking up the envelopes, Allingham quickly
sifted through them. There were several more bills, including one
from his tailor. Remembering that he had just ordered several new
suits, he wondered if he should try to have the order canceled. But
then, why bother, he thought grimly. It was too late to start econo-
mizing now.

As he continued through the pile of envelopes, he was somewhat heartened to find one of them was a letter from his cousin,
Lady Caroline Ashby. However, quickly perusing it, he found
that his cousin's purpose in writing him was a thinly veiled request for money. He threw down the letter and suddenly laughed
at the irony. Poor Caroline. She had certainly come begging to the
wrong relative.

Getting up from his desk, Allingham walked over to one of the
bookshelves that lined the wall. He ran his hand along a row of
gilt-edged volumes and sighed. It appeared he had no choice. He
would have to sell his entire book collection and God knew what
else.

Going back to the desk, the viscount's eye suddenly fell on the
letter he had received three days ago from Peter Grey. Picking it
up, he reread it. The fellow certainly was impudent, he thought.

Allingham sat for a time, staring at the letter and wondering
what Grey had had in mind. It suddenly occurred to him that he
might have been too hasty in dismissing Grey's offer out of hand.
After all, he had no idea what the man had in mind.

The viscount looked thoughtful. Perhaps he should go and see this Grey just to satisfy his curiosity. Certainly there was no harm in talking with him.

A short time later, Allingham was driving his stylish high-perch phaeton through the congested streets in the hub of the city. Turning his chestnut horses onto Hamilton Street, the viscount pulled up in front of a large, handsome Georgian red brick building that proclaimed "Grey Shipping, Ltd." After handing the reins to his groom, he jumped down and looked about him. A gang of street urchins had quickly gathered at the sight of the magnificent horses and equipage.

"Lud, Jem," cried one dirty-faced boy to his equally grubby companion. "Look at them horses and that bloomin' rig! I wish I was a nob and could bloody well ride about like that!" His friend, a ragged eleven-year-old, nodded in wide-eyed agreement and the two youngsters enviously watched Allingham as he made his way inside the building.

As the viscount entered the shipping company, he found himself in a large, spacious room lined with desks. Men sat at each desk, furiously scratching pens against paper. Allingham was unused to the feverish activity of a busy workplace and he just stared with some amazement at the sight before him. He was interrupted by a gangly red-haired youth who sat at the desk nearest to the doorway.

"Might I be of assistance, sir?" asked the clerk, eyeing the viscount with considerable interest. It was obvious from the gentleman's clothes and bearing that he was a man of considerable wealth and importance.

Allingham made an almost imperceptible nod and grandly handed the youth his card. "I wish to see Mr. Peter Grey," he said in an imperious voice.

The clerk looked down at the card. Written in ornately scripted letters was "Viscount Allingham." The young man looked up in amazement. So this was the Viscount Allingham! While the clerk could hardly be expected to know the elite members of the *ton*, he certainly had heard of the great Allingham! Blushing, he stammered, "I will tell Mr. Grey, my . . . my lord." He then rushed off to his employer's office.

When he appeared breathless at Grey's door, that gentleman regarded him with some alarm. "What the devil is the matter, Walter?"

The clerk gulped and handed him the viscount's card. He was surprised when his employer did not seem to share his awe of the great man. "So, the fellow has decided to see me after all, has he?" said Grey, smiling cynically. "I thought he would change his mind. Well, send him in, Walter."

Without a word, the clerk rushed off and returned a moment later with the viscount. Grey stood up. "Lord Allingham. I am Peter Grey." He held out his hand.

The viscount shook Grey's hand and then stood eyeing him with his usual arrogant expression. The businessman promptly sat down at his desk. "Sit down, my lord," he said and Allingham took the leather chair facing him.

"I received your letter, sir," began the viscount coolly, "and although I do not appreciate such an intrusion into my personal affairs, I must admit to some curiosity."

While Grey did not much like Allingham's haughty demeanor, he nodded amiably. "I know it was bold of me to send you such a letter, my lord. Indeed, my family thought it was a cork-brained thing for me to do. . . . "

Allingham raised his eyebrows. "Your family?"

"Indeed, my lord. My family knows all about it. I mean, about your situation."

The viscount frowned and said icily, "You and your family were discussing *my* situation?"

Grey nodded and leaned toward the viscount. "You see, my lord, this involves my family. That's why I came up with this scheme of mine—to help them. Of course, it would help you in the bargain."

"Help me?"

"Indeed so. I am confident that you will find my scheme mutually agreeable."

Allingham raised his eyebrows once again. "Indeed? Then I suggest you cease beating about the bush and tell me what you are talking about."

Grey, who was unused to being addressed in such an insolent manner, bristled a bit, but continued. "Very well. I shall get to the point. You see, my lord, I know all about your financial troubles. This is my proposal. I shall take care of your debts if you will use your influence to have my family accepted by society."

The viscount regarded him as if he had not heard correctly. "Take care of my debts if I use my influence to have your family accepted by society?" he repeated.

"It would not be difficult for you, Lord Allingham. I am told you have considerable position in elite circles. All that I am asking is that you see that my family gets invited to all the important society affairs. You know, vouchers to Almack's and that sort of thing. And that my wife and my children are received by your friends in the *ton*."

Allingham shook his head. "I fear, Mr. Grey, that what you ask is impossible. If I may be blunt, sir, society is very selective about embracing new members." He regarded Grey with a frown. "You must realize that persons engaged in trade are not considered suitable. I do not think that even I would have the power to arrange for *your* admission to society."

Surprised at his visitor's insulting tone, Grey's face reddened in anger. "You do not have to get me accepted by society!" he said. "I have no desire to join your pack of wastrels and snobs! No, indeed, it is my family that is to be accepted—my wife, my son, and my daughter.

"My wife comes from the gentry. She was a Chesterton before her marriage. They are an old and respected family in Devonshire. My wife is a lady, sir. There is no finer lady in any London drawing room! She should not be denied entry to your damnable society just because she is married to me!"

The viscount crossed his arms in front of his chest. "I fear it is out of the question, Mr. Grey. As a gentleman, I do not sell my influence."

"Then you are a great bottlehead, Allingham," said Grey, "for that is apparently the only commodity you have to sell. You are a fool if you do not accept my offer."

Although the viscount was offended at Grey's words, he restrained himself from getting up and leaving the room. He was in a very serious financial predicament. Perhaps he should set aside his pride and consider Grey's proposal. After all, he used his influence in society all the time at the behest of friends and relations. If Grey's wife and family were presentable, there may be no harm in taking them up. Allingham looked thoughtful. "Are you aware of the extent of my debts, Mr. Grey?"

"Not precisely," returned Grey.

"They amount to more than twenty thousand pounds." Watching Grey's reaction, the viscount was surprised that the older man did not even blink an eye.

"I am a very wealthy man, my lord. Such a sum is easily managed."

"Indeed?" said Allingham, staring at Grey. He found himself thinking that the man must be rich indeed if he could so easily part with more than twenty thousand pounds. The viscount paused and then continued. "You say your wife was a Chesterton before her marriage?"

"Yes," said Grey, pleased that the viscount now seemed to be mulling over the matter.

"Is she related to Sir Ronald Chesterton?"

"Distantly I believe."

Allingham appeared thoughtful. "And you have a son and daughter?"

"Yes, my daughter is Phillipa and my son is Albert."

"And their ages?"

"Pippa—we call her Pippa, my lord—is four-and-twenty and Albert—we call him Bertie, you see—is three years younger."

"Is your daughter married?"

"No."

The viscount frowned at this information. Unmarried at four-and-twenty? She was doubtlessly bracket-faced and dowdy. He certainly did not want to make a fool of himself attempting to foist such a person on society.

Grey seemed to know what he was thinking. "If you would but meet my wife and children, you would see that they would do well in society. Why don't you come to my house for tea tomorrow? After you meet them, you can make up your mind."

The viscount hesitated for a moment. "Very well," he said finally. "I shall come. What is your address?"

"Fifteen Grosvenor Square."

Allingham was somewhat encouraged by this. At least Grosvenor Square was a suitably exclusive address. The viscount rose from his chair. "I shall see you tomorrow then, Grey."

Grey got to his feet, considerably heartened at his lordship's willingness to call on them. He knew how excited his wife and son would be at hearing the news. "Very good, my lord."

Allingham nodded and took his leave. When he came into the outer office, Walter, the clerk, rushed to get the door for him. Not acknowledging the young man's presence, the viscount stepped out onto the street.

"Out of my way, you," said Allingham to the assembled urchins loitering by his high-perch phaeton. They quickly jumped back and watched as the viscount climbed up into his vehicle, took back his reins and pulled his horses away from the curb.

The moment Peter Grey arrived home that evening he quickly sought out his wife. Finding her seated on the sofa in the drawing room, he rushed toward her. "Louisa, my dear!" he cried, taking her into his arms and kissing her soundly.

When their lips parted, Mrs. Grey regarded him in surprise. "Good heavens, Peter, you appear in a boisterous mood tonight."

He grinned. "Indeed, I am, my darling," he said. "I have some news that will please you."

At that moment, Pippa and Bertie entered the room, followed by Patches. The dog, elated at the sight of Mr. Grey, ran over to that gentleman barking excitedly. "Patches, my girl, what a good dog you are." Petting the dog, Grey looked up at his children. "I am glad you two are here. I was just about to tell your mother about something that concerns you as well."

Mrs. Grey nodded. "Yes, your father has said that he has some good news, so do sit down so he can tell us what it is."

Pippa and Bertie took chairs across from their parents and looked expectantly at their father. "Yes, Papa?" said Pippa. "Pray do not keep us in suspense."

"Very well. It is only that I saw the Viscount Allingham today."

"What?" cried Mrs. Grey. "You called upon Allingham?"

Grey grinned again. "No, my dear. He called upon me."

Bertie regarded his father with an incredulous expression. "The viscount called upon *you*, Papa?"

Grey laughed. "I can see I have confounded you. Yes, Allingham did me the great honor of visiting me at my office. At least, *he* considered it a great honor."

"But, my dear," said his wife, "why did he pay a call upon you at your office?"

"Well, I knew he would not deign to receive me if I called upon him. So I wrote him a letter instead, telling him that I had an idea that would be profitable for both of us. I asked him to stop by my office to discuss it. I had hoped that his curiosity would get the better of him and it did."

Pippa eyed her father in surprise. "Oh, dear, Papa. You cannot mean that you told this Allingham about your scheme to have him sponsor us in society?"

"I most certainly did, my girl."

Bertie looked horror stricken. "Papa, how could you do such a thing?"

"Yes, Peter, how could you?" cried his wife.

"Now don't go into the high fidgets," said Grey soothingly. "It worked out splendidly."

"You cannot mean that Allingham agreed to your proposal?" asked Pippa in amazement.

Grey put a hand on his chin. "Well, not exactly."

"Whatever do you mean, Peter?" asked his wife.

He leaned back on the sofa. "Well, I suggested he meet you first. He was quite agreeable to that." Grey grinned. "I daresay his lordship wishes to find out whether you are presentable enough to bother with."

"Oh, Papa!" cried Pippa, her blue eyes flashing. "So we are to be paraded before this Allingham like livestock at an auction? And he will decide if we are presentable enough?"

Grey laughed. "Calm yourself, my dear. I daresay you cannot expect him to agree to help us without meeting you. He is coming to tea tomorrow and then he will decide."

Mrs. Grey appeared ready to swoon. "Allingham is coming to tea tomorrow! Oh, dear, how shall we have time to make preparations?"

"Don't be absurd, my dear," said Grey. "It is only tea, after all."

Bertie suddenly appeared eager. "Allingham coming for tea!" he cried. "Can you believe it? I shall wear my new green coat. Or perhaps the blue striped one would be better." He looked over at his sister. "What do you think, Pippa?"

"I think you are bird-witted, Bertie, to care so much about what you are wearing," she said scornfully.

Bertie looked offended. "But it is Allingham, Pippa!" he protested.

Pippa shook her head in disgust. "Good heavens, Bertie, it is not as if the Duke of Wellington were coming for tea!"

Her father laughed. "I can see that Pippa is not overwhelmed by the idea of our august visitor. I daresay you will have to show a little more enthusiasm tomorrow, my girl. The fellow expects lesser mortals to be awestruck by his magnificence."

"Really, Papa, he sounds perfectly odious," said Pippa. "I do not understand why we must bow and scrape to this Allingham. Surely he is not very honorable if he would consider taking money from you for such a thing."

Mrs. Grey regarded her daughter with some concern. "Pippa! Lord Allingham is one of the most influential gentlemen in society, and we are very fortunate that he would agree to call upon us. I do hope you will try to make a good impression."

Pippa frowned but did not reply. As her family continued to talk excitedly about the upcoming visit of the illustrious viscount, she told herself that Allingham's approval or disapproval did not signify to her in the least.

4

Mrs. Grey was in a flutter the next day as she went about supervising her servants. Rising much earlier than was her habit, she wanted to make absolutely sure that everything would be up to Allingham's standard of perfection.

She followed her maids around, checking to be certain that they had spotlessly cleaned the entire house. Then, after a lengthy discussion with the cook on whether to have lemon sponge cake, cherry scones or strawberry tarts for tea, Mrs. Grey decided that the best solution would be to have all three. After certifying that the silver was gleaming and the table linens were suitably pressed, the nervous hostess retreated to her room to dress.

Peter Grey, returning home early so that he would be on hand for their exalted visitor, was quite impressed with the preparations that had been made for tea. Filching a strawberry tart from the kitchen, he went upstairs to get dressed.

After having spent an inordinate amount of time in front of his mirror, Bertie had finally decided to wear his new green coat that boasted a double row of shiny gold buttons. Making sure that his ivory pantaloons were without a crease and that his red hair was carefully combed into place, the young gentleman made his way downstairs to await his lordship.

When he entered the drawing room, he found his sister sitting on a sofa reading a book, Patches lying as usual at her feet. She looked up as he came into the room. "Don't you look splendid, brother. I daresay, you will outshine Allingham in that coat."

Bertie, who could not help but be pleased by this remark, sat down on the sofa next to her. "Bosh, Pippa," he said. "He looked down at the large dog at his sister's feet. "I do think we had better banish Patches to the kitchen. It would not do to have her about when Allingham arrives."

Although Patches seemed to take no offense at this remark, Pippa appeared irritated by her brother's suggestion. "Oh, I do not doubt that his lordship would be horrified by Patches's lack of a pedigree."

"Do not be ridiculous, Pippa. You know Patches is not the most well behaved of dogs. The minute the food would arrive, she would be begging shamelessly."

Pippa nodded. "That is true. But then, are we not going to be begging shamelessly at this tea ourselves?"

"Whatever do you mean by that?" asked her brother.

"Why, what else are we doing but begging for this Allingham's good opinion? I find it quite dreadful!"

Bertie sat back, carefully smoothing his pantaloons to avoid wrinkles. "Do not be a goose, Pippa! You do not seem to understand what Allingham's approval means. Why, we would be able to enter into the first circles of society!" Bertie, like his mother, was most eager to gain entry into such elite company. The young dandy was dazzled by the glittering social world and very desperately wanted to be a part of it.

"Oh, hang society!" cried Pippa, in a most unladylike fashion.

Bertie gave her a disapproving look. "I hope you do not intend to speak like that in Allingham's presence."

"Oh, do not worry, little brother. I do not want to ruin things for you and Mama. I shall be as good as gold."

Bertie looked somewhat unconvinced by this, but he nodded. "I am glad to hear it, Pippa." He looked at the clock over the mantel. "But, don't you think you had better go change?"

"What do you mean? I am wearing this."

Bertie eyed his sister's blue muslin frock critically. "But, Pippa, surely that is not your nicest dress. What about that new dress that you just had made, the white one with the little flowers on it?"

Pippa regarded her younger brother in annoyance. "I am sorry if you do not think I am quite up to snuff, Bertie, but I think this dress is just fine." She stood up. "If you will excuse me, I need to get some air. I'm going to take Patches out for a walk."

"A walk? You cannot mean that you are going out now?" asked her brother in astonishment.

"And why not?"

"Because it is nearly three o'clock! Allingham could arrive at any time!"

"Oh, nonsense!" said Pippa. "Allingham will certainly appear fashionably late. Do not worry, Bertie, I will be back in plenty of time to await the great tulip." Ignoring her brother's pleading look, she called down to Patches. "Come on, girl. Do you want to go for a walk?" The large canine jumped up and barked excitedly.

"Well, do not go very far, Pippa," warned her brother. Ignoring him, she walked from the drawing room with Patches following happily at her heels.

After putting on a gray pelisse trimmed in blue satin and donning a wide-brimmed leghorn hat, Pippa made her way to the door. Attaching a lead to Patches's collar, she stepped outside.

It had rained steadily that morning, but the sun had finally broken out of the clouds. As she walked down the sidewalk, dodging the occasional puddle, Pippa smiled. It was good to be outside and away from the house. She was quite tired of hearing about Lord Allingham and the preparations for his visit. Indeed, she had half a mind to stay away as long as possible in the hope that she would miss the viscount.

Of course, considered Pippa, as she walked briskly along, she could hardly do such a thing. Her mother would never forgive her. She sighed. No, she would have to go home and try to be charming to the dreadful Viscount Allingham.

There was a large park just a few blocks from the Greys' residence, so Pippa decided to take Patches there. As she stepped inside the iron gate that marked the entrance to the park, Pippa smiled and looked about at the beautiful expanse of green trees before her. "Come, Patches," she said, "we shall take a quick turn in here and then we had best return home."

Patches barked agreeably and they began strolling along one of the paths that led into the park. As they walked along, Pippa began to think again about Allingham. She had to admit that she was somewhat curious to meet the viscount after everything that her mother and Bertie had said about him. It might be interesting to meet the so-called arbiter of fashion in person. Pippa was so intent on these thoughts that she did not recognize trouble ahead in the shape of a small red dog.

An elderly gentleman was throwing a stick to the little dog in an open area of grass when it suddenly spied Patches approaching. The small dog, sensing more fun in the offing, quickly ran over to the much larger dog, barking furiously. Patches, never one to pass up an opportunity for a good time, barked in reply. Before Pippa realized what had happened, her dog had lurched away in a mad run, causing her to drop the lead.

"Patches!" she cried, watching her begin to chase the small red dog.

"Nipper!" shouted the elderly gentleman. "Come back here, you little rascal!"

Both dogs ignored their master and mistress, and gaily ran about in circles. The small dog then made a beeline right for a large mud puddle. He splashed through the puddle, followed by a jovial Patches.

Pippa and the elderly gentleman were now making a dash after the two recalcitrant canines. Fortunately, the two dogs had apparently had enough of a run. They stopped and seemed content to stand there, amicably sniffing each other.

Grabbing Patches's lead off the ground, Pippa regarded her dog sternly. "Look at you, Patches! Good heavens, what a mess!" The wet, mud-covered Patches looked up at her mistress and then, giving a mighty shake, sent a large amount of muddy water flying from her fur.

Pippa gave a cry as she was splattered with the dirty spray. "Oh, Patches!" she cried. "Bad girl!" Looking down at her pelisse, Pippa was horrified to see large blotches of mud on it.

The elderly gentleman, who had quickly fastened a leash on the small red dog, regarded Pippa with an apologetic expression. "I am sorry, miss. I fear my Nipper here is a great one for getting into mischief."

Pippa looked first at the fox-faced Nipper and then back at Patches. Both dogs had silly grins on their faces as if they had enjoyed every moment of their escapade. Despite the sorry condition of her poor pelisse, Pippa could not help but laugh. She looked over at the elderly gentleman. "It appears, sir, that our dogs have very much in common."

The gentleman, looking at his small dog and Pippa's large one, laughed along with her.

Although Pippa had predicted that the Viscount Allingham would arrive fashionably late for tea, that gentleman pulled his stylish high-perch phaeton up to the Greys' house just shortly after she and Patches had departed for the park. Eager to have the whole business of tea at the Greys' over with, the viscount strode up to walk to the front entrance.

Bertie chose the moment of Allingham's arrival to look out the drawing-room window. He had hoped to see his sister and Patches returning from their ill-timed walk. "Oh, no," he said, "it's Allingham!"

"Oh, dear!" cried his mother, who had joined her son and husband in the drawing room to await their company. "It cannot be he! Why, Pippa has not yet returned." She wrung her hands in consternation. "How could the girl have gone off like that, knowing that we were expecting Lord Allingham?"

Her husband smiled. "I daresay that is why she went off—to avoid meeting the fellow."

"Really, Peter!"

"Oh, do not worry, my dear. She told Bertie she would be back directly."

The butler entered the room. "Lord Allingham is here, sir."

"Yes, Hawkins," said Grey, "do send his lordship in."

Nodding, the servant left and returned a moment later. "Lord Allingham," he intoned and the viscount appeared before them. As usual, his lordship was dressed to the nines in a fawn-colored coat of superfine, buff-colored pantaloons and spotless black boots. Bertie was nearly overcome at the sight of such grandeur.

"Lord Allingham," said Grey amiably. "How good of you to come. May I present my wife, Mrs. Grey, and my son, Albert?"

The viscount gave Bertie a slight nod and taking Mrs. Grey's hand, he bowed. "I am pleased to meet you, madam," he said.

Mrs. Grey smiled charmingly at him. "Thank you, my lord. Will you please sit down?"

The viscount walked over to an armchair and flipping up the tails of his coat, sat down. His first impression of Mrs. Grey was favorable. She was quite good looking, he decided, and seemed to have tolerably good manners. As for the boy, he was presentable in appearance, despite his unfortunate red hair and abominable green coat.

"I am sorry that my daughter is not here, Lord Allingham," said Mrs. Grey. "She had to go out for a moment. I do hope that she will return shortly. I know that she would be very disappointed to miss your lordship's visit."

The viscount frowned slightly at this information. So the daughter was not in attendance. No doubt he had been right about her and Grey was keeping her away on purpose. "I should be disappointed as well," replied the viscount with some irony.

Allingham's critical gaze took in the drawing room, noting the furniture and decoration. Except for a painting of a child that he found cloyingly sentimental, Allingham quite approved of the rest of the room. He turned to Mrs. Grey. "Your husband has told me that you come from Devonshire, madam." As the viscount had intended, this remark provoked much conversation concerning Mrs. Grey's background and family connections.

After satisfactorily learning all he could about Mrs. Grey, the viscount was ready to focus his attention on Bertie. That young gentleman was almost speechless when the great Allingham asked him a question about what he thought of London.

Before he could reply, there was a sudden commotion in the hall-way. Looking toward the door, Allingham was startled when a huge black-and-white dog came bounding into the drawing room. The ca-nine did not hesitate, but went directly to the viscount. Barking excit-edly, she jumped up, placing her muddy paws on the viscount's lap.

"What the devil?" he cried, leaping up from his seat. Bertie, quite appalled by the scene, pulled Patches away from his lord-ship. Allingham looked down in horror to see big muddy prints on what had been his immaculate pantaloons.

"Oh, no! Patches!" cried a female voice which made the vis-count glance back up. Standing before him was a tall young woman with disheveled auburn hair. She was wearing a mud-covered pelisse and was regarding him with the loveliest pair of blue eyes that he had ever seen. Allingham was temporarily stunned. It was as if he had been suddenly struck by a thunderbolt.

As a man who prided himself on being immune to feminine charms, the viscount's reaction to Pippa was most uncharacteris-tic. Scores of ladies in society had long ago despaired of captur-ing Allingham's heart. In truth, many had decided that the handsome viscount had no heart at all.

Although the rational Allingham would have scoffed at the ridiculous notion of being the victim of Cupid's arrow, it did ap-pear that Pippa had provoked sensations in his lordship that he found quite disturbing. He stood there staring at her as if transfixed.

Finding herself somewhat disconcerted under the intense gaze of the viscount's gray eyes, Pippa quickly began to explain what had happened. While her mother and brother listened to this story with anguished expressions, Pippa's father could hardly refrain from laughing at the sight of the popinjay Allingham in his mud-died pantaloons.

"I am so dreadfully sorry," Pippa was saying. "When I brought Patches inside, she broke away from me, and dashed in here. Oh, dear, she has gotten you quite muddy! Oh, I am sorry!"

To her surprise, a slight smile appeared on the viscount's coun-tenance. "It is of no great import, Miss Grey," he said. "You are Miss Grey, are you not?"

"Yes," said Pippa, regarding the viscount curiously. She thought that he was very handsome and grand looking.

"This is my daughter, Phillippa, Lord Allingham," said Grey. "And that ill-mannered creature is our dog, Patches."

The viscount bowed over Pippa's hand and then gazed down into her blue eyes. "Charmed, Miss Grey," he said. His lordship, who was very fond of dogs, gave Patches a pat on the head. The dog responded by wagging her tail furiously and straining at her leash to get at the viscount again.

"It appears you have an ardent admirer, Lord Allingham." Pippa took the dog's leash from her brother. "I will take her away before she disgraces herself further. Do excuse me. And I am so sorry about Patches, Lord Allingham." With these words she left the drawing room, leaving his lordship to gaze thoughtfully after her.

Coming into the entry hall with the reluctant Patches, Pippa handed the dog over to a footman. She then hurried up to her room to change.

"Oh, miss!" cried her lady's maid, eyeing her with a startled expression.

Pippa looked beyond the servant to her reflection in the dressing table mirror. Her pelisse was mud-splattered and her auburn hair was tousled in wild disarray. Pippa frowned. She looked a complete fright! What must the viscount have thought of her!

Quickly rushing to help her mistress rid herself of the pelisse and dress, the maid looked questioningly at her. "What do you wish to wear, miss?"

Pippa did not hesitate. "I think I will wear my new dress, Betty, the white one with the flowers."

The maid smiled. "Yes, miss, that is quite lovely." As Pippa got dressed, she thought of her disastrous meeting with the viscount. And Mama had said that I should try to make a good impression, she thought wryly. Well, I certainly made an impression in any case, she decided with a smile.

Thinking of Allingham, Pippa grew reflective. Although at first he had seemed rather formidable, staring at her with those intense gray eyes, Pippa suspected that the viscount might not be quite as bad as she had imagined. After all, he had taken the incident quite well and he had seemed to like dogs.

When she had finished buttoning her mistress's dress, Betty hurriedly attempted to fix Pippa's auburn locks into some semblance of order. When the servant had finished, Pippa scrutinized herself in the mirror again. "You have worked a miracle. Thank you, Betty." Taking one last glance at her reflection, Pippa got up to return to the drawing room.

Ever since Pippa had left the room, Allingham had tried to turn his attention back to the other members of the Grey family. However, he seemed to have trouble concentrating on the conversation. It was quite vexing, but he could not stop thinking of Pippa and wondering when she would reappear.

Fortunately for the viscount, Pippa's absence was of short duration. When she reentered the room, Allingham and the other gentlemen rose to their feet. Staring at her, the viscount found himself thinking that she was even more lovely than he had remembered. Attired in a fashionable white dress ornamented with violets, Pippa was quite striking. Her auburn hair was now neatly coiffed with small curls surrounding her face. She smiled over at Allingham and he experienced the same troubling sensations as before.

Mrs. Grey, relieved by her daughter's presentable appearance, smiled. "Ah, Pippa. Now that you are here, I think we should go ahead and have tea."

Pippa, what a delightful nickname, thought his lordship, his eyes still fastened upon her. She was not in the least what he had expected. His critical gaze swept over her, and he noted her excellent figure, lovely smile, and extraordinary blue eyes. With some difficulty he managed to turn his attention back to Bertie. He must not sit gaping at the girl like some silly mooncalf, he told himself.

Although she was aware of his scrutiny, Pippa could not have imagined the turmoil she had created in the viscount. After ringing for tea, she sat down in an armchair next to her brother. This put her directly across from their illustrious guest.

Bertie, having recovered from his acute embarrassment, was listening to Allingham as if he were dispensing the wisdom of the ages. In actuality, his lordship was informing the young man about the best bootmakers in the city. Although this topic was of infinite interest to Bertie, Pippa was somewhat disappointed.

When the subject continued on to the matter of tailors, Pippa began to grow slightly bored. She was glad when the servants appeared with the diversion of tea. Mrs. Grey, pleased that things were going so smoothly now, poured out the tea and instructed Pippa to hand the first cup to the viscount.

When Pippa handed the teacup over to Allingham, his lordship scarcely glanced at her. The viscount was, in fact, quite aware of that lady's disturbing presence, but he was determined to put on an appearance of polite indifference.

As Pippa handed her brother his teacup, Bertie was just telling the viscount about his tailor. "I go to Harrington on Cherry Street," said Bertie proudly. "He made this coat for me."

Pippa noted the disdainful glance the viscount cast at the garment. "I fear, Grey, I would not waste another farthing on this Harrington," he said, lifting his teacup to his lips.

Bertie looked totally crestfallen. "You do not like this coat, my lord?"

The viscount took a sip of his tea and gave a slight shrug. "It is a mediocre coat from a mediocre tailor." Pippa was amazed at Allingham's bluntness. He continued. "Do not fear, young man. I shall introduce you to my tailor."

"Would you, sir?" asked Bertie, who at that moment reminded Pippa of an eager puppy. Allingham nodded slightly and the young man seemed elated.

Grey, who like his daughter, had been uninterested in the talk of boots and tailors, suddenly perked up by this exchange between Allingham and his son. "You would take my son to your tailor, Allingham? Does that mean that you intend to take him up in society as well?"

Allingham hesitated, putting down his teacup. It did seem that Mrs. Grey and her children were respectable enough, despite their unfortunate connection to trade. Surely it would do no harm to introduce them into society. And there was, of course, a considerable financial imperative for doing so.

Turning to Grey, he nodded. "Yes, Mr. Grey, I shall do what I can to introduce your family into society." He glanced over at Pippa. Although he was disturbed by the feelings that that young lady had engendered in him, the prospect of a more intimate connection with her was not unappealing.

"Oh, Lord Allingham!" cried Mrs. Grey, clasping her hands together joyfully. "You are very kind."

"That is splendid!" cried Bertie, who could hardly contain his excitement.

Grey, although much less effusive than his wife and son, smiled. "I am glad to hear it, Allingham."

The viscount smiled slightly, as if he were a benevolent monarch dispensing the royal largesse. He glanced at the Greys as if they were his grateful subjects. However, when his gaze fell upon the lovely Pippa, he was surprised to find that that lady did not look overcome with joy. Allingham turned back to her father. "I must make a condition to this arrangement, Mr. Grey."

"Condition, my lord?"

"My condition is this," said the viscount. "If your family is to be accepted by society, each family member must agree to do what I say. It is very important that my advice be taken in all things—what to wear, to whom to speak." He paused. "And whom to avoid. Indeed, there will be much for you to learn."

Pippa regarded the viscount rather indignantly. Having had earlier revised her opinion of his lordship, she now found herself thinking that her original estimation of Allingham was much more on the mark. He seemed able to talk of nothing but boots and clothes, and it was clear he considered them bumpkins in dire need of instruction.

"Oh, of course, Lord Allingham," said Mrs. Grey. "We should be honored to have the assistance of a gentleman such as yourself."

Raising her eyebrows at her mother's shameless flattery, Pippa frowned again. She was quite glad when the viscount announced that he must take his leave. As he made his farewells, he stopped before Pippa. "Good day, Miss Grey," he said, his eyes regarding her once again with an intense expression.

Pippa, assuming that the viscount was scrutinizing her for faults, felt her face reddening. "Lord Allingham," she said coolly. Nodding slightly, he left the room.

The moment he had gone, Mrs. Grey went to her husband and gave him a hug. "Thank you, Peter! It is everything that I could ever hope for! To have Allingham take us under his wing! I can scarcely believe it!"

Bertie smiled. "And he is allowing me to accompany him to his tailor tomorrow!"

His father grinned at him. "Good lord, my son, the nonesuch!" He looked over at Pippa. "You are unusually quiet, my girl. What did you think of the great tulip?"

"I will say that he seemed an expert on boots and tailoring," said Pippa. "Indeed, now that I have met the great man, I can understand why we must all fawn upon his every word."

Her daughter's sarcasm was not lost on Mrs. Grey. "Why, Pippa," she said, "I thought Lord Allingham was quite charming. I daresay, he showed considerable restraint over Patches getting mud all over him. I was so mortified! And you, Pippa, coming in looking like some wild gypsy!"

Grey grinned. "Come now, Louisa, it was not as bad as all of that. Pippa looked enchanting. I think Allingham was quite impressed with our mud-covered daughter." He winked at Pippa.

"Oh, Papa," she smiled, "don't be absurd."

Grey laughed. "I'm not absurd, my girl. But I am famished. I'm going to have another piece of Cook's excellent lemon sponge cake."

Pippa smiled and they all went back to the tea table to further discuss the viscount's visit.

5

The morning after his visit to the Greys, the viscount was in a peculiarly restless mood. After pacing about the drawing room for a time, he sought out the solace of his library. However, even his beloved books were unable to hold his lordship's attention for long. His mind kept wandering back to the lovely Pippa.

Finding his turbulent feelings for the tradesman's daughter most unsettling, Allingham chided himself for behaving as if he were some silly schoolboy in love for the first time. The viscount frowned. In truth, he had never been silly as a schoolboy and he had never been in love, either. He had always considered himself above such nonsense.

Walking over to the bookshelf, the viscount selected a volume on astronomy. He then sat down in a leather armchair and opened the book, hoping that a rational scientific discussion would distract him from his romantic notions. However, he soon found his thoughts straying from the constellations back to Pippa Grey.

Frowning, he stared gloomily into space. Allingham had been somewhat perplexed by the young lady's apparent coolness toward him. She had seemed friendly enough at first, he thought. However, during the course of tea, he had noted a distinct chill, as if he had said or done something to displease her. Allingham grew reflective. He could not remember doing or saying anything that would have offended Pippa. Yet it appeared that the lady had not had a favorable opinion of him.

The viscount was not accustomed to women disliking him. After all, he was society's leading gentleman. The ladies, well aware of Allingham's lofty position, were eager to have him take notice of them. They usually followed him about, eager for a word from him. Even receiving criticism from the viscount was considered a mark of distinction.

"My lord?" came a voice and Allingham looked over to find his butler had entered the room. The servant was carrying a salver and presented it to the viscount. "A messenger delivered this letter for your lordship."

Allingham picked up the missive. "Thank you, Morris," he said and the butler nodded and left the room.

Opening the envelope, the viscount found a short note and a check for twenty-five thousand pounds. He stared at the check for a moment and then read the brief note from Grey. "My lord," it said. "I believe this sum is sufficient. With sincere appreciation, Your Servant, Peter Grey."

The viscount pushed the letter aside and looked again at the check. It was more than enough to pay off the string of creditors that had been plaguing him.

The viscount frowned again, wondering if he were doing the right thing in accepting Grey's money. He was not happy at having agreed to sell his influence in such a way. Surely it was hardly the act of a gentleman. But what choice did he have?

His lordship looked down at Grey's note. So now he had sold himself for twenty-five thousand pounds. An ironic smile came to his face. Well, certainly men had sold themselves for much less, he reflected. Now he was in Grey's service and he must start at once to get the man's family accepted by society.

The viscount placed the check in the breast pocket of his coat. He must do his duty and get right to work. He was planning to take young Albert to his tailor that afternoon. That would be a considerable first step. He must also write down some advice that would be quite useful for entering the somewhat choppy waters of the London social scene.

Taking out some paper and a quill pen from his desk, the viscount began to write hastily. After a time, he stopped and carefully studied the page before him. He smiled slightly, quite pleased with his catalog of how to succeed in the *ton*.

Having finished writing his advice, the viscount pondered the best way to introduce the Greys to elite company. Perhaps the Fairfields' ball, he thought. However, he quickly dismissed the idea. It would be better to have them get their feet wet first at a smaller function. Allingham suddenly had an idea. Of course, he thought, the duchess! Calling for a servant, his lordship ordered his carriage brought round. After taking care of some financial matters, he would pay a visit to the Duchess of Northampton.

Some time later, the viscount pulled up his vehicle in front of the residence of the Duke and Duchess of Northampton, which was one of the grandest houses in all of London. He was quickly

ushered to a small sitting room where her grace was ensconced on
a sofa, a large tortoise-shell cat sitting on her lap.

The duchess, a plump, matronly lady of sixty, who had silver
hair under a lace cap, regarded his lordship in surprise. "Allingham, my dear boy. Whatever brings you here at such an hour? I
did not think you ever rose before noon."

The viscount graciously took the hand that she held out to him.
He bowed gravely. "Perhaps I am reforming, Duchess."

Her grace laughed. "I shan't believe that, young man. Now do
sit down." She eagerly patted the seat next to her. "I am so glad
that you have come. I have not had any diverting company or
fresh gossip all week."

The viscount smiled and sat down on the sofa. "It appears that
Claudia is in fine fettle," he said.

The duchess smiled and fondly petted the furry creature on her
lap. "She has been a very naughty cat, stealing a kipper from the
sideboard at breakfast. The duke was not amused."

Allingham appeared to agree with his grace. He regarded the
cat sternly. "I fear you are a most rag-mannered feline, Claudia."
The cat appeared indifferent to the viscount's rebuke, merely
snuggling closer to her mistress.

Her Grace grinned over at him. "It looks as if everyone is not
crushed by your disapproval, Allingham."

He ignored this remark and glanced about the room. "But
where is Chloe?" As if on cue, a smaller gray-striped cat suddenly
appeared from a hiding place behind a large potted palm. "Ah,
there she is." The cat made her way over to the viscount. Staring
up at him with large blue eyes, she suddenly jumped up onto his
lap. He then proceeded to stroke her gently, causing the small cat
to purr contentedly.

The duchess shook her head. "You do have a way with the
creature, Allingham. Chloe usually hides under the furniture
when anyone else is about."

"Yes, well, Chloe always shows remarkably good judgment,
Duchess. I daresay, some of your acquaintances make me want to
dive under the sofa as well."

Instead of being offended, the duchess laughed. "You are
dreadful, Allingham." She paused and regarded him with interest.
"Now, do tell me what you have come to see me about. It is obvious that you have something on your mind."

Allingham hesitated. The duchess was an old and dear friend of
his. One of the leading hostesses of society, her grace had taken
an immediate liking to the young Allingham when she had first

met him almost ten years ago. The viscount was very fond of the duchess, viewing her much as one would a slightly eccentric, favorite aunt.

A private man, Allingham did not often reveal very much of himself to others. Her grace was one of the few persons with whom Allingham would occasionally let down his guard. However, since he did not wish for her to know his true connection with the Greys, the viscount decided he had best be careful in what he said about them.

"I must confess, Duchess, that I did come to ask you a favor," he said finally. "It's about your soiree."

"Oh, dear," she said. "I knew you would be upset when you found out. I do hope you will still come, Allingham."

He eyed her with a puzzled expression. "I do not know what you mean. Found out what?"

"Then you did not know about Seagrave?"

As usual, Allingham frowned when he heard that gentleman's name. "What about Seagrave?"

"It is only that I had to invite the odious man to my soiree. My husband was quite adamant about it. I fear he is quite mutton-headed where young Seagrave is concerned. But, you know that the late baron was a good friend of his."

The viscount nodded. He was well aware that the Duke of Northampton liked Seagrave and disliked him. Since he did not want to be a bone of contention between the duchess and her husband, he shrugged. "It does not signify if Seagrave is there, ma'am. He shall not keep me away."

She smiled. "I'm glad to hear it, Allingham." She paused and regarded him curiously. "But what is this favor that you are talking about?"

The viscount tried to appear nonchalant. "I wondered if you might invite some additional persons to your soiree. A Mrs. Grey and her two children."

Her grace raised an eyebrow. "Indeed? Mrs. Grey? Do I know her?"

"I am sure you have not had that pleasure, Duchess. I have just recently made her acquaintance. She is a charming lady."

"She is not one of Lord Darlington's cousins? The one who married George Grey, the black sheep of the family?"

"Certainly not."

"Well, I cannot imagine who she might be. I thought I knew everyone, Allingham."

The viscount smiled. "You do not know her, my dear duchess. No one does. She has come from Portsmouth."

"Oh, dear," said the duchess. "Does anyone come from Portsmouth?"

"I daresay the Greys do."

"You must tell me about them. Do not be mysterious. Is this Mrs. Grey a widow?"

Allingham shook his head. "No, she is married."

"And who is her husband?"

"His name is Peter Grey." He paused. "He has made an enormous fortune in shipping."

Her grace looked surprised. "I believe I have heard of him. But I must say, I cannot understand how you should know such persons." The duchess shook her head. "My dear Allingham, you are asking a favor that I cannot grant. Why, the duke would be furious at the idea of having this Mr. Grey in his house."

"But it is not Mr. Grey who wishes to come. It is his wife and children. They are perfectly acceptable. Mrs. Grey is a Chesterton—they are respectable Devonshire gentry. Her family was not happy at her marrying Grey although the fellow is now as rich as Croesus. The duke could have no possible objections to Mrs. Grey and her children."

The duchess appeared thoughtful. "I should very much like to know why you wish to have them come to my soiree."

The viscount put on an expression of bored indifference. "Oh, it is just a whim of mine, Duchess."

The elderly lady regarded him with a hawk-like expression. "You are not a whimsical man, Allingham. I find this very odd." She paused. "You said there are two children?"

"Yes, a son and a daughter."

"A daughter?" asked the duchess, suddenly appearing enlightened. "An unmarried daughter?"

"Yes."

The duchess smiled. "And is she pretty?"

The viscount, who was well aware of the direction her grace was heading, nodded. "Tolerably pretty," he said, glancing down at the cat on his lap to avoid the elderly woman's penetrating gaze.

"My dear Allingham, I would not have believed it!" cried the duchess. "You have a *tendre* for this tradesman's daughter!"

His lordship scowled. "Do not be ridiculous."

Her grace smiled knowingly. "Very well, I shall not say another word. And, indeed, I shall be more than happy to invite this young lady and her mother and brother to my soiree. I will be most eager to meet the girl. What is her name?"

"Pippa," he said and then quickly corrected himself. "I mean to say, Phillippa is her actual name."

"Pippa. How charming." She smiled again. "It appears my soiree promises to be most entertaining."

Allingham pretended to ignore her insinuations. "Thank you, Duchess." After providing her with the Greys' address, he somewhat hastily took his leave, much to the disappointment of her grace and the cat Chloe. After he departed, the duchess wondered about the young woman who had so apparently captivated her friend Allingham.

Pippa sat at a small table in the drawing room, writing a letter. Her mother sat nearby on the sofa, halfheartedly working at a needlework design of yellow and purple pansies. Every so often Mrs. Grey would glance somewhat impatiently in her daughter's direction.

"It does appear that you have much to tell Agnes, Pippa," the older woman said finally.

Pippa looked up and smiled. "Yes, I fear I shall run out of paper before I run out of news."

Mrs. Grey nodded. "Well, I do not doubt that Agnes shall be glad to hear from you, even if the girl can hardly help but be envious when she hears of your life in town."

Pippa did not reply, but returned to the letter. She knew that her mother would not be pleased to find out that she considered her friend Agnes the fortunate one. How she wished she could be back in Portsmouth with her!

Although Pippa would have had to admit that London was an exciting and fascinating place, she would have given much to return to her former home. She very much missed her friends and the pleasant life she had had there. Unlike her mother and brother, Pippa was not at all eager to enter the glittering social whirl of London.

After writing a few more paragraphs to her friend, including the wish that Agnes would visit her at first opportunity, Pippa finished her letter. As she addressed the missive, her brother entered the room. Dressed in ivory pantaloons, a blue-striped coat, and a canary-colored waistcoat, Bertie appeared nervous as he sat down on the sofa next to his mother.

That lady smiled brightly at him and happily put down her needlework. "You look very handsome, Bertie."

"Do you really think so, Mama?" he asked. "I did want to appear well dressed for Lord Allingham." He appeared doubtful. "Do you think he will approve of this waistcoat? And I fear my neckcloth is not quite the thing."

"Good heavens, Bertie," said Pippa, getting up from the table and walking over to the sofa, "why do you care what you look like? I thought Allingham was taking you to his tailor to rectify all the grievous faults of your wardrobe."

Bertie frowned and Mrs. Grey quickly jumped in. "It was quite kind of his lordship to offer his assistance."

Pippa frowned. "Kind? Is he not getting paid for his assistance? I am sure Lord Allingham would not even deign to speak to us if it weren't for Papa's money."

Her mother shook her head. "Really, Pippa, you must watch that tongue of yours. Now, Lord Allingham should be here shortly and you must promise you will be on your best behavior."

"I shall do something even better, Mama," said Pippa. "I will not be here when he arrives. I have my letter to post. And I wanted to go to the bookstore . . . "

Mrs. Grey interrupted her daughter. "You shall do no such thing, my girl! You will stay here until Lord Allingham arrives and you will be civil to him! Do you understand?"

"Oh, very well, Mama. I shall try to be civil to him."

"Try?" repeated her mother, regarding her with a disapproving expression. "You had better do more than try, Pippa."

Pippa sighed in resignation and sat down in an armchair to await the great tulip's arrival. Fortunately, Allingham was once again punctual as he appeared at the Greys' door precisely at two o'clock.

As the viscount was ushered into the drawing room, Bertie rushed over to him. "Lord Allingham." To his chagrin, he thought that gentleman was eyeing his canary waistcoat with disfavor.

"Grey," said Allingham, nodding condescendingly at the young man. He glanced over at Mrs. Grey and made a slight bow. "Madam." His eye then fell upon Pippa. Trying to seem disinterested, the viscount gave her a slight nod. "Miss Grey."

Noting his haughty expression, Pippa frowned. It appeared that Allingham thought she was hardly worthy of his consideration. She would have liked to respond to him in an equally haughty fashion. However, thinking of her mother, she managed to smile. "Lord Allingham," she replied politely.

It would have quite shocked Pippa if she had known the viscount's true thoughts at that moment. His air of indifference was once again masking his rather agitated feelings. He thought Pippa looked quite lovely in her simple lilac-colored dress, her auburn hair piled up in a knot on top of her head.

"Do sit down for a moment, Lord Allingham," said Mrs. Grey. The viscount smiled slightly and took the chair next to Pippa.

"My brother is quite excited about making the acquaintance of your tailor, my lord," said Pippa. "It is a very great honor for Bertie, I'm sure."

Although he thought he detected some irony in Pippa's tone, the viscount nodded. "Weston is an artist without equal, Miss Grey."

Bertie agreed enthusiastically. "I daresay your coat is proof of that, my lord. It is all the crack!"

Allingham glanced at Pippa and found she was eyeing his coat with considerable interest. When he met her gaze, she smiled mischievously at him. "Indeed, Lord Allingham. Your coat is a veritable masterpiece." Allingham was not quite certain how he should take this remark and he regarded Pippa with slightly raised eyebrows.

Mrs. Grey directed a warning look at her daughter. Pippa seemed in one of her flippant moods and one never knew what she might say. Mrs. Grey turned to the viscount. "I am so pleased that you are assisting Bertie, Lord Allingham. It is so important that he makes the right impression in society." She paused and looked again at her daughter. "That we *all* make the right impression."

The viscount was relieved to turn his attention back to Mrs. Grey and the topic of their entrance into society. "That is very true, madam." He paused. "And, you will soon be able to make that impression. You will shortly be receiving an invitation from the Duchess of Northampton for a soiree she is hosting."

Mrs. Grey could hardly contain her excitement. "The Duchess of Northampton! Oh, but that is wonderful, Lord Allingham!"

"Oh, yes," said Bertie, "that is simply splendid news, my lord!"

The viscount seemed gratified by their response. "Yes, the duchess is highly regarded in society. Only a select company receives invitations to her soirees. And I have reason to believe that a certain royal personage might be attending."

Pippa's mother clutched at her bosom. "You cannot mean that His Royal Highness may be there?"

Allingham shrugged. "One can never be certain. But I thought it was best that you be forewarned so you would not be too surprised."

"That is so good of you, my lord," said Pippa, regarding him with an amused expression. "I should not want to swoon in His Royal Highness's presence."

The viscount decided that the lady was enjoying some sort of sport with him. He managed to smile slightly. "You do not appear to be of a swooning nature, Miss Grey."

Pippa's mother, worried that her headstrong daughter would offend Allingham, attempted once again to attract his attention. "We are so pleased to receive such an invitation, Lord Allingham. When is the soirée to be held?"

"Thursday next," said the viscount. "So it does not allow very much time for preparation." He reached inside his coat and retrieved some papers. "I have taken the liberty, madam, of writing down some advice that I think you will find useful."

As Mrs. Grey took the papers, Pippa eyed Allingham curiously. "What type of advice, my lord?"

"I have written some important rules of etiquette, Miss Grey. And I have also included a list of the names of certain persons. Some of them may be at this soirée. Some of them most certainly will not. I thought you should know how to behave if you should chance to meet any of them."

Pippa could scarcely believe her ears. She got up from her armchair and went over to glance at the paper over her mother's shoulder. Written in an elegant hand was a long list of names with brief comments written next to them. Pippa read the first name "Richard Mannerling, the Marquess of Sheffield" and the remark next to it, "a leader of the *ton*, treat with proper deference." There were several names following this, all indicating a highly placed person worthy of attention. However, as the list continued there were certain names that contained remarks such as "you may safely ignore" or "snub with impunity."

As she read through the list, Pippa did not know whether to be angry or amused. It just confirmed her suspicion that Lord Allingham was the most pompous, supercilious man in the kingdom. Her eye alighted on one name and she glanced up at his lordship. "You have written next to an Isabelle, Lady Granville, 'do not under *any* circumstances have anything to do with this woman.' You seem quite emphatic, my lord. What is this lady's crime?"

Allingham crossed his arms in front of his chest. "I fear that is not a fit subject for a lady to hear," he said. "Let it suffice to say that the woman is quite notorious."

"Quite notorious?" said Pippa.

The viscount nodded. "I do not consider her fit company for

you, Miss Grey. If you are so unfortunate as to make her acquaintance, you must shun her company."

Pippa frowned at his sanctimonious attitude, but made no reply. Instead, she resolved that if she ever met the notorious Lady Granville, she would be very eager to be friendly with her.

Mrs. Grey, who had silently prayed that her daughter would not make a terrible blunder, was relieved that Pippa remained quiet. "Thank you, my lord," said Mrs. Grey, putting down the paper, "we shall make a study of this."

Bertie, who had also been afraid of his sister insulting the viscount, hurriedly chimed in. "Yes, Mama, we certainly shall do that. Now, I think Lord Allingham and I had better be off. We would not want to keep his lordship's tailor waiting."

The viscount nodded and rose from his seat. However, before he could take his leave, Pippa stood suddenly before him. "And do you not have any advice for me as well, my lord?" she asked, a mocking look in her beautiful blue eyes.

Allingham raised a dark eyebrow. "Advice for you, Miss Grey?" he asked.

"Yes, I daresay, I could not possibly meet with your approval. Indeed, I find it hard to believe that anyone could. Come, what are my faults, my lord? What should I change so that I might be considered deserving of notice by exalted persons such as yourself?"

"Pippa!" cried Mrs. Grey in alarm. Bertie could only eye his sister in horror.

Allingham glanced down at her, eyeing her slowly from head to foot. His intense scrutiny made her blush. His ice-gray eyes met her angry blue ones. "I should not change a thing, Miss Grey," he said simply. Pippa was so surprised that she found herself without a reply.

The viscount turned to Mrs. Grey. "Good day, madam," he said and without a further word, he left. After glancing disapprovingly at his sister, Bertie hurried out after him.

"Oh, Pippa," said Mrs. Grey, "how could you do such a thing? What must Lord Allingham think?"

Pippa was unrepentant. "I do not care a button what that insufferable man thinks, Mama!" Mrs. Grey could only shake her head and wish that she had a more manageable daughter.

6

After receiving a lecture from her mother about her disgraceful behavior toward the Viscount Allingham, Pippa appeared somewhat more contrite. Realizing how upset her mother was, she apologized to her and promised that she would be more civil to Allingham in the future.

Although far from satisfied with her daughter's sudden penitence, Mrs. Grey decided it was best to let the matter rest for the time being. However, she was determined to have a word with her husband about Pippa. Surely he would be able to make the girl behave more sensibly.

Mrs. Grey was well aware that her daughter thought more of her husband's opinion than her own. Since Pippa had been a child, she had adored her papa. In truth, the girl was very much like her father, strong-willed and stubborn.

Deciding that it was best for Pippa to be absent when the viscount returned, Mrs. Grey was more than happy when her daughter announced that she wished to go out for the afternoon. Pippa, very glad to escape, hurriedly put on a lilac-colored pelisse that matched her dress. Then, donning a bonnet trimmed in white satin and pink ribbons, she took up her reticule and left the house, accompanied by her maid Betty.

Walking along the street, Pippa had much time to reflect upon her second meeting with Lord Allingham. As she thought of the viscount's list, she frowned. She was certain that if he were not under obligation to her family, Allingham would feel no compunction in snubbing them as well. She imagined a new entry on his list, "Peter Grey and family—provincial nobodies. In trade. Pretend they do not exist." Pippa smiled at the thought.

After posting her letter to Agnes, Pippa and her maid walked on until they came to a row of shops. Pippa had found a number of excellent bookstores since moving to London. She had to admit that it was one advantage that London had over her beloved Portsmouth.

Pippa was particularly pleased with Eaton and Son, Booksellers, a small, crowded establishment that had a splendid assortment of titles. As she and Betty approached the shop, Pippa was filled with eager anticipation. Entering the bookstore, Pippa began to peruse the shelves that were packed with newly published volumes.

Betty, who could not understand her mistress's excitement over books, stood at a discreet distance. The worthy servant found it much more entertaining to study the interesting, and in some cases, eccentric-looking patrons browsing in the bookstore.

Unlike her servant, Pippa was quite unaware of the people around her. Feeling like a child in a candy shop, she happily picked up one book after another. After studying the bookseller's wares for a considerable time, Pippa decided to purchase a volume of poetry by the scandalous Lord Byron, a book on Greek mythology, and a political tract condemning the government's apathy toward the city's homeless and impoverished children.

As she made her way down the narrow aisle toward the clerk, a rather stout gentleman barged past her, causing one of her books to fly out of her arms. Before she could make a move, another gentleman appeared beside her. "I shall retrieve it for you, ma'am," he said gallantly, bending over and picking up the book. He studied it carefully. "It appears unharmed," he said, smiling amiably at Pippa.

"Thank you, sir," she said, returning his smile. Approximately thirty years of age, the young gentleman standing before her was quite handsome with blond hair, blue eyes, and a charming smile. Pippa thought he could very well have been a hero who had stepped out from her volume of Greek mythology.

Taking another glance at the book he held in his hand, the gentleman handed it back to her. "I must say, ma'am, you have excellent taste in your choice of books."

"I'm glad you approve," said Pippa with an amused expression as she took the book back from him.

He laughed. "You see, I would have to approve since I published that particular volume."

Pippa regarded him in surprise. "You are the publisher of this book?" she asked.

He nodded. "Allow me to introduce myself, ma'am. I am William Cartwright of Cartwright Publishing."

Pippa was quite impressed by this information for she remembered seeing the Cartwright name on several of the books she owned. "I am so glad to meet you, Mr. Cartwright. I am Miss Pippa Grey."

Taking the hand that she offered him, Mr. Cartwright reflected that Miss Grey was a very attractive young woman. Betty, seeing the handsome young man with her mistress, watched their meeting with considerable interest.

"I believe you have also published another book I have just read," said Pippa, "one by Mr. Josiah Kent."

Cartwright grinned. "Indeed, I have. I must say, Miss Grey, I am most gratified to find someone who has purchased our books. I fear that you are in a very select company."

Pippa laughed. "I very much hope that is not the case, Mr. Cartwright. It is quite admirable that you publish works on such important issues."

"Then you are interested in social causes, Miss Grey?" asked Cartwright.

"Oh, yes," said Pippa eagerly. "I do think there are so many injustices in society that need to be rectified, such as those Mr. Kent spoke of in his book."

"Yes, the problems can seem overwhelming, Miss Grey. But one must do what one can to bring about solutions."

Pippa nodded. She was developing a very favorable opinion of the young publisher as he continued to discuss the problems described by the reformer Josiah Kent. Their conversation then turned to the many authors Cartwright knew. They stood talking for a considerable time, causing Pippa's maid to wistfully imagine that a romance was blossoming between her mistress and the handsome stranger.

Although she could have talked to Cartwright much longer, Pippa finally announced that she really must take her leave. The young man seemed very disappointed. "It has been a great pleasure to speak with you, Miss Grey," he said. Pausing, he regarded her hopefully. "I wonder if I might be able to call upon you?"

"I should very much like that, Mr. Cartwright," said Pippa. The young publisher smiled and handed her his card. Pippa reciprocated by pulling a calling card from her reticule.

Glancing down at the card, Cartwright read the address. He did not fail to note that Phillipa lived in one of the most exclusive neighborhoods in the city. She was obviously a young lady of wealth and privilege. While Pippa might be interested in his causes, Cartwright doubted that she could be interested in a man of limited means like himself.

Still, as Pippa took her leave of him, Cartwright smiled hopefully. As he watched her pay for her books and then depart from the bookstore, William Cartwright resolved that he would visit the lovely and intelligent Miss Grey at first opportunity.

Arriving home quite late in the afternoon, Pippa was greeted by the butler. "Good afternoon, Miss Grey."

"Hawkins," said Pippa in a conspiratorial whisper. "Are there callers in the drawing room?"

Hawkins tried not to smile. "No, miss. Lord Allingham was here, but he has gone. Master Albert is alone in the drawing room."

"I see," replied Pippa, relieved to hear that the viscount had departed.

Taking off her pelisse and bonnet and handing them to Betty, Pippa made her way to the drawing room, where she found her brother seated on the sofa with Patches lying at his feet.

The black-and-white dog got up and hurried over to Pippa, her tail wagging furiously. While Patches was clearly overjoyed by her mistress's arrival, it was obvious that Bertie was still annoyed with Pippa. He eyed her with considerable disapproval as he watched her pet Patches and then come and join him on the sofa.

"So, Bertie, were you suitably awed by the great Weston?" asked Pippa, ignoring his censorious expression.

He frowned. "I fear I do not find your sarcastic comments very amusing, Pippa. And I daresay, neither did Lord Allingham."

Pippa shook her head. "I'm sorry if I offended you, Brother. But, truly, I do not understand how you can think Allingham is such a paragon. I find him haughty and insufferable."

"Insufferable?" said Bertie. "Why, he is nothing of the kind. He was quite good about everything. When I tried to apologize for your rudeness . . . "

Pippa's eyes grew wide. "You apologized for *my* rudeness?"

Bertie nodded vigorously. "I tried to, in any case. But Lord Allingham would not hear of it. He said the matter was of no consequence to him."

"Of no consequence to him?" repeated Pippa indignantly.

"Yes," said Bertie, "although I could tell he had been very much offended. Really, Pippa, it was too bad of you to say such things to him."

"It was too bad of me? And what of Allingham? Writing that list of names, telling us which people we should snub! You cannot believe that he would condescend to take any notice of us if Papa had not paid him to do so."

Bertie stubbornly crossed his arms in front of him. "You may think of him what you will, Pippa. I find Allingham a most agreeable gentleman. He was quite solicitous toward me at his tailor's."

"I do not doubt that, brother. He doesn't want you to disgrace him among his snobbish friends."

Bertie stood up. "I shall not listen to any more of this, Pippa. You are being totally unreasonable about Allingham. He can do much to assist you."

"I do not want his assistance," said Pippa. "Indeed, I dearly wish Mama did not have her heart set on our entering society. Why should we wish to be part of such an odious institution?"

Bertie regarded his sister incredulously. That anyone would not wish to be part of London's glittering society seemed unbelievable. "I do not think there's any point in further discussion if that is how you feel," said Bertie. Frowning at her, he walked out of the room.

Pippa frowned in return. She wondered how she and her brother could differ so profoundly. Bertie seemed to hero worship Allingham and want nothing more than to follow in his footsteps. Shaking her head, Pippa decided that Bertie could sometimes be a great blockhead.

A few moments later, she looked up as her mother entered the room. "So, you are back, Pippa. I must say you stayed away a very long time."

"Well, I didn't want to see Allingham again, Mama," said Pippa.

"I cannot understand why you have taken such a dislike to him. Lord Allingham is a delightful gentleman."

"Delightful? Oh, Mama, he is so dreadfully proud. It was very clear he thinks himself far above us."

"I don't know why you would say such a thing, Pippa. He was perfectly charming. Now you must promise me that you will be civil to him in the future. Do not forget that his influence is enormous."

"I am well aware how influential he is, Mama," replied Pippa. While she wanted to add that she did not care at all about Allingham's influence, Pippa did not wish to vex her mother any further. "I shall try to be civil."

Rather encouraged by this, Mrs. Grey smiled. "That is all I ask, my dear. But where have you been all this time? You cannot have spent the rest of the afternoon in a bookstore?"

Pippa smiled. "As a matter of fact, that is exactly what I did. Oh, Mama, I had a very enjoyable afternoon. I met the most charming gentleman."

Her mother eyed her with sudden alarm. "What? You met a gentleman?"

"Yes, in the bookstore. You see, I dropped one of my books and he picked it up for me."

"Oh, Pippa," said her mother. "you did not encourage a strange gentleman to speak with you?"

"He was perfectly respectable, Mama," insisted Pippa. "His name is William Cartwright. He gave me his card. Here it is."

Mrs. Grey studied the card with disapprobation. "Cartwright Publishing? This gentleman was in the publishing business?"

Pippa bristled a bit at the uncomplimentary way in which her mother made this remark. "Yes. He publishes very serious and important books, Mama. I found him a very admirable gentleman."

Mrs. Grey did not like the sound of this at all. "Was he an older gentleman, Pippa?" she asked, hoping this Mr. Cartwright was a balding man with a stooping posture.

"Oh, no, Mama. I should not think he was more than thirty." She smiled. "And he is very handsome."

Mrs. Grey was rather disturbed by her daughter's enthusiasm. Pippa was usually quite critical of the male sex. Her reaction toward this Mr. Cartwright was worrisome. "My dear, I hope you haven't formed any foolish attachment."

"Foolish attachment, Mama?" Pippa burst into laughter. "Really, Mama, I only just met the man. And you know me well enough to know that I do not form 'foolish attachments.' If you fear that I shall elope with him to Gretna Greene tonight, you may rest assured that I shall not do so. I believe a girl should know a gentleman for at least a week before thinking of elopement."

Mrs. Grey did not appear amused. "Why must you always be so flippant?"

"Oh, Mama, I'm not always flippant. But you must admit it is absurd to think I should fall in love with a man I only just met in a bookstore scarcely two hours ago."

"Why is it absurd? Girls fall in love with men they meet every day."

"Not I, Mama," said Pippa with a smile. "But if I did fall in love, I daresay it might be with someone like Mr. Cartwright. He is such an admirable gentleman. And his company publishes such admirable works."

Mrs. Grey did not like the sound of this remark. "I do hope you realize such a man would be totally unsuitable."

"I don't see why Mr. Cartwright should be considered unsuitable. He appears to be a very nice and charming man. I'm sure he is hardworking and respectable."

"But, my dear, he's not the sort of man that you should marry."

Pippa laughed. "Marry? Truly, Mama, I'm hardly thinking of marrying Mr. Cartwright." She paused for a moment. Then, smiling mischievously, she added. "Not yet in any case."

"Pippa!"

"Oh, Mama!" said Pippa, laughing again. "But who is the sort of man I should marry, Mama? I suppose you imagine it is someone like Lord Allingham?"

Her mother sighed. "You have formed a dreadful prejudice against that gentleman, Pippa. But, yes, I want you to marry a man in society, a man with a title and position. I don't believe I should be faulted for wishing my daughter to marry well."

"Good heavens, Mama, I don't understand you. After all, you married Papa, a man who had neither title nor position, and who made his fortune in trade. Surely, you couldn't have found a better man than Papa!"

Mrs. Grey nodded. "You are right about your father, my dear. I could not have a better husband. But, marrying him was not easy. You know well how my family disapproved of the match. They thought I was marrying beneath me. And while I've been very happy with your father, I have had to suffer such humiliation. I don't want you to suffer the slights that I have had to endure. No, indeed, I want you to be accepted anywhere." She paused and took her daughter's hand. "I know it's hard for you to understand, Pippa, but I only want what is best for you."

"Oh, Mama, I know you do," replied her daughter fondly. "But let us talk no more about the sort of man I should marry. In truth, I think I should be much happier as an old maid."

"Pippa!" cried her mother in horror. "You mustn't say such a thing!"

Pippa laughed. "Oh, very well, Mama. Let us speak no more of marriage. But I must tell you more about Mr. Cartwright. He is such a fascinating gentleman."

Although her mother was far from pleased at her daughter's apparent interest in Mr. Cartwright, she expressed no further disapproval. After all, Mrs. Grey always found it so alarming to hear her daughter express a preference for spinsterhood that the idea of Mr. Cartwright did not seem quite so bad.

7

Shortly after arriving at his club, Allingham decided that he had made a mistake in coming there that day. He had hoped to find a peaceful haunt to sit and read the latest issue of his favorite magazine. Instead, a boisterous group of gentlemen had gathered there, loudly recounting the glories of past hunts. As he sat in a large, comfortable armchair, his lordship cast some disdainful glances over at the crowd as they laughed and regaled one another with their exaggerated tales.

The viscount had an unusual aversion toward blood sports, considering them barbaric and cruel. When he was a child of eleven, he had once gone so far as disrupting the local foxhunt by putting down other lures to confuse the hounds. Several gentlemen in the county had thought that the young man should have been horsewhipped for such a heinous offense. Although he no longer took such an active role in discouraging hunting, Allingham still considered it an unworthy sport for a gentleman.

Since it appeared the hunting-mad members of his club intended to stay for some time, Allingham decided to leave. However, just as he was about to get up from his chair, more congenial company arrived in the person of Sir Henry Lonsdale. That gentleman greeted the loud gathering of sportsmen and then made his way over to his friend.

"Jack," he said, a broad smile on his face, "what great good fortune finding you here."

Allingham stood up and shook his friend's hand. "You would have not have found me if you had arrived a moment later, Harry." He glanced contemptuously over at his fellow club members. "I was finding myself growing exceedingly weary of listening to those braggarts."

At that moment a loud voice that they both recognized as belonging to Sir Frederick Ridley was heard to say, "The cunning little creature thought he had us outfoxed, but my Raffles was more than a match for him! By God, we got that fellow all right!"

The gentlemen around him all guffawed and one of them slapped Sir Frederick on the back.

Allingham looked disgusted. "I do wish that there were a pack of bloodthirsty hounds chasing after that buffoon, Freddie Ridley."

Sir Henry, knowing well his friend's opinion of hunting, smiled. "It does conjure up a most edifying picture, Jack. But do sit down, my friend, and we shall talk of more pleasant subjects."

The viscount obliged and returned to his armchair. The baronet took the chair next to him. "Very well, Harry," said Allingham with a slight smile. "I daresay any subject is more pleasant than foxhunting."

Sir Henry motioned to the waiter and asked for a glass of wine. He then looked at his friend. "I have heard that you plan to attend the Duchess of Northampton's soiree next week."

Allingham eyed Sir Henry a trifle warily. "You must have been speaking to her grace. Yes, I told her that I will be in attendance."

"The duchess said you had made a rather peculiar request—that she invite a certain lady and her two children. She said you were quite mysterious about the whole business. You can imagine my surprise when she said this lady was a Mrs. Grey." He paused dramatically. "A Mrs. Peter Grey."

Allingham frowned. "Really, Harry, what the devil is so peculiar about my asking the duchess to invite someone to her soiree?"

"I do find it odd, my friend, that you had just asked me about this Peter Grey a few days ago. You pretended that you just wished to know about him out of idle curiosity."

"Well, I was curious about him," said the viscount, frowning.

"Come, Jack, why are you so secretive about this?" said Sir Henry. He grinned. "The duchess had a very interesting theory . . . "

"I can guess what her theory is," replied the viscount. "She has the cork-brained notion that I have a grand passion for Grey's daughter. It is total nonsense." Allingham put on a mask of bored indifference, but Sir Henry was not so easily fooled. He sensed that his friend was not as disinterested in the lady as he pretended.

"I daresay the duchess is wrong then," said the baronet. He paused. "But you have met this daughter?"

"Yes, I have," said the viscount irritably.

"And is she pretty?" asked Sir Henry.

"Dammit, Harry, I'm sure in your little chat with the duchess she already informed you that I said the girl was tolerably pretty."

"And charming, too, I'll warrant," said the baronet, grinning.

"She was far from charming to me, Harry," said Allingham grimly. "Indeed, she took great pleasure in being rude to me."

Sir Henry looked genuinely surprised. "Rude to *you*? I must say, Jack, this story does seem deuced strange. Why are you taking up this Grey family if it's not because of the daughter?"

Allingham eyed his friend for a moment and then shrugged in resignation. "Oh, very well, I suppose I can tell you, Harry, but I'm not very eager to have the truth of my connection with the Greys bandied about town."

"Your connection with the Grey family? Good God, Jack, you cannot mean they are some sort of relations?"

"Certainly not," said his lordship, rather affronted that his friend would make such a ridiculous assumption. "I have a business connection with Mr. Grey."

"Business?" said Sir Henry. "Whatever can you mean, Jack?"

The viscount shrugged. "You were right the other day in suspecting that I was in financial trouble. My debts were considerable."

Sir Henry regarded him in surprise. "My dear fellow, I did not know that matters were that serious." A look of enlightenment appeared on the baronet's face. "You cannot mean you have some financial arrangement with Peter Grey?"

Allingham nodded. "To be frank, I'm in his service."

"In his service? What the devil do you mean, Jack?" asked Sir Henry.

Allingham smiled, "You see, Harry, I received an impudent letter from Peter Grey suggesting some sort of mutually beneficial arrangement between us. Of course, I wanted nothing to do with him. But then upon reflection, I thought it would do no harm to see him and find out what he meant.

"When I met with the fellow, he made a rather interesting proposal. He offered to settle my debts if I helped his family succeed in society. At first I was very much affronted at the suggestion, but after a good deal of thought, I decided to accept his offer."

"Good God!" cried Sir Henry, quite astonished.

"Yes, I've become Peter Grey's hireling. In return for his money, I shall establish the Greys in society. Of course, you see why no one must ever find out about this."

"Of course," said Sir Henry.

"It is quite humiliating to find oneself in such a position."

Sir Henry shook his head sympathetically. "Poor old Jack. But I daresay it is not so bad. Indeed, it seems a highly beneficial arrangement for both parties. Why, I see nothing wrong in your assisting these Greys."

"You've always been more democratic than I, Harry," said Allingham.

His friend laughed. Before the baronet could make a reply, their conversation was interrupted by the sudden appearance of a new gentleman in the room. Tall and muscular, the newcomer was handsome in a rugged sort of way. He nodded to some of the other men as he entered the room.

"Seagrave!" shouted one of the foxhunting gentlemen, apparently overjoyed at seeing the baron.

Both Sir Henry and Allingham exchanged a glance as Seagrave greeted the others. Catching sight of Allingham and his friend, the baron made his way over to them. "Lonsdale," he said, acknowledging the baronet with a slight nod. He then turned to the viscount. "Allingham, I must thank you for paying your debt to me. I was damned surprised, I must say." He paused and grinned. "You must have located some buried treasure. Or perhaps you found a genie's lamp."

The viscount stared up at him with haughty expression. "My affairs are of no concern of yours, Seagrave. You have your money. I suggest we have no further need of conversation."

"I suppose not," returned the baron with a disdainful smile. He hesitated, not knowing what to say next. Looking down at the viscount, Seagrave thought of how he had bullied the young Allingham while at Eton. In those days he had answered Allingham's insolence with his fists.

Now, however, the viscount was a man of considerable influence in society. Seagrave regretted that one could no longer simply pummel him into submission. While the baron was also in the Prince Regent's circle, he was not so popular with the Prince. Although he hated the fact, Seagrave could not help but admit that Allingham was His Royal Highness's favorite.

It had given Seagrave a good deal of satisfaction to think that the viscount was in financial difficulty. He had been quite disappointed when Allingham had paid him the considerable sum of money he owed. It was apparent that the viscount had run into some good fortune.

Seagrave frowned at the thought. Then, making a mocking bow, he took his leave of Allingham and the baronet. Going over to the group of boisterous gentlemen who had been talking about hunting, the baron was soon engaged in loud conversation.

"How I despise the man," said Sir Henry. "I cannot see him without thinking of those horrible school days. I was utterly terrified of him."

The viscount frowned. "He hasn't changed from those days. He is still an ignorant bully."

The baronet nodded. "Did you hear that he has taken up with Lady Granville?"

Allingham regarded his friend in surprise. "Isabelle? Good God, I hadn't heard."

"I had thought she had better taste. I daresay, since she was unable to snare you, my friend, she decided to latch on to Seagrave. Everyone knew that she had been attempting to bring you to heel. It was the talk of the town all last season."

Allingham, who did not like to think of himself as the object of such gossip, ignored this. He glanced over at the baron. "Seagrave has taken Isabelle as his mistress?"

"Yes, they have both been rather indiscreet. Granville doesn't seem to care what his wife does. I daresay he is well accustomed to the role of cuckold."

Allingham frowned to think of Isabelle. One of society's great beauties, she exhibited deplorable morals. Married to an aged, doting husband, she had taken a number of lovers over the years.

Last season Isabelle had fancied herself in love with Allingham. She had thrown herself at him in a most shameless way, hoping to become his mistress. The viscount had been rather blunt in his rejection of her, and she had not taken it at all well. Indeed, his lordship was well aware that the lady now hated him with a passion as fervent as her former infatuation.

So now she had become Seagrave's mistress. Allingham did not doubt that she had done so to antagonize him. After all, she was well aware of the animosity between them.

Noting his friend's expression, Sir Henry decided that he should change the subject. "Let us speak no more of Seagrave, Jack. You must tell me if I can help you in any way. If you need any money . . . "

"My dear Harry, you are hardly in a position to spare any blunt."

"Indeed, you are right," returned the baronet, who had many debts of his own.

Allingham smiled. "You are a good friend, Harry, but I assure you I'm quite flush thanks to Grey's assistance."

"Then it is I who will be putting the touch on you, Jack," said Sir Henry with a grin.

The viscount laughed. "You can assist me in seeing that the Greys are accepted by society, Harry."

"I daresay you will not need my assistance for that," said the baronet. "The blessing of the great Allingham is all that is needed."

Allingham smiled. "We shall see," he said, smiling at his friend. "Now let us get out of this damnable club, Harry. I have no wish to spend another minute in the same room with Seagrave." The baronet agreed and the two friends left the room to their old adversary and his jovial huntsmen companions.

That afternoon Pippa sat on a bench in the garden, trying not to dwell on Allingham. It was vexatious to her that the unpleasant viscount occupied even one moment of her thoughts. Indeed, she did not know why he seemed to come to mind so frequently.

Pippa would have been quite amazed to learn that she had been the frequent object of Allingham's thoughts. Not having the slightest inkling that the viscount was attracted to her, she was convinced that his lordship disliked her every bit as much as she disliked him.

Turning her attention to the flowers, Pippa contemplated the small walled garden with its colorful profusion of primroses and violas. Patches wandered lazily about the flowers, stopping every so often for a curious sniff.

"Pippa!" cried an excited voice, disturbing Pippa's peaceful revery. Looking up, she saw her mother advancing toward her, waving a piece of paper in her hand. "There you are, my dear. I did not know where you had gone."

Pippa smiled. "It is such wonderful weather I could not bear to be inside, Mama. Are the flowers not lovely?"

Her mother quickly glanced over at the garden. "Yes, they are quite pretty." She took a seat next to her daughter on the stone bench. "My dear," she said in a triumphant voice, "it has come!"

"What has come, Mama?" asked Pippa.

Her mother pushed the paper that she was holding in her hand toward her daughter. "It is the invitation from the Duchess of Northampton! Is it not wonderful!"

Pippa looked down at the invitation which included a handwritten note from the duchess. Although she did not share her mother's enthusiasm, she nodded. "Yes, Mama, it was very good of the Duchess of Northampton to invite perfect strangers to her soiree."

"Well, of course, it was all Lord Allingham's doing," said Mrs. Grey. "Oh, Pippa, I'm so nervous! All manner of important people will be there. Perhaps even His Royal Highness!"

"Do not worry, Mama. I'm sure you will charm everyone, including the prince."

Her mother smiled. "Thank you, my dear." She looked down again at the invitation. "It is so important that we make a good first impression. I don't know what I should wear. Oh, I do wish we had more time so I could have a new dress made!"

Pippa could hardly refrain from smiling at this remark. Her mother was quite extravagant about her wardrobe. In fact, Mrs. Grey had so many dresses, hats, shoes, and other articles of clothing, that her daughter did not know how she ever kept track of them. Fortunately, Mrs. Grey had a very competent lady's maid for the task.

"Oh, Mama," said Pippa. "I'm certain you can manage to find something to wear."

Mrs. Grey grew thoughtful. "I suppose the green evening gown might do well enough. You know, the one with the lace overlay?"

"That is an excellent choice," said Pippa, nodding.

However, her mother seemed uncertain. "But then there is the peach-colored satin. Or perhaps the lavender silk with the pearl embroidery?"

Pippa, realizing that her mother would be debating the matter right up until the soiree, smiled. "You will look lovely in whatever you wear, Mama."

Mrs. Grey still looked uneasy. "And what of you, my dear? What shall you wear?"

"Oh, I'm sure I have something, Mama. Perhaps my blue silk dress."

"Your blue silk dress!" exclaimed Mrs. Grey in alarm. "But, Pippa, that's at least three seasons old. You have worn it countless times."

Her daughter smiled. "But I don't think any of the guests at the duchess's soiree would have seen me in it, Mama. And it is my favorite. I very much doubt they would have been at any of the social occasions we attended in Portsmouth."

"That is true," said Mrs. Grey. "But, really, Pippa, you must wear something else. You must wear one of your new gowns. I'm sure Lord Allingham would not approve of you wearing such an old dress."

Pippa regarded her mother with a mischievous expression. "Do be careful, Mama. Such a comment may make that old dress seem irresistible to me."

"Pippa!"

Pippa laughed and then listened to her mother for some time as Mrs. Grey continued to lament the sorry state of her wardrobe.

8

It was Allingham's usual custom to arrive very late at social functions. In fact, his lordship often occasioned much consternation on the part of society hostesses who feared that he might one day make the ultimate breach in etiquette by appearing after the Prince Regent.

Despite his well-known propensity for lateness, the viscount was among the first guests to arrive at the Duchess of Northampton's soiree. Her Grace, suspecting that she knew the reason for her friend's punctual behavior, smiled as she greeted him.

"Allingham, my dear boy, what a surprise to see you at this hour. Does your early appearance indicate an eagerness to see a certain young lady who is to be in attendance this evening?"

The viscount bowed and took the hand that the duchess had offered him. "Dear Duchess, I do hope you cease this nonsensical talk," he said, regarding her with a practiced look of ennui. "I assure you that you are quite mistaken if you think I have the slightest interest in Miss Grey."

"Then you are not at all anxious to see the young lady?" she asked, her eyes twinkling.

Allingham frowned. "No, I am not. I'm sorry if I disappoint you, ma'am."

The duchess smiled again. "You cannot blame me for hoping you will fall in love. My dear Allingham, it would make me very happy to see you finally lose your head over a woman."

The viscount shook his head. "That is one thing, Duchess, that I shall never do. Now, if you will excuse me, I must say a few words to the duke." Bowing again, Allingham left the duchess and made his way over to her husband. Her Grace watched him go with an amused expression on her face.

As the evening progressed, a number of well-dressed ladies and gentlemen congregated in the Northamptons' drawing room. The duchess was well known in society for her excellent parties and those in attendance felt themselves most fortunate. They were pleased to see that that pink of the *ton*, Lord Allingham, was one of the company. The guests were even more excited by the rumor that an even more illustrious royal guest might be attending the gathering.

The viscount spent most of his time surveying the guests with a look of either hauteur or boredom. Despite his demeanor and his earlier disavowals to the duchess, his lordship was actually quite eager to see Miss Grey and her family. Waiting impatiently for their arrival, he was growing quite frustrated by their failure to appear.

Feeling very much like a solicitous parent, the viscount felt responsible for seeing that the Greys made a creditable start in society. He had not seen them since he had taken young Albert to his tailor the previous week. The admirable Weston had promised to have a new suit of clothes for that gentleman in time for the soiree so Allingham was certain that Albert would look quite presentable. Indeed, since young Albert was a handsome young man with pleasing manners, Allingham had little concern about him.

Although his lordship had thought the Grey ladies might also need his advice in the matter of their clothes for the party, he was reluctant to suggest such a thing in light of Pippa's sarcastic behavior toward him. Since Mrs. Grey and her daughter had been dressed quite well in his earlier encounters with them, he decided that they would be attired in an acceptable enough fashion.

Pulling his watch from his pocket, he cast a look at the time and frowned. Where were they? Almost everyone had arrived by now.

Folding his arms across his chest, Allingham looked toward the door to see Sir Henry Lonsdale and his wife enter the room. The viscount watched the Lonsdales greet their hostess and host and then make their way into the throng of people. Happy for a diversion, Allingham walked over to them.

"Harry," said the viscount, bestowing a rare smile on his oldest friend, "I am glad to see you." He bowed to the baronet's wife. "Lady Lonsdale, how charming you look. That rose-colored gown suits you to perfection."

Sir Henry's wife, a petite and attractive blonde, was quite pleased at receiving a compliment from the arbiter of fashion. She smiled up prettily at him. "Why thank you, Allingham. And I must say that you look splendid as always."

"I do not hear anyone commenting on my dashing appearance," said Sir Henry with mock indignation.

Lady Lonsdale smiled adoringly at her husband. "You, my darling, are the most handsome man in the room." She glanced back at the viscount. "If you will forgive me for saying so, my lord."

Allingham smiled slightly. "They do say that love is blind, ma'am." Both the lady and her husband laughed.

Although his lordship took a rather dim view of marriage, he had to admit that matrimony appeared to suit his friend Harry. Of course, he considered the baronet's case to be exceptional.

"So, Jack," said Sir Henry, glancing around at the ladies and gentlemen who stood chattering in groups about the large room, "where are the Greys?"

"Oh, yes," said his wife, "I'm quite looking forward to meeting them. Harry has told me all about them." She paused and smiled. "I hear the daughter is 'tolerably pretty.'"

Allingham frowned over at the baronet, wondering just what his friend had told his wife about the Greys. "They have not yet arrived," he said in some irritation.

Sir Henry looked over at the entranceway where the duke and duchess stood welcoming their guests. "Well, it looks as if Lady Granville has just come in."

The viscount followed his friend's glance and saw the lady making a rather grand entrance into the gathering. A very attractive woman, Lady Granville had fashionably dark curls and striking green eyes. She also had an admirable figure which she showed off to good advantage that evening in a revealing white gown.

Accompanied by her elderly husband, the Earl of Granville, the countess walked regally into the room, bestowing nods of recognition upon those of the company worthy of her attention. In gazing about the room, her glance fell upon Allingham. Frowning at him, she tossed her head and abruptly turned away.

Sir Henry smiled. "It appears, my friend, that the lady is giving you the cut direct. I daresay she is still furious with you for your rejecting her."

"I would say that is very much to your credit, Allingham," said the baronet's wife, who quite detested Lady Granville.

Sir Henry smiled. "Indeed, it is. Not many men could have resisted the beautiful Isabelle." When he saw his wife's expression, he hurriedly added, "Of course, I find nothing appealing about the lady in the least."

Lady Lonsdale regarded her husband skeptically. Sir Henry was glad when his wife's attention was taken up by a new arrival, Seagrave.

Dressed in dark evening clothes and a snowy white cravat, the baron looked quite handsome in a rough-hewn way. Coming in alone, he quickly made his way over to where Lady Granville was standing with two other ladies. He proceeded to lean toward her, whispering in her ear. The lady listened with a seductive smile and then she laughed appreciatively.

Lady Lonsdale watched them in disgust. "Seagrave is a scoundrel. Look at how he flaunts his newest mistress. I think it is despicable!"

Allingham regarded Seagrave and Lady Granville with a scornful look. From their behavior, it was clear that the gossip was right and the two of them were involved in an affair. Since he despised Seagrave and considered Lady Granville a female shark, he thought they very much deserved each other.

Watching them, his lordship was rather surprised at their indiscreet conduct. Such blatant, reckless behavior was not tolerated in society. It appeared that Seagrave felt his position so well assured that he could flaunt convention.

Turning his attention away from the baron and his new amour, the viscount changed the subject, politely inquiring after Lady Lonsdale's parents. They then stood discussing several other topics, including the latest gossip concerning His Royal Highness and his estranged wife, Princess Caroline.

As the evening went on, Allingham continued to glance toward the door. By now it was beginning to grow late and the viscount began to wonder if the Greys would ever appear.

Excusing himself from his friends, he walked over to the duchess, who stood conversing with two young gentlemen. Seeing the viscount's dismissive look, the gentlemen obligingly took their leave of the duchess, allowing the great Allingham to speak with her.

"Ah, Allingham," said Her Grace, "I do hope you are enjoying yourself. The orchestra should be starting at any time now for the dancing."

The viscount stared out indifferently at the crowd. "You know that I detest dancing, Duchess."

She nodded. "Yes, everyone knows that. You seem in a bad temper, Allingham. Is anything the matter?"

He frowned. "The Greys have not appeared yet. I cannot believe that they would be so late in arriving."

"Well, I can believe it, dear boy, since I wrote down a later time for them on their invitation."

He raised his dark eyebrows. "You did what?"

She laughed. "Do not look so disapproving, Allingham. I

wished to assist these Greys of yours in making a great success. That is why I decided to have them come late. As you know very well, it is the latecomers who arouse the most attention."

"Good God, Duchess, what have you done?" said Allingham. "It is one thing to be rather late. It is quite another to arrive when the party is nearly over."

Her Grace appeared amused. "Why, my dear Allingham, I believe you are worried. It is so very diverting seeing you in such a state."

"I'm not in a state," said Allingham ill-temperedly.

"Well, I assure you that your Greys will be here shortly. Why don't you go and have some punch? It is quite excellent."

Exceedingly vexed with his friend, the viscount bowed stiffly and retreated. Taking the duchess's advice, he went over to the punch bowl and poured himself a glass. As he raised it to his lips, his eyes went back to the doorway. His glass suddenly stopped in midair as he witnessed the arrival of the Greys.

His lordship was not the only guest at the soiree whose attention was suddenly riveted on the arrival of the new guests. Several heads craned toward the entranceway and watched with considerable interest as the duchess went over to greet the latecomers.

Allingham barely noticed young Albert Grey. Having just obtained his new suit from the inestimable Weston that very day, Bertie looked a nonpareil in his dark evening clothes.

The viscount also paid little attention to Mrs. Grey despite the fact that she appeared quite fashionable in a peach-colored silk gown with a hem adorned with white roses. Allingham's gaze was reserved for Pippa, who was attired in a magnificent gown of vivid crimson satin.

"Good God," muttered Allingham, who could scarcely believe his eyes. "She is wearing red!" It was a well-known rule of the viscount's that a lady should never wear red. He would never have imagined that Pippa would have made such an egregious mistake.

While Allingham was experiencing a shock at seeing Pippa, that lady was at her mother's side, greeting her hostess. Mrs. Grey expressed her undying gratitude to the duchess for Her Grace's kindness in inviting them. Her Grace smiled graciously and assured Mrs. Grey that she was very pleased that she could attend.

While making polite small talk, the Duchess of Northampton viewed Mrs. Grey and her family with keen interest. She noted that Mrs. Grey was a pleasant-enough woman and that her son seemed a handsome, well-spoken young man. But it was Pippa who commanded her attention.

Her Grace fixed her eyes upon the young lady who had apparently captivated Allingham. She was a very pretty young woman, concluded the duchess, eyeing Pippa's dress with some amusement. She knew well that the viscount had declared red an unsuitable color. All of the ladies in society accepted this declaration as gospel and would never consider wearing such a dress. "Miss Grey," said the duchess, smiling at Pippa. "I'm so glad you could come to my party."

"It was very good of you to invite us, ma'am," said Pippa. She looked out at the gathering and noticed that they seemed to be attracting much attention. "There appears to be a great number of people here already."

The duchess nodded. "And I'm sure they are all eager to meet you, my dear. Indeed, I know of one gentleman who has been most anxious to see you." When Pippa regarded her with a puzzled expression, the duchess smiled broadly. "I'm speaking of Allingham, of course." She leaned over and said in a confidential tone, "He appears to be quite enchanted with you."

Pippa's puzzlement was replaced by astonishment. "Lord Allingham enchanted with me?" She suddenly laughed. "I fear, Your Grace, you are very much mistaken."

"Am I?" asked the duchess, still smiling. "Then perhaps you can tell me why Allingham is at this moment hurrying over to us?"

Pippa looked out at the crowd and saw the viscount advancing toward them. However, as he moved slowly and languidly, Pippa could hardly describe his progress as "hurrying." Pippa could not help but note how handsome he looked, but his unsmiling expression hardly indicated an eagerness to see her. She was certain that his lordship viewed his shepherding them into society as a most unpleasant duty.

Bertie did not disguise his pleasure at seeing the viscount. He smiled broadly at his approach. "Lord Allingham," he said enthusiastically.

"Grey," replied Allingham. Eyeing Bertie's evening clothes with a critical eye, he gave a slight nod of approval. "It appears Weston did very well indeed."

Bertie grinned and looked down at his coat. "I'm so glad you think so, sir. It is a splendid coat, is it not, Lord Allingham? I daresay, my friends in Portsmouth would be quite envious to see me rigged up like this."

His lordship did not have a chance to reply to this for at that moment Mrs. Grey, the duchess, and Pippa joined them. The viscount bowed to the ladies. "Allingham," said the duchess, "here are your Greys. I do agree with you. They are a most charming family." Pippa almost burst into laughter at the ludicrous expression that appeared on the viscount's face at this remark. Her Grace, seemingly unaware of this, continued on, turning toward Mrs. Grey. "I must say, that dress of yours is very lovely, Mrs. Grey. Is it not, Allingham?" she asked, glancing over at his lordship.

The viscount nodded. "It is a most attractive dress, Mrs. Grey."

The duchess looked over at Pippa and then smiled slyly at his lordship. "And does not Miss Grey look positively enchanting, Allingham?"

The viscount's gaze fell upon Pippa. Despite the garment's unfortunate crimson color, Allingham could not help but note that the low-cut satin gown provided a most gratifying display of the lady's voluptuous charms. Although he was suddenly seized with some rather erotic fantasies concerning Pippa, his lordship attempted to appear unmoved. "Indeed," he murmured. "Most enchanting."

The duchess gave Pippa a triumphant smile. "You should be very pleased, Miss Grey. Lord Allingham does not offer praise lightly. If he does not like a lady's dress, he does not hesitate to say so." She grinned impishly at his lordship. "Is that not true, Allingham?"

The viscount pointedly ignored this remark and turned to Mrs. Grey. "Might I introduce you and your family to some of the other guests here, madam?" he asked, offering his arm.

Pippa's mother appeared thrilled. "Oh, that is very good of you, my lord."

Allingham turned to Her Grace. "If you will excuse us, Duchess." The elderly lady nodded and smiled as she watched her young friend escort the Greys away.

The viscount proceeded to introduce Pippa and her family to a number of the persons assembled there. Bertie was particularly pleased at being introduced to several charming matrons who had pretty daughters in tow.

When it was time for dancing, Bertie wasted no time in asking one of the young ladies, a Miss Fanny Carlisle, to dance. Mrs. Grey beamed at her handsome son and conversed with Lady Carlisle.

Pippa smiled as she watched her brother escort the lovely Miss

Carlisle out to join the other dancers. She was so intent on Bertie, that she did not at first realize that the viscount was staring at her solemnly.

Looking over at him, she was a bit taken aback at the intensity of his scrutiny. "Is something wrong, Lord Allingham?"

"No, indeed, Miss Grey."

"I feared that my hair was coming undone."

"No, your hair looks . . . splendid."

Pippa was surprised at the compliment. "Thank you, my lord," she replied with a smile.

Allingham appeared to hesitate for a moment. "Miss Grey," he said finally, "would you care to dance?"

Pippa regarded him curiously. "Thank you, my lord, but you mustn't feel an obligation to dance with me."

Allingham frowned. "I do not feel any such thing, Miss Grey. I hope you will do me the honor of this dance?"

"Very well, my lord," she said, taking the arm he offered to her. As they walked toward the dance area, Pippa noticed that they were being watched with keen interest by the onlookers in the crowd. Had she been aware that Allingham never danced at such gatherings, she would have better understood the fascinated looks of the ladies and gentlemen in attendance.

She looked over at Allingham. "It is very kind of you, my lord, to lend me such countenance by dancing with me." She smiled mischievously. "But are you not fearful that you may be lowering your own exalted standing in this company by choosing such a partner? Your willingness to descend from your lofty heights is truly admirable."

A frown appeared on his face. "It appears that you seem determined to vex me, Miss Grey."

She laughed. "While it was not my intention, I confess I rather enjoy vexing you, my lord."

He frowned again. "I'm glad I am providing you with amusement, madam," he said stiffly.

Pippa was somewhat surprised to realize that she had offended him. "In truth, I did not mean to provoke you, Lord Allingham," she said, smiling up at him. "I promise that I shall try not to provoke you any further."

He met her gaze and a slight smile appeared on his face. "Why am I doubtful that you will be able to keep that particular promise, Miss Grey?"

She laughed again and they proceeded to join the other couples for the dance. The viscount was pleased when the orchestra's selection was a waltz. Despite his claim that he detested dancing, Allingham found it quite enjoyable to put his arm around Pippa's waist and whirl her about the room.

Waltzing past her brother and Miss Carlisle, Pippa smiled. "It appears Bertie is having a wonderful time."

The viscount glanced over his shoulder at the couple. "As does Miss Carlisle," he said with some satisfaction. "She is from one of the best families. Your brother could scarcely do better."

Pippa's eyebrows arched slightly. "I did not realize, my lord, that your arrangement with my father included acting as a matchmaker. You seemed to have found a bride for Bertie already."

"A good match could be very advantageous to your brother," replied Allingham.

"Oh, yes, I'm sure that is true," said Pippa, suppressing a smile. She looked up at the viscount with a serious expression. "But I daresay a good match could be advantageous to me as well. I was wondering, my lord, why you did not introduce me to any eligible gentlemen. Surely there must be some in attendance. Really, my lord, if you are finding a bride for Bertie you may as well seek a husband for me."

Allingham glanced down at her in some surprise. He suspected that she was joking, but her expression remained solemn. "I shall rectify my failing as soon as possible," he said.

"Good," replied Pippa, trying hard to refrain from bursting into laughter. "I was afraid that you considered me too firmly on the shelf to bother about my marital prospects."

Allingham frowned. "You are far from on the shelf, Miss Grey." He was silent for a moment as they continued to dance. "Of course, you should be thinking of a husband," he said finally. "There are some gentlemen here who might suffice."

Pippa tried hard to maintain her pose of seriousness. "Really, my lord? I do wish you would point them out to me."

He looked at her a moment and then glanced around the room. "There. Do you see that gentleman talking to the duchess? That is Sir Francis Sedgewick."

Pippa glanced over in that direction. "You do not mean that gray-haired man with the spectacles? Is he not rather . . . grandfatherly for marriage?"

Allingham shrugged. "Sir Francis is somewhat older than you, of course."

"Somewhat?" said Pippa.

The viscount smiled. "A good deal older than you, Miss Grey. But the Sedgewicks are a very ancient, respected family and Sir Francis is recently widowed. And his fortune is enormous. He is considered a very great prize."

"Sir Francis?" asked Pippa. "I imagine he is a baronet?"

Allingham nodded. "Yes, his estates are in Gloucestershire."

Pippa pretended to be disappointed by this news. "A mere baronet? Oh, I fear that will never do, my lord. I was hoping to marry a duke, or a marquess at the very least."

This remark caused Allingham to regard her in such a way that she burst out laughing. He smiled. "So you were gammoning me, Miss Grey?"

"Yes, I confess I was. You don't have to worry about hunting me a husband. I have no wish for one."

"Nonsense," he said, "every woman wants a husband."

"Just as every man doesn't want to be married," she said. "What a vexatious state of affairs. You, my lord, have thus far avoided matrimony."

"Yes, I have been fortunate in that regard."

She laughed. "It appears we are alike in our cynical view of the married state. While you find my admission difficult to believe, I assure you I am not eager to marry." She shook her head. "Why should I relinquish my freedom only to be miserable by marrying some gentleman who cares only for my fortune?"

The viscount's gray eyes regarded her intently. "Surely, Miss Grey, you have had many suitors who were not only interested in your fortune."

"I am hard-pressed to name any, Lord Allingham."

"Then you have met only fools," returned the viscount, directing a look of such intensity at her that she was completely taken aback.

Flustered by this surprising remark, Pippa could only look away. She was relieved when the dance ended a short time later and the viscount returned her to her mother.

Allingham regretted his words the moment he had said them. He had always felt himself in complete control of his emotions. Yet now when he was holding Miss Grey in his arms, he had felt oddly off balance. Indeed, he warned himself, he had been treading on dangerous ground dancing with her.

The viscount led Pippa back to Mrs. Grey. Before he could make any further remark, they were besieged by a number of gentlemen eagerly seeking Pippa for the next dance. Allingham bowed stiffly before retreating across the room. He then stood watching with a frown as Pippa and a new partner began to dance.

While the viscount was vaguely aware that he was being observed by the company, he did not realize that his behavior that evening was unleashing a frenzy of gossip. Allingham's comings and goings were of great interest to most of the ladies and gentlemen in attendance since he was a personage of enormous consequence.

Many of the guests had noted with some astonishment how he had rushed up to greet the Greys. Those watching him while he led Pippa and her family around the room were amazed at his solicitude in introducing them about. But most surprising of all was seeing Allingham, who never danced at such occasions, waltzing with the striking Miss Grey.

Allingham's unusual attentions to them made the Greys the subject of great interest. Learning that Mrs. Grey was the wife of a wealthy businessman, many of those at the duchess's exclusive party were quite amazed that the viscount would have taken them up with such enthusiasm.

The sight of Allingham and Pippa dancing together fueled the speculation that his lordship was wooing the young lady. Since the viscount had hitherto resisted all the overtures from a legion of female admirers, it had been thought that Allingham was immune to feminine charms. Therefore, the company was fascinated by Allingham's apparent *tendre* for Pippa.

Two persons who were especially interested in the matter were Seagrave and Lady Granville. That couple would have provided most of the gossip for the evening if it had not been for Allingham and Pippa. The company's preoccupation with the viscount and the young lady in the crimson dress lessened the interest in Seagrave and his mistress who spent the entire evening at each other's side, behaving in a most flagrant manner.

Seagrave, who had no fear of the lady's elderly husband, was quite proud of his conquest of the raven-haired beauty. He was very happy to flaunt their relationship to the company, knowing that most of the gentlemen there would be extremely envious of him.

Lady Granville was also eager to show her new lover to society. Imagining that she could use Seagrave to annoy the viscount, Isabelle was most anxious that Allingham would see them together. When Allingham appeared totally uninterested in them both, she was considerably disappointed.

"I do believe the duchess has lowered her standards in the most appalling way," said Isabelle, addressing Seagrave, who was seated beside her on a sofa at the far end of the room, practically nibbling on her ear.

"What did you say, my dear?"

"I said the duchess has lowered her standards," repeated Isabelle.

Seagrave grinned. "You mean, of course, these Greys whom Allingham has taken up."

Isabelle nodded as she watched Pippa dancing with a ruddy-faced gentleman. "Good heavens, that is the most hideous dress I have seen since Charlotte Fitzmaurice wore that dreadful gown at her presentation."

The baron looked at Pippa. He very much approved of her auburn tresses and admirable figure, but thought it best to keep this opinion to himself. "By God, it looks as if Allingham is charmed by the female, hideous dress or no. See how he stands there regarding her with such a serious look."

Lady Granville frowned as she caught sight of Allingham. The man who was renowned for his cold heart and indifference to the female sex was staring at Miss Grey with a decidedly interested expression. "Do not be ridiculous, Seagrave," said Isabelle. "Allingham would not give such a creature a second look."

"It appears to me that he has taken a third and fourth look at the very least," said Seagrave. "We saw him dragging her and her family about introducing them. And he danced with her. In truth I never thought he knew how. I don't believe I have ever seen him dance until now."

Isabelle frowned again. Since she had been so lamentably unsuccessful in her attempts to charm the viscount, she was far from pleased to think that another lady had so easily captured his attention.

"I think it highly amusing if Allingham has taken a fancy to this little nobody. I am told she is nothing but a tradesman's daughter."

Seagrave shrugged. "But a very rich tradesman. Grimsby has told me that he is one of the richest men in the kingdom. I should not be surprised if Allingham does not find the lady's fortune of great interest."

While it seemed quite inconceivable to Isabelle that Allingham could be indifferent to Pippa's lowly origins, she could not deny that the viscount was acting very strangely. Perhaps Seagrave was right. Perhaps the viscount was interested in the young woman's fortune. The idea irritated Isabelle who decided that she would like to make Miss Grey's acquaintance.

Oblivious to Isabelle's scrutiny, Pippa was enjoying herself very much. Unlike Allingham, she had always adored dancing, and she was also a person who loved parties.

It was a pleasant surprise to Pippa that the company at the duchess's soiree was so agreeable. Indeed, while she had expected the elite company to be toplofty and distant, Pippa found most everyone she met to be perfectly charming. She knew that it was Allingham's influence that assured her family such a warm welcome. For her mother's sake, she was glad of it.

After finishing a lively mazurka with the ruddy-faced gentleman, Pippa was once again surrounded by a crowd of eager applicants. One rather stout gentleman spoke out, "My dear lady, do say you will dance with me next."

"Really, Baxter," came a feminine voice, "you mustn't exhaust the young lady." Pippa looked over to see an elegant dark-haired lady in a white dress standing before her. When the unlucky Mr. Baxter began to protest, the lady smiled at Pippa. "Would you not care to rest for a moment, my dear? I should be very glad if you would consent to sit with me."

Pleased with the dark-haired lady's friendly tone, Pippa smiled. "I should like that very much, ma'am." She smiled apologetically at Mr. Baxter and the other gentleman. "I'm sorry, gentlemen, but I should like to rest for a time."

Although there were some grumbles from the gentlemen gathered about them, the woman in the white dress took Pippa's arm and led her away. Finding an empty sofa at one side of the room, she motioned for Pippa to sit down.

"I know that it is very bold of me, but I so wished to make your acquaintance, Miss Grey. Why, you are the sensation of the evening. I am Lady Granville."

"How do you do, Lady Granville?" said Pippa, regarding Isabelle with keen interest. So this was the woman Allingham had advised her to shun! She seemed so pleasant and refined, thought Pippa. And she was certainly beautiful.

"I do hope you will forgive my taking you away from the dancing," said Lady Granville once they were seated on the sofa, "but I did save you from that oafish Baxter. I fear the fellow is notorious for treading on his partner's feet. Poor Catharine Hamilton was lame for days after dancing with him."

Pippa smiled. "Oh, dear. Then it appears you have rescued me, Lady Granville."

Isabelle smiled. "Yes, I daresay I have, Miss Grey. But I shall not keep you long. I should not dare to disappoint all the gentlemen. Now do tell me about yourself. I believe you are new to town."

Pippa smiled in return, thinking that Lady Granville seemed quite charming. "I have not been here long. The duchess was so very kind to invite me."

"Yes, she is a dear," said Isabelle, smiling disingenuously. "But you have had such success this evening, my dear. Everyone is talking about you and your lovely mother and handsome brother. They are saying, 'Who are these new people who have so captivated Allingham?' I thought I must find out. I told Lady Harley that I thought you might be a cousin of the Earl of Rathdowne. His mother was a Grey, of course."

"No," replied Pippa, "I am no relation."

"Then I was mistaken. You are perhaps one of the Greys of Suffolk, Lord Wilmot's family?"

Pippa shook her head. "My father is Peter Grey of Portsmouth. He has a shipping business in the city."

"How very interesting," said Isabelle. "Is Mr. Grey here? I should love to meet him."

"Oh, he doesn't like society very much," said Pippa, pleased at Isabelle's reaction to her admission of her father's connection to trade. It seemed that the notorious Lady Granville was not in the least snobbish.

"Men oftentimes detest society," said Isabelle. "My husband much prefers staying home in the country. But you must introduce me to your mother and that dashing brother of yours."

"I should be pleased to do so," said Pippa, wondering why Allingham had warned her against the lady. She seemed very nice.

Isabelle picked up her fan and waved it in front of her. "I saw your dancing with Allingham. What a triumph for you. You will be the envy of everyone, my dear." She smiled. "Everyone but me, of course." When Pippa did not seem to know how to reply to this, Isabelle laughed. "You see, Miss Grey, the great Allingham and I are not on friendly terms. I would not doubt that he has said all manner of dreadful things about me."

Again Pippa did not know how to respond. Her hesitation made Isabelle laugh once again. "Well, you mustn't believe a word of what he says about me. He is a man of unaccountable whims. If he takes a dislike to a person, he has no hesitation in doing his best to use his influence to undermine one in society.

"Of course, I do not enjoy speaking ill of anyone, so I shall say nothing more. But do beware of Allingham, Miss Grey. He can be such a dreadful man. I daresay he gave you quite a scolding tonight about your dress."

Pippa regarded Isabelle with a puzzled expression. "My dress? Whatever do you mean?"

"Oh, my dear, then he did not mention it?" asked the countess with a startled expression. "I am sorry. I just assumed he would have said something to you. Usually Allingham is quite rude about such things."

"But what is wrong with my dress?"

The countess stopped fanning herself and smiled. "There is nothing wrong with it, Miss Grey. It is the most beautiful dress here. But Allingham is such a tyrant. He has proclaimed that no lady should ever wear red. He has said that it is an esthetic affront and most painful to him."

Pippa raised her eyebrows. "Is it, indeed?"

"I fear so, Miss Grey," replied Isabelle, shaking her head. "And we all slavishly adhere to his commands as if he were the absolute monarch of fashionable society. It is really quite wearisome." She smiled brightly at Pippa. "I'm so glad that you are wearing that lovely crimson dress, Miss Grey. By wearing it, you have given Allingham a well-deserved set down."

"While that was certainly not my intention, Lady Granville, I must confess that I am not concerned what Lord Allingham thinks of my dress."

"That is splendid, my dear. I shall tell the other ladies and we will take courage from your example. I'm so glad you have come to town, Miss Grey, and I so look forward to knowing you better. I should very much like to call on you."

"That would be very kind," said Pippa.

"I know that we will become friends," said Isabelle. "Oh, look. The prince is arriving!"

"The prince?" said Pippa, glancing toward the entranceway. An excited murmur rose among the crowd as the Prince Regent strode into the company.

Lady Granville quickly stood up and then made a deep curtsy as the prince looked out at the gathering. Following her ladyship's lead, Pippa curtsied gracefully and then cast a curious gaze on Royal George. To her surprise, the portly prince stared right back at her. Smiling, he made a slight nod in her direction. After exchanging a few words with the duke and duchess, who were standing at his side, His Royal Highness began to make a progress across the room in order to accept the greetings of the company. He seemed eager to make his way over to where Pippa and Lady Granville were standing.

Both ladies made another curtsy and the prince smiled charmingly at them. "Ah, Lady Granville, you look delightful as ever," he said. Before the countess could respond to this royal compliment, the prince turned his attention on Pippa. "I do not believe I have been introduced to this lovely young lady."

Isabelle chimed in. "May I present Miss Pippa Grey, Your Royal Highness?"

Pippa made another curtsy. "I am honored to meet Your Royal Highness."

The prince extended his hand and raised her to her feet. "By my word, you are a wondrous sight in that dress, Miss Grey," he said, regarding her with admiration.

"Thank you, Your Royal Highness."

The prince was still eyeing Pippa's figure appreciatively. "Dashed magnificent gown, my dear. I think I should fancy a waistcoat of that color."

Pippa smiled. "I had some of the material left over, sir. I would be pleased to give it to Your Royal Highness."

"Would you, Miss Grey? That would be splendid. You are new to town, I believe?"

"Yes, sir."

"How very delightful to have such a charming addition to our society here. And Lady Granville has taken you under her wing, has she?"

"She has been very kind, Your Royal Highness."

"Good. Well, I should be happy to introduce you about, Miss Grey." The Prince Regent held out his arm. "If you would care to accompany me."

Pippa maintained her poise at her prince's extraordinary courtesy. "You are too kind, sir." Smiling at him, Pippa put her hand on his arm and they proceeded across the room.

The entire company watched in unison as the Prince Regent escorted Pippa about the room. It was quite amazing to everyone that the young lady in the crimson dress had so quickly captured royal attention. No one was more surprised by this development than Allingham.

His lordship had been observing Pippa's success that evening with a mixture of pleasure and chagrin. He had had little doubt that he had helped the lady considerably by dancing with her. Allingham knew that by lending his countenance to Pippa he had guaranteed her acceptance in the gathering. However, he had found her enormous popularity somewhat astonishing. It was obvious, he had thought grimly, that he was not the only one affected by the lady.

Continuing to keep his eye upon Pippa, he had been somewhat disturbed at seeing Lady Granville steer her away from the dance floor. Knowing the countess as he did, the viscount could not think that she had friendly intentions toward Pippa. As he had watched the two ladies involved in a tête-à-tête, Allingham had frowned. The viscount had almost been ready to go and rescue Pippa from Lady Granville when the prince had appeared and performed that duty for him.

As Allingham stood watching His Royal Highness chatting amiably with the Greys, he smiled slightly to himself. Certainly there was little doubt now that Pippa and her family would be much sought after in society. He had achieved his mission with apparent ease.

An unwelcome voice interrupted the viscount's musings. "Well, Allingham," said Seagrave, coming to stand beside him, "it appears your Miss Grey has made quite a sensation this evening."

The viscount turned around and scowled at the baron. "She is not 'my' Miss Grey, Seagrave."

That gentleman grinned. "Really? It seemed to me that you have been watching the lady all evening with a rather proprietary look on your face." He paused. "But, I'm glad I'm mistaken—for the lady's sake as well as my own. She is a damned pretty girl."

Allingham crossed his arms in front of him and cast a contemptuous gaze on the baron. "I know you think you are irresistible, Seagrave, but Miss Grey is too sensible to have anything to do with you."

The baron laughed. "We shall see about that. Of course, I shouldn't dare to pay my attentions to a lady, whom His Royal Highness so obviously fancies. What good luck that Lady Hertford is not here. Miss Grey has every opportunity to charm the prince. I'll warrant she would think herself most fortunate to receive such royal favor." The words "royal favor" were spoken in an insinuating tone calculated to anger the viscount.

"You are an ignorant fellow, Seagrave," said Allingham, directing a disdainful look at the baron. "I suggest you find company that will appreciate your conversation. I most certainly do not."

Seagrave grinned. "By God, Allingham, you are in a damned foul mood. Of course, I can understand that you would be upset by the prince's attention to your lady. It is clear you are very interested in this Miss Grey. I cannot blame you. I'd fancy a chance to bed the wench myself."

The viscount scowled ominously, his famous self-control vanishing. "You damned bastard, Seagrave," he said, glowering at the baron. "Get out of my sight or, by God, you will have cause to regret it." These last words were spoken loudly enough to be heard by a good number of those present. Several ladies and gentlemen turned in their direction, quite astonished to see the usually dispassionate viscount looking as if he were ready to do bodily harm to the baron.

"Gentlemen!" cried a voice and both Allingham and Seagrave looked over to see the Prince Regent regarding them with an expression of royal displeasure. A startled Pippa stood at his side. "Do remember where you are," chided His Royal Highness.

Allingham, who had been dangerously close to grabbing Seagrave by his collar, seemed to regain control of himself. He bowed to the prince. "I am sorry, Your Royal Highness. Seagrave and I were having a slight disagreement."

The prince looked from Allingham to the baron. He shook his head like a disapproving schoolmaster. "We must have no such disagreements here. There are ladies present. I advise you gentlemen to behave as such. Now shake hands."

Allingham frowned, unhappy at his public reprimand. He hesitated, unwilling to do as the prince commanded. "Allingham," said the prince sternly. The viscount looked over at His Royal Highness and then grudgingly shook Seagrave's hand.

"That is better," said the prince, pleased that he had taken control of the situation. He turned to Pippa. "You have said that you know Lord Allingham, Miss Grey?"

Pippa nodded. "Indeed, we are acquainted, Your Royal Highness."

"Have you been introduced to Seagrave?"

"No, Your Royal Highness."

"Then I must present him. Miss Grey, Baron Seagrave. Seagrave, this is Miss Grey."

The baron took Pippa's hand and bowed over it. "I am delighted to meet you, Miss Grey," he said, looking up at her with a bold, appraising look.

"Thank you, my lord," returned Pippa, nodding politely to Seagrave. She glanced over at Allingham and found he was regarding them both with a sullen expression.

"Now if you will excuse us, gentlemen," said His Royal Highness, offering his arm to Pippa. After casting a quizzical look at the viscount, Pippa took the prince's proffered arm and walked away with him.

Seagrave smiled as he watched them go. "I can understand your jealousy, Allingham. Miss Grey is a devilishly pretty girl. I do hope that you do not have cause to quarrel with Prinny over her."

The viscount did not deign to reply. He merely directed a withering look at the baron and then stalked off.

9

It was very late when the Greys finally returned home from the soiree. Mrs. Grey excitedly hurried to the drawing room with Bertie and Pippa following after her. As she had hoped, her husband was sitting on the sofa waiting up for them.

"Oh, Peter," she cried, rushing over to him, "you will never believe it! We had such a wonderful time tonight!"

Grey looked up at his wife and smiled. "I'm glad to hear it, my dear. Now do sit down, all of you, and tell me about it."

Mrs. Grey perched herself next to him on the sofa while Bertie and Pippa obediently took the chairs across from their parents. "I hardly know where to begin, Peter," said Mrs. Grey excitedly.

"Perhaps you should start with the part about the Prince Regent, Mama," suggested Pippa, casting an amused look over at her brother.

"Oh, of course!" said Mrs. Grey turning eagerly to her husband. "My dear, we were actually introduced to the prince himself! Can you imagine it? I daresay, I felt as if I might faint! But he was a most amiable gentleman. Yes, he was very charming. Although, I fear he is rather too fat, poor man."

Grey smiled broadly. "So you all met the Prince Regent? That is most gratifying."

"Oh, it was very gratifying, my dear," said Mrs. Grey, vigorously nodding her head which caused the ostrich feather in her hair to bob back and forth. "And, Peter, both Bertie and Pippa were great successes! Bertie danced with all manner of eligible young ladies. . . . "

Grey interrupted her. "So, you were popular with the ladies, my boy?" he asked, grinning over at his son.

Bertie blushed. "Tolerably so, sir. But not so popular as Pippa was with the gentlemen."

"Oh, yes, my dear," burst in Mrs. Grey, beaming over at her daughter. "Pippa was a triumph! She was swarmed by gentlemen all evening! And His Royal Highness was absolutely delighted with her."

Grey grinned over at his daughter. "So you were a triumph? I'm not in the least surprised. And you did not even wish to enter society, my girl. I daresay you find it more to your liking than you thought."

Pippa smiled. "I must confess I did enjoy myself, Papa. And the company was quite agreeable."

"And Allingham?" said Grey. "Did he do his duty in introducing you about?"

"Indeed, yes," cried Mrs. Grey. "Lord Allingham could not have been more solicitous. He introduced us to everyone. And he danced with Pippa!"

"Well, then," said Grey, winking at his daughter, "it appears the fellow is certainly working hard for his money. Why dancing with Pippa! Who could imagine it?"

"But it was extraordinary," said Bertie. "Not that anyone would not wish to dance with Pippa. She was simply deluged with partners after her dance with Allingham. But I mean that I heard it said a number of times that Allingham never dances."

"Yes, I heard that as well," said Mrs. Grey. "Was it not good of him to go against his usual custom? And to think that Pippa did not even like him overmuch."

"Indeed?" said Grey, grinning at his daughter. "And what do you think of our friend Allingham now?"

Pippa shrugged. "I scarcely know, Papa. I will admit that he was very civil to me even though I tried to vex him."

"Pippa!" cried her mother, horrified.

She laughed. "Do not worry, Mama, I wasn't so very bad." She paused, remembering the scene between the viscount and Seagrave. "At least I wasn't the one who made him so angry tonight."

"Allingham angry?" said Grey, very much interested.

"Oh, yes," said Mrs. Grey. "Everyone was talking about it. Pippa witnessed their altercation."

"Altercation?" said Grey. "Did they resort to fisticuffs?"

"Do not be ridiculous, Peter," said Mrs. Grey. "Do tell your father what happened, Pippa."

"Oh, it was only that Allingham and another gentleman, a Baron Seagrave, were exchanging words. Allingham looked very angry. The prince told them to behave and made them shake hands. Allingham did not look at all pleased."

"It must have been horribly embarrassing for poor Allingham," said Mrs. Grey. "I'm told that there is no love lost between the two gentlemen."

Bertie nodded. "I wonder what they were speaking of. Did you hear, Pippa?"

"No, I heard nothing."

"Lord Allingham seems such an even-tempered man," said Mrs. Grey, "but gentlemen will have their quarrels occasionally."

"Yes," said Grey, nodding, "they were probably arguing over a horserace or some other equally weighty matter." He turned to his wife. "Now, do tell me more about this party, Louisa." Since Mrs. Grey was more than happy to tell about the soiree in minute detail, they sat up for some time before retiring to bed.

The following morning, Mrs. Grey and her children all slept much later than was their usual custom. Mr. Grey, resigned to the idea that the members of his family were destined to become great slugabeds now that they were in society, went off to his office.

When Mrs. Grey rose, she was in an exceedingly cheerful mood. Still excited about the previous evening, she could not stop talking about it. Although Pippa had enjoyed herself at the party, she soon began to find the subject of the soiree rather wearisome. One could only listen to her mother's enthusiastic descriptions of the event for so long before wishing that there was some other topic to occupy her.

After having a light luncheon, Mrs. Grey urged both Pippa and Bertie to dress with special care since they would receive callers. Mrs. Grey was certain that they would be besieged with visitors after their triumphant evening.

Although Pippa did not share her mother's certainty that they would be inundated with eager guests, she dutifully went to her room to change. Assisted by Betty, Pippa dressed in an attractive dress of pale green muslin with a high collar and long, close-fitting sleeves.

Making her way to the drawing room with Patches, Pippa found her mother at the window, an expectant look on her face. Mrs. Grey turned and glanced approvingly at her daughter. "You look quite lovely, my dear. Now you must have Patches go to the kitchen, Pippa." The black-and-white dog looked up sorrowfully at Mrs. Grey as if she knew of her impending banishment. "I'm sorry, Patches," said Mrs. Grey, putting her hands on her hips, "but you cannot be trusted with company. You demonstrated that with Lord Allingham."

Pippa laughed. "Poor Patches, I fear Mama doesn't think your manners are fit for guests. Come on, my girl, I will take you to the kitchen where I'm sure Cook will have a nice bone for you." The large dog seemed more agreeable now and happily trotted out of the room after Pippa.

When she returned to the drawing room, Pippa found that her brother had appeared. He looked quite dapper in a beige coat and buff-colored pantaloons. "I do hope we have some callers," he said. "I don't wish to spend all afternoon waiting about. It will be a great waste of time if no one comes."

"Of course we will have callers," said Mrs. Grey confidently. "We were a great success last night. I daresay, we shall get scores of people coming to visit us today."

Pippa smiled doubtfully. However, she was soon to find that her mother's prediction was right on the mark. Shortly after they had settled themselves in the drawing room, the butler arrived to announce their first caller, Lord Thomas Keith. After that gentleman paid his respects, a steady stream of visitors kept them occupied all afternoon.

All of the excitement was finally too much for Mrs. Grey. At teatime she told her children that she had a horrible headache and retired to her bedchamber. Bertie also took his leave, telling Pippa that he had promised to meet some gentlemen late that afternoon.

Left alone, Pippa decided that she had seen enough visitors for one day. Indeed, it seemed that all London Society had appeared on their doorstep. When the butler entered the room, she informed him that she would not be receiving anyone else. Hawkins looked rather disappointed. "But there is a young gentleman here, miss." The servant extended the silver salver toward Pippa, who took the calling card from it.

Pippa looked at the card. "The Marquess of Ravensly?" she said.

Hawkins was obviously pleased at having such an illustrious caller. "Yes, miss."

Pippa appeared thoughtful. She remembered the marquess very well. A handsome young man of four-and-twenty with curly brown hair and a charming smile, Ravensly had made a very favorable impression upon her at the soiree.

"Oh, very well, I shall see him. But he will be the last."

Hawkins vanished, returning with the visitor. Finding Pippa alone, his lordship could hardly believe his good fortune.

"Do sit down, Lord Ravensly," said Pippa.

The marquess was only too happy to do so. He began chatting

about the soiree. Pippa, thinking Lord Ravensly a very amiable man, was enjoying her conversation with him, when the butler once again entered the drawing room. "Pardon me, miss. But the Viscount Allingham is here."

Pippa frowned at the servant. Had she not distinctly told him that she would not receive any other callers? It was clear that Hawkins did not think it possible that she would refuse to see the great Allingham.

Ravensly, although thinking the viscount's visit very ill-timed, jumped to his feet. Too timid to risk offending Allingham, he thought it best to take his leave. "I really must be going, Miss Grey," he said. "I do hope I may call upon you again?"

She smiled in return. "Of course, my lord." Bowing politely to Pippa, the marquess then took his leave.

A moment later, the butler returned followed by the viscount. She noted that as always, he was dressed to perfection in a dove gray coat and ivory pantaloons. "Miss Grey," he said, making a polite and very formal bow to her.

"Lord Allingham," she said. "Please sit down."

His lordship took a chair across from her and glanced around him. "Where is Mrs. Grey?"

"She retired to her room with a headache."

"Then you received Ravensly alone?" he said with a censorious look. "I think that most unwise, Miss Grey."

She raised her eyebrows. "Really, my lord? Then I daresay I should not have allowed Hawkins to admit you. I'm receiving you alone. And if you find it too shocking that I do so, you have only to leave."

"Do not be ridiculous," replied Allingham. "I wasn't speaking of myself, but of Ravensly."

"Yes, of course, it is a different matter altogether," said Pippa, smiling at his frowning expression. "Lord Ravensly is a very disreputable character."

"While he may be as pure as the driven snow, it is not altogether proper for a young single lady such as yourself to entertain him alone."

"I stand rebuked and I shall endeavor to behave in a more seemly fashion, Lord Allingham."

The viscount frowned again at her smiling expression. "I do wish you would take things seriously. I suppose you think Ravensly very charming."

Pippa nodded. "I do indeed, my lord."

Allingham tried to appear indifferent. "Ravensly is a most eligible fellow. In fact, he is one of the greatest prizes of the marriage mart. He is the heir to a dukedom. You may secure the catch of the season if you play your cards right."

Pippa shook her head. "I have told you, my lord, that I am not interested in a husband. And from what I've heard, you should not be advising anyone on cards."

Allingham, looking quite affronted by this remark, abruptly stood up. "I shall waste no more of your time, Miss Grey."

"Oh, do sit down, my lord," said Pippa. "I didn't mean to insult you. It is only that you must not speak to me as if I were a child. I cannot be expected to enjoy having someone telling me what to do or how to behave. I'm a grown woman, Lord Allingham, and I should like to be treated as such."

The viscount hesitated and then sat down again. "I only wish to offer you advice that may be of assistance. You are not familiar with society, after all. You do not want to make a blunder."

"Oh, most certainly not, my lord," said Pippa. "And do know that I shall give all of your advice the consideration it deserves."

Allingham frowned. "It is clear how you regard my advice. I saw you speaking with Lady Granville last evening even though I expressly told you that she is a person to avoid."

"I could hardly not speak with her," said Pippa with a frown. "She introduced herself."

"Yes, that is exactly the sort of ill-mannered thing she would do," said Allingham. "I was very serious in telling you to avoid her. Association with such a female will do you no good."

"Good heavens, Lord Allingham," said Pippa, "I found Lady Granville to be a charming person. I don't know what she has done to cause you to label her as 'notorious,' but I do not doubt that you judge her too harshly."

"I judge her as she is, madam," said the viscount irritably. "And you are well advised to stay away from her. She is not admitted to a good many drawing rooms."

"But she was invited to the duchess's soiree."

"Yes, but her grace detests her. She only invites her in consideration for Lord Granville. They are cousins, you know. If she calls here, you should not admit her."

Pippa regarded him with a disapproving look. "Lord Allingham, we are most appreciative of your efforts to steer us through the rocky shoals of society. Your assistance has already assured my family a place in society. While I myself care little for that, I am well aware that it has made my mother very happy.

"But while I shall consider your advice, my lord, you must not expect me to blindly do as you say. If I wish to speak to Lady Granville, I shall do so. I know you will disapprove just as I know you disapproved of the dress I wore last night."

Allingham regarded her in surprise. "What do you mean, Miss Grey?"

"I was told that you disapproved of the dress I wore to the soiree last night."

"Who would have told you such a thing?"

"Lady Granville."

"I might have known."

"You cannot deny that you were horrified by my dress?"

"I would not say I was horrified," said the viscount.

"But you did not like my dress?" she asked.

Crossing his arms in front of him, he nodded. "Very well, I admit I did not like it. Or it is more accurate to say that I did not like the color."

"Lady Granville said that you had declared that a lady must never wear red."

"Indeed, I have said as much many times. I find crimson a most unacceptable color, Miss Grey. Ladies should never wear it. And most especially ladies of your complexion."

"But, Lord Allingham," said Pippa with mock dismay, "red is my favorite color. You wouldn't be so cruel as to say I should never wear it."

The viscount nodded. "I would most emphatically say that you should never be seen in that color again, Miss Grey. You should wear flattering shades such as sea green or canary yellow." Allingham's gray eyes regarded her closely. "Or perhaps a pale blue that would match those remarkable eyes of yours." Pippa was somewhat taken aback by this last remark and the obvious look of admiration in Allingham's expression.

The viscount, realizing he had spoken incautiously, quickly adopted his usual indifferent pose. "Many colors would suit you," he said. "But, crimson, Miss Grey, is not one of them." He paused a moment. "If you should like, I might be able to assist you with your wardrobe. I could recommend an excellent dressmaker. Madame Dupre on Cavendish Street. I would be happy to accompany you to both the linen draper's and Madame Dupre's to advise you on what clothes would best suit you."

Pippa frowned. "I'm quite capable of dressing myself, my lord," she said irritably. "I do not need your assistance." Realizing what she had said, she blushed.

Allingham smiled slightly and then he shrugged. "Very well, Miss Grey. I just hope you take my advice to heart."

"Oh, I shall," said Pippa with a sudden smile. "I shall, indeed, my lord."

10

The following morning Mrs. Grey and Pippa sat at the breakfast table. Mrs. Grey was once again lamenting on how she had missed Lord Allingham's visit the previous afternoon. Pippa reassured her mother that his lordship would no doubt call upon them again.

"I do hope you are right, Pippa," said Mrs. Grey. "He is such a dear man."

Pippa regarded her mother strangely. "Allingham a *dear* man, Mama?"

"Now, Pippa, you still seem to be prejudiced against Lord Allingham. We owe him a very large debt for gaining us entry into society."

"Indeed, Mama, do not forget that his lordship is being well rewarded for his services."

"Must you remind me of that?"

"I feel one should keep it in mind rather than wrongly imagine that Allingham is assisting us due to his kind heart."

"Well, I should prefer to believe so," said Mrs. Grey with a sigh. "But in any case, Lord Allingham has already helped us immeasurably." Mrs. Grey smiled at her daughter. "Oh, my dear, I still cannot believe all that has happened! I sometimes think I must be dreaming!"

Pippa smiled and began to put marmalade on a slice of toast. "I'm glad you are so happy, Mama."

"Indeed, I am. It was my dearest wish that you and Bertie should be accepted in society. But I could not have imagined that you both would be such great successes! To think that the Marquess of Ravensly paid a call upon you. My dear, he is the heir to a dukedom! If you should marry him, you would one day be a duchess! Imagine, my Pippa a duchess," she said wistfully.

Pippa laughed. "Really, Mama, do not be ridiculous. I hardly know Lord Ravensly."

Mrs. Grey smiled knowingly. "You will be better acquainted in time. But even if Lord Ravensly doesn't make you an offer, there are many other acceptable gentlemen who will."

Pippa, who had no desire to discuss suitors, decided to change the subject. "It appears my brother is sleeping late again."

Her mother nodded. "Yes, but he was out late last night with the new friends that he met at the soiree. Oh, I'm so glad Bertie has found some congenial company."

Unlike her mother, Pippa was not so pleased at the idea of her brother gallivanting about town. She knew that young gentlemen were often addicted to drinking and games of chance. She only hoped that Bertie's new friends would not be a bad influence on her impressionable younger brother.

After taking a bite of her toast, Pippa glanced over at her mother. "I thought I might go out this morning, Mama. Would you wish to accompany me?"

"Thank you, my dear, but I do think it wise for me to stay at home and rest. I do not doubt that we will have more company this afternoon. But where do you plan to go?"

"Oh, I thought I should go to the linen draper's to get some new material. And perhaps I might visit a dressmaker."

"The linen draper's," said Mrs. Grey, her eyes lighting up. "And a dressmaker! That is a splendid idea, Pippa. You could use some new gowns, my dear. Oh, I should like to go, but I feel so very tired. I feel I should rest if I am to receive visitors."

"We could go another time, Mama."

"Oh, no, my dear. You mustn't change your plans. Betty will go with you. You must take the carriage." Happy that her daughter was expressing interest in new clothes, Mrs. Grey began to chatter on about the latest designs she had seen in one of the fashion magazines.

After the morning meal was finished, Pippa prepared to go out on her shopping expedition. Attired in a blue spencer with military trim and a jaunty blue bonnet trimmed with white feathers, Pippa made her way to the awaiting carriage.

She was followed by Betty. The servant was quite eager to accompany her mistress, especially when she heard that their destination was to be the linen draper's. Betty considered such an establishment infinitely more interesting than a bookstore.

When they arrived at Ackerman's Linen Draper's Shop, Pippa was quickly assisted by a shopgirl, who, noting Pippa's fine clothes, pegged her for a lady of quality. "May I help you, madam?"

"I'm looking for some material for a new gown." Pippa gazed

at the bolts of fabric on the shelves behind the clerk. Her eye fell upon a roll of crimson-colored cloth. "I should like to see the crimson silk if you please."

The clerk, a short middle-aged woman with spectacles, turned to fetch it. "A very fine choice, madam."

Pippa examined the material. "I shall take the entire bolt."

The shopgirl appeared surprised. "Very good, madam."

"And do show me what else you have in this color."

"In the same color, madam?" asked the clerk. "There is some very fine satin, I believe. Yes, I shall fetch it, madam.

The woman hurried to bring another bolt of red cloth to Pippa. "This should do nicely, too," she said. "I shall take it as well."

"All of it, madam?"

"Yes, all of it," said Pippa. "Now do you have a velvet in a similar shade?"

The clerk, who thought the young lady was acting rather strangely in buying such huge quantities of red material, merely nodded and went to find the crimson velvet. After all, it was not her place to question the whims of ladies.

Pippa's purchases were quickly deposited in her carriage. She then informed her driver to take her to the dressmaking establishment of Madame Dupre on Cavendish Street.

Arriving at the dressmaker's, Pippa walked into the elegant front room of the exclusive shop. A well-dressed young woman quickly approached her. "May I be of assistance, madam?" she asked.

Pippa nodded. "I am Miss Pippa Grey. Lord Allingham suggested that I come here."

Before she could say another word, the woman spoke excitedly. "Lord Allingham? Oh, yes, madam. Do please sit down. I shall fetch Madame Dupre." Making a curtsy, she quickly hurried out of the room.

Pippa was amazed by the effect of Allingham's name on the woman. She took a seat on a sofa covered with rose-colored velvet and glanced about the room. It was only a moment before an attractive middle-aged woman with henna-dyed hair appeared before her.

"Ah, Mademoiselle Grey, I am so pleased that you have honored me by coming to my establishment," said the woman in a pronounced French accent. She paused, eyeing Pippa with great interest. "My assistant said Lord Allingham recommended me to you."

Pippa nodded. "Indeed, he did, madame. Lord Allingham praised you most highly."

Madame Dupre beamed with pleasure. "His lordship is very kind. But, what might I do for you, mademoiselle?"

"I was hoping you could make me some new dresses, Madame Dupre. I was thinking perhaps two evening gowns and three walking dresses. And I should like a riding habit as well."

The dressmaker seemed overjoyed at the prospect of such a lucrative order. She clapped her hands together. "*Oui*, mademoiselle, I shall be delighted to do so." She smiled at Pippa. "It shall be a pleasure to have such a lovely young lady show off my creations, Mademoiselle Grey." She hurried over to a fat book sitting on an ornate cherry table. "Here are some designs you may care to look at." She turned to a page in the book and presented it to Pippa. "I do think, mademoiselle, that this gown would look magnificent on you."

Looking down at the sketch of the dress, Pippa nodded approvingly. "It is quite splendid, madame."

The dressmaker nodded. "Oh, yes, mademoiselle, and you would suit it to perfection. I would suggest making it in a white gauze."

Pippa glanced up at Madame Dupre. "I fear I do not wish to have the dress in white, madame."

"Ah, but white is always the most elegant choice," protested the dressmaker. She shrugged. "But if mademoiselle prefers another color."

"Yes, in fact, I just purchased some material at the linen draper's," said Pippa. She looked at Betty who was standing near the door. "Do have Will bring in the material, Betty." The maid nodded and hurried out. She quickly returned, followed by the burly coachman.

"Here it 'tis, miss," said Will, hefting the bulky package into the shop.

"Do put it down on the table," commanded the dressmaker imperiously. The servant nodded and, after depositing the package as instructed, he left.

Pippa went over to the package and pulled off the brown wrapping paper around it. Madame Dupre stared down at the bolts of crimson-colored material in astonishment. "But it is red, mademoiselle," she said.

"Yes," said Pippa.

"But, mademoiselle," protested the dressmaker, "you cannot be serious. You wish to have all of the dresses in this color?"

Pippa nodded. "I most certainly do."

Madame Dupre shook her head. "I do not think it a good idea, mademoiselle. Lord Allingham would never approve of such a color."

"But, madame, it is because of Lord Allingham that I'm having these dresses made in this color," said Pippa, trying to retain a serious expression. "You see, I wore a gown of this shade the other evening. His lordship said I looked positively enchanting in it. He said that although he had previously thought crimson a most unacceptable color, he had been altogether mistaken. I'm certain he thought the color most flattering."

The dressmaker regarded Pippa with a curious expression for a moment. Then she sighed. She knew all too well that wealthy young ladies had to be catered to. "Oh, very well, Mademoiselle Grey. I shall do as you wish."

Pippa smiled. "Thank you, madame. Now do show me what other designs you think would suit me." The dressmaker took up the book and began to peruse it for other sketches to bring to Pippa's attention.

While Pippa was busy deciding what dresses to order at Madame Dupre's, Allingham was involved in the equally serious business of deciding what to wear. After settling on a coat of olive superfine and tan-colored pantaloons, the viscount began to dress.

As his lordship's valet was assisting him with his coat, the butler entered the room. "Pardon me, my lord, but Sir Henry Lonsdale is here to see your lordship. He is in the drawing room."

"Very good, Morris," said Allingham and, taking one last look at his reflection in the mirror, he went to greet his friend.

"Harry," he said, entering the drawing room. The baronet jumped up from his chair.

"Jack, old man," said Sir Henry with a smile, "I'm happy that I have found you at home."

"Where else should I be at such an hour?" said the viscount, sitting down on the sofa.

The baronet grinned. "I suppose it is rather early to pay a call, Jack, but I was most eager to talk to you. When I came here yesterday afternoon to see you, I was told you were out."

Allingham regarded his friend curiously. "You seem devilish eager about something, Harry. What is it you wish to speak with me about?"

"I was most curious to discuss the events of the other evening with you."

"Which events?" asked Allingham with seeming disinterest. "Which evening?"

"Come now, Jack," said Sir Henry, "you know very well I am referring to the duchess's soiree. I never had the chance to speak to you after the Greys arrived."

"Yes, well, I don't think there is very much to discuss about the matter."

The baronet laughed. "You are modest, Jack. Surely, you must have been quite pleased to see what a success the Greys were. They were the talk of the company." He paused. "But then, my friend, so were you."

Allingham regarded his friend with a frown. "What do you mean, Harry?"

Sir Henry grinned again. "Why, the company was quite interested in your behavior toward the Greys—especially your behavior toward a particular member of the Grey family. Indeed, the way everyone talked about you and the young lady, I felt that I would soon be wishing you joy."

"Good God, Harry," muttered the viscount, "quit spouting such nonsense. I daresay you were listening to the duchess again." He frowned. "You know very well why I was helping the Greys."

His friend nodded. "I do indeed, Jack. And yet . . ."

"What?"

The baronet smiled. "Well, you did seem rather partial to the girl, Jack. Diana told me that when you were dancing with Miss Grey you were regarding her with what my wife called 'a most passionate gaze.' "

"You know I am fond of your wife, Harry," said Allingham, shaking his head, "but she can sometimes be a great goose."

"Yes," agreed the baronet, "an adorable goose, to be sure. However, I find Diana is seldom wrong when it comes to affairs of the heart. She thinks you are in love with Miss Grey."

"Dammit, Harry," said the viscount. "That is nonsense."

"Is it, Jack?"

Allingham stood up and paced back and forth. He stopped and looked at his friend. "I don't know, Harry. I seem unable to get her out of my thoughts. It is quite disturbing. I have never felt this way about any woman before."

"My dear old friend," said the baronet, "I believe you are in love."

"Don't be absurd," said Allingham.

His friend only laughed. "I should never have thought it possible. But, I must say I do approve. Although I just met the lady briefly, she seemed quite charming. I'll warrant she'd make you an admirable wife, Jack."

The viscount looked down at his friend and shook his head. "Wife? Don't be an idiot, Harry. I could not marry Miss Grey."

"Whyever not? Of course, I daresay it is her family. It will not do with her father being in trade."

"That is not it," said Allingham. "First of all, I scarcely know her."

"Well, you will soon know her better."

"And then there is the fact that she seems to dislike me. That is rather an impediment to wedded bliss."

Sir Henry laughed. "Perhaps so, but surely you are mistaken. I cannot believe that she would dislike you."

"The idea that anyone would dislike me is so incredible?"

"Well, no," said Sir Henry with a grin. "I do admit there are a few misguided souls who do not see you as I do."

"And Miss Grey is apparently one of them. And then there is the matter of my lack of fortune. She is well aware of my financial state and her father is so damnably rich. If I offered for her, she would think me nothing but a fortune hunter."

"Then you must convince her otherwise. Indeed, my dear Jack, I believe Miss Grey is the girl for you."

Allingham shook his head. "There is no point in discussing the matter any further, Harry."

"Very well," said Sir Henry. "Well, you have done the Greys a great service. They were a great success and Prinny seemed totally charmed by Miss Grey."

The viscount frowned. "I did not like his paying her so much attention. Seagrave implied that Prinny's interest was more than polite curiosity."

"How absurd!" said Sir Henry. A flash of recognition came to his face. "Then that is what your words with Seagrave were about."

Allingham nodded. "I lost my temper. Indeed, I nearly planted him a facer."

"Thank God, you didn't," said Sir Henry. "It was bad enough as it was."

"I wish Prinny had not interfered," said Allingham with a frown. "It was bad luck he had to be about."

"My dear Jack, one cannot resort to violence at the duchess's soiree."

"I suppose not," said Allingham with a faint smile. "But since I succeeded in creating a scene, I should have preferred having the opportunity to pummel the fellow." Sir Henry laughed and the viscount continued. "But I do not wish to spend any more time talking of Seagrave or Miss Grey. Surely you have something else we might discuss, Harry."

Sir Henry nodded, launching into an amusing story about his wife's uncle. As the baronet began his tale, Allingham found himself perversely wishing that they were still discussing Pippa.

11

Pippa was surprised when a week went by without any sign of Lord Allingham. She had expected him to call upon them with additional advice for their forays into society. But when he did not appear, Pippa decided that the viscount was apparently too vexed with her to wish to call on them. While one might have expected that Pippa would have been pleased by the viscount's absence, she found herself strangely disappointed that he did not appear.

It did seem that the Greys did not need further help from Allingham. They had already been quite successful in entering London's elite circles. Since the duchess's soiree, Pippa's family had received numerous callers. They had in return been graciously received at houses from which they had previously been turned away.

Lady Granville had called and had been warmly welcomed by Pippa. Although Mrs. Grey had been rather reluctant to encourage the acquaintance with a lady whom Allingham thought unacceptable, she had to admit that Lady Granville seemed charming. Pippa, who was eager to have a new female friend, found herself liking Isabelle very much. Since she could not understand Allingham's antipathy toward her, Pippa suspected that Allingham had been most unfair in his judgment of the lady.

Pippa and her family also were the recipients of numerous invitations to dinners, parties and, most important, the Huntingdon's ball. Mrs. Grey knew that an invitation to this ball was very much coveted in society. She was extremely pleased that they were to be in the select company attending the gala event.

Although Pippa was enjoying the attention that they were receiving, she was beginning to get a bit weary of the constant social calls. One afternoon when her mother was intent on paying visits to several prominent hostesses, Pippa begged off, saying that she preferred an afternoon to herself. After some protests, her mother finally relented.

Watching her mother leave in the carriage, Pippa decided that it would be a pleasant day to take a walk in the park. Going upstairs to her room, she hesitated in front of her wardrobe. She suddenly decided that she would wear one of the new walking dresses that she had received that very morning from Madame Dupre.

As Betty assisted her with her clothes, Pippa glanced at herself in the mirror. She was very pleased with the dressmaker's handiwork. The crimson pelisse was decorated with matching braid and accentuated Pippa's figure to perfection.

Betty stood back and regarded her mistress admiringly. " 'Tis quite lovely, miss. What hat would you care to wear?"

"I should think the straw bonnet, Betty. The one with the white roses."

The maid hastened to retrieve it. She then handed it to Pippa who quickly donned the broad-brimmed bonnet. "Well, what do you think?" she asked the servant as she tied the hat's red ribbon under her chin.

Betty nodded her approval. "It is perfect, miss."

Pippa smiled. "Thank you, Betty." At that moment, there was a knock on the door and the maid went over to open it.

Bertie came into the room and stopped when he spied his sister. "Good lord, Pippa, what a bang-up outfit!"

"I'm so glad that you like it, brother," she said. "I went to a new dressmaker to have it made. Madame Dupre." She paused, smiling. "She was recommended to me by Lord Allingham."

Bertie appeared surprised. "So, Pippa, you actually took Allingham's advice. That is quite remarkable. But it was dashed fortunate that you did. I daresay you will cause quite a stir in that rig."

Pippa took up her gloves and glanced back at her brother. "I was going to take Patches out for a stroll, Bertie. Would you care to accompany me?"

He nodded. "Yes, I would. I should think being seen with such a fashionable female may raise my reputation considerably."

Pippa laughed and taking her brother's arm, she went downstairs with him. A short time later, with Bertie in charge of Patches's leash, they set off for the park.

"I'm glad you agreed to go with me, Bertie," said Pippa as they walked along. "I have scarcely seen you in the past few days. You seem to be spending much time with these new friends of yours. Indeed, you have been coming home near dawn and sleeping until noon."

He stole a sidelong glance at her. "Do I detect some censure in that remark?"

She shook her head. "Oh, I do not wish to be a scold, Bertie. It is only that I do not wish you to fall in with the wrong company."

Her brother grinned. "Wrong company? Don't be such a cabbage head, Pippa. My friends are from the best families. Mama is quite impressed."

Pippa frowned. "Mama is overcome by anyone with a title, Bertie. But there is many a lord who spends his time drinking and carousing. Indeed, I fear most of them have little else to keep them occupied."

Bertie laughed. "Do not be such an old stick, Pippa."

She sighed. "Oh, very well. I shall not lecture you any further." They continued on until they reached the iron gate which marked the entrance to the park. Patches was quite thrilled at finding herself in a place full of such exciting smells. She pulled eagerly at the lead.

"Do slow down, Patches, old girl," said Bertie. "Running through the park is not at all the thing to do. We must stroll in a leisurely fashion." The wayward canine did not take heed of this remark, continuing to happily pull at the leash."

Walking along with her brother at a rather brisk pace, Pippa was the object of much attention. Several gentlemen riding their horses through the park cast admiring glances at the young lady dressed in the stunning red outfit. Well-dressed ladies driving by in fancy curricles craned their heads to get a better look. And Lady Jersey, one of society's most influential patronesses, went so far as having her driver stop so she could exchange a few words with Pippa and her brother.

As he watched her ladyship drive away, Bertie turned toward his sister and grinned. "I said you would create a sensation in that outfit, Pippa. I would not be surprised if Lady Jersey is on her way to Madame Dupre at this very moment to order a dress in that same shade of red."

Pippa thought of Allingham's reaction to Lady Jersey in crimson and smiled. "I do hope you are right, Bertie."

They continued their walk. Patches was still having a lark. Suddenly spying a squirrel, the large dog lunged and began barking furiously. It took all of Bertie's strength to hang on to her leash. The terrified squirrel made a mad dash up a giant oak tree and then, once safely in the upper branches, chattered angrily down at them.

Patches was still straining at the leash to go after the bushy-

tailed creature. "Come now, girl," said Bertie, holding the leash
with all of his might, "you must know by now that you cannot
climb trees."

Pippa laughed. "Indeed, I don't think she has realized that unfortunate fact yet, Bertie." She and her brother were so intent
upon Patches and the squirrel that they did not notice that another
vehicle was approaching them. At the last moment, Pippa turned
her head and saw the high-perch phaeton and its occupants. "It's
Allingham," she said.

"Allingham," said Bertie. He quickly turned his head to see his
idol.

The viscount, who was driving the phaeton, did not fail to no-
tice Pippa and her brother at the side of the path. His friend Sir
Henry, sitting in the seat next to him, motioned over to them.
"Why look, Jack! It's Miss Grey and her brother."

"I see them," said Allingham coolly. Having immediately observed the red outfit that Pippa was wearing, he was rather irked
with the lady. So that I how she regarded his advice, he told himself.

Allingham pulled up his horses, bringing the phaeton to a stop.
"Miss Grey," said Sir Henry, smiling at Pippa. "And good day to
you, Grey."

Bertie hurried over to them, pulling Patches along with him.
Recognizing Sir Henry, whom he had met at the duchess's soiree,
he smiled. "Good day, Sir Henry. And good day to you, Lord
Allingham. What good fortune to meet you here."

Allingham acknowledged this enthusiastic greeting with an indifferent nod. He then turned his cool gaze toward Pippa, who
had stopped next to the phaeton. Knowing what his lordship
would think of her crimson walking dress, she smiled brightly at
him.

"Good afternoon, my lord. Good afternoon, Sir Henry."

The baronet tipped his tall beaver hat. "Miss Grey," he said
with a charming smile. "I'm delighted to see you again. I did not
have much chance to talk to you at the duchess's soiree since you
were so occupied."

"Thank you, sir," said Pippa. "I did enjoy meeting you and
your wife that evening."

The baronet regarded her with an admiring look. "I must say,
Miss Grey, you look quite lovely. It appears you are partial to
red."

Pippa saw the viscount scowl and tried not to laugh. "Thank
you, sir. It is my favorite color."

"Well, it looks splendid on you, Miss Grey. Does it not, Jack?"

The viscount met Pippa's amused gaze and shook his head. "The lady knows what I think of that color. I daresay, that is why she chose it."

Pippa smiled brightly up at him. "You are a very perceptive man, my lord," she said.

Allingham regarded her silently for a moment and then a slight smile appeared on his handsome face. "And you, Miss Grey, are a vexatious female." She laughed while Bertie and Sir Henry regarded them with perplexed faces.

Patches, on hearing the viscount's voice, was most eager to get near that gentleman. She jumped up, resting her paws on the side of the phaeton. Bertie pulled at her leash. "Oh, do get down, Patches. Down!" Patches took no notice of the young man's commands, but continued to keep her paws perched on the side of the phaeton as she grinned up eagerly at the viscount. "I'm sorry, my lord," said Bertie, glancing up apologetically at Allingham, "but Patches is a strong-willed creature and doesn't always mind."

The viscount gave Pippa a meaningful look. "She must take after her mistress in that regard." Setting his reins aside, Allingham leaned over and patted the dog on the head. Patches seemed quite pleased by this attention and gazed up adoringly at the viscount.

"Jack does have a way with animals," said Sir Henry, smiling as he watched his friend pet the dog. "When he was a boy, he had a menagerie of pets—dogs, cats, rabbits, even a pig."

Pippa regarded the viscount curiously. "A pig, my lord?"

When Allingham did not immediately reply, the baronet continued. "Oh, yes, Miss Grey, a pet pig named Claudius. It was a lucky creature, too, since Jack wouldn't hear of having Claudius made into pork cutlets."

Pippa and Bertie both laughed. Casting his friend a warning look, Allingham gave Patches a final pat and then sat back up in the seat. Picking up the reins, he looked down at Pippa. "Would you care for a ride home, Miss Grey?"

"No, thank you, my lord," she said. "It is very kind of you to offer, but we are enjoying our stroll. It is such a marvelous day and the park is so lovely."

Sir Henry nodded. "Indeed it is, Miss Grey. Have you seen the swans on the pond over there?"

Pippa shook her head. "I wasn't aware there was a pond here."

"Oh, yes," replied the baronet enthusiastically. "It is just through those trees there. It is really quite exceptional." Sir Henry turned to his friend. "It is but a short distance, Jack. Why do we not show the pond to Miss Grey?"

Although the idea of strolling with Pippa through the wooded glade toward the pond seemed strangely appealing to his lordship, Allingham shrugged indifferently. "There are the horses to consider, Henry. You go ahead and I shall wait here."

"Oh, I should be glad to watch them for you, my lord," said Bertie. "If you would care to go." He smiled up at Allingham. "Perhaps you might take charge of Patches?"

The viscount looked from Bertie to Pippa. That young lady was smiling up encouragingly at him. "Do you not wish to see the swans, Lord Allingham?" she asked.

He finally nodded. "Oh, very well," he said, nimbly climbing down from the vehicle's lofty seat. He handed the reins to Bertie who seemed most eager to trade him Patches's leash. Sir Henry followed his friend down from the phaeton and then offered his arm to Pippa. Smiling, she took it and they proceeded toward the small grove of trees. Allingham trailed behind with the large black-and-white dog at his side.

Pippa could not fail to note that Patches behaved exceedingly well as she walked at the viscount's side. The enormous dog walked along in such a well-mannered fashion that Pippa was very much surprised.

As Sir Henry had promised, they had gone but a short distance through the trees when the pond appeared before them. "Oh, it is beautiful, Sir Henry," said Pippa as she looked out at the water. The branches of willow trees arched gracefully over the edge of the pond and the blue sky was reflected on the shimmering surface.

The viscount, instead of enjoying the scenic view of nature before him, was content to fix his gaze on Pippa. Seeing her had once again aroused his desire for the lady. He suddenly wished that he was there alone with her and that he could take her into his arms.

Pippa, unaware of the thoughts she was engendering in the viscount, was still looking out at the water. "I do not see the swans, Sir Henry. Wait, there is one!" Watching the lovely white creature as it glided over the pond, Pippa's eyes suddenly alighted on a woman standing near the edge of the water. The woman was dressed in a plain, sacklike dress that could not disguise the fact that she was pregnant. Her dark hair was disheveled and she seemed to have a rather wild look on her face.

"Oh, dear," said Pippa, watching the stranger with concern.

"Do you see that woman there? She looks quite distraught. We must go and see if we can help her."

The viscount's pleasant musings were quickly cut short by this speech. He followed Pippa's gaze toward the edge of the pond where he spotted the woman in question. He frowned at seeing the woman's condition. "You cannot be serious, Miss Grey," he said. "You mustn't concern yourself with such a person."

Pippa eyed him with a disgusted look. Without another word, she started to make her way toward the other side of the pond. Allingham and Sir Henry exchanged a glance and then followed after her.

As she came nearer to the woman, Pippa suddenly gave a cry. Allingham followed her horrified gaze and saw that the woman had left the edge of the pond and was beginning to wade into the water. The viscount shouted to her, but the woman appeared totally oblivious to their presence.

Realizing the woman's desperate intent, Pippa began to run. Allingham, dropping Patches's leash, began to take off after her. Sir Henry and the dog also proceeded to join in the chase. Quickly overtaking Pippa, the viscount was the first to reach the water. After tossing off his hat, his lordship quickly took off his coat and threw it on the ground. Then, without any hesitation, he waded into the pond. Patches, her Newfoundland blood coming to the fore, quickly jumped into the water after him and began to swim out to the woman.

Pippa and Sir Henry stopped at the pond's edge and watched as Allingham called out to the woman who was now in waist-high water. She looked back, a frantic expression on her face. "Leave me alone!" she cried. She then continued plodding along into deeper water.

The viscount muttered a curse and continued trudging after the woman. As he caught up to her, he reached out and grabbed her arm. Turning around, the woman began to struggle fiercely, but Allingham was able to hold her in a tight grasp. Suddenly she burst into tears and collapsed against the viscount's chest.

Pippa watched the scene with a mixture of horror and amazement. She was quite astonished by the viscount's valiant behavior in rescuing the woman. Even more surprising was how he now had an arm around the woman, speaking to her in a low, comforting voice.

After some minutes, the woman seemed to gain control of herself and Allingham led her back slowly through the water. Patches, who had been swimming around them in considerable agitation, followed close behind. When Allingham and the woman reached the shore, Pippa and Sir Henry were there to meet them.

"There now," said Allingham gently, as he steered the woman onto the bank. Patches, climbing up out of the water, barked excitedly and then gave her wet fur a tremendous shake.

Pippa could now see that the woman before them was a mere girl of sixteen or seventeen. The girl gazed at her with sad brown eyes. "I am sorry, miss, but I had nowhere to go. They threw me out, you see. Because of . . . because of . . ." The young woman stopped and gazed pitifully at Pippa.

"Oh, my poor dear," said Pippa, reaching her arms toward her. The girl did not hesitate but, bursting into tears once again, hurried into Pippa's embrace.

Sir Henry quickly took off his coat and placed it around the girl's shoulders. He then clapped his friend on the back. "Well done, Jack," he said in a low voice. The viscount did not reply but kept his attention on Pippa and the girl.

The young woman had quit crying and was wiping her eyes with one hand. Pippa gently pushed an unruly strand of dark hair from the girl's face. "You must get out of those wet clothes. Come, you will go home with me."

The girl looked up at her and appeared close to tears again. "Go home with you, miss?" she asked in disbelief.

Pippa nodded, smiling at her. "Yes, you shall. I am Miss Grey. What is your name?"

"Lizzy, miss," said the girl. "Lizzy Claypool."

"Well, Lizzy, we should go now. Are you all right?"

Lizzy managed a weak smile. "Yes, miss."

Pippa turned to the viscount. "Could you drive us, my lord?"

"Of course, Miss Grey," he said.

On hearing Allingham addressed, Lizzy regarded him with some astonishment. "M'lord?" she repeated in a small voice.

Pippa turned back to her. "Yes, Lizzy, this gentleman is Lord Allingham. And the other gentleman is Sir Henry Lonsdale."

Lizzy regarded them both with a shamefaced expression. "I'm sorry, m'lord, sir, to cause so much trouble." She looked down at the viscount's feet. "And your poor boots, m'lord."

Allingham glanced down at his drenched boots. He shrugged. "It is of little importance, my girl," he said. The viscount turned to Pippa and found that lady was regarding him with an odd expression. "Shall we go, Miss Grey?" he asked.

Pippa suddenly smiled at him. "Yes, my lord, I think we

should." She glanced at the girl. "Come, Lizzy, it is but a short distance to his lordship's phaeton." The young woman nodded and they began walking toward the woods. As Sir Henry picked up Patches's lead, Allingham reclaimed his hat and coat from the ground. They then proceeded to follow the two women back to the phaeton.

12

Bertie was quite astonished when he observed his sister returning from the pond with the bedraggled Lizzy at her side. Noting that the viscount and Patches also appeared to have taken a soaking, the young man quickly climbed down from the phaeton and hurried toward them.

"Whatever has happened, Pippa?" he asked.

Pippa, who was leading Lizzy along by the arm, looked over at her brother. "I shall tell you all about it later, Bertie. But first, we must return home. Lord Allingham is going to drive us."

Bertie gave his sister a quizzical look but obediently followed after her to the phaeton. After helping Lizzy and Pippa up into the vehicle, Bertie turned to the viscount. "But what of Patches, my lord? You cannot want her to ride in your phaeton. She is a frightful mess."

Allingham glanced down at the wet dog. Patches barked and grinned up at him. The viscount smiled slightly and looked back at Bertie. "She can sit on the floor. If you think you can manage her well enough."

Bertie nodded. "Come, girl. Up here." Patches needed no other invitation, but jumped eagerly up into the vehicle. Bertie then got into the phaeton and squeezed in beside his sister and Lizzy. He watched as the coatless Sir Henry climbed up into the high seat, followed by the viscount.

Although he was dying of curiosity, Bertie remained quiet during the short journey back to their house. It was obvious to him that the young woman with his sister was very upset and very pregnant. Keeping a firm grasp on Patches, Bertie could only sit and wonder what had occurred.

After the viscount pulled up to the Greys' residence, he quickly descended from the driver's seat. He then assisted Lizzy and Pippa down from the vehicle and solicitously escorted them into the house. Bertie, Sir Henry, and the rambunctious Patches followed along behind.

Although the butler was rather surprised by the appearance of Pippa with the young woman in the sodden dress, he did his best not to show it. "Hawkins," said Pippa, "this is Lizzy Claypool. She needs some dry clothes. And I am sure she could also use something to eat. Could you have Mrs. Fox see to it?"

The butler nodded and looked at Lizzy. "If you would come this way."

Lizzy regarded the servant with some trepidation. She glanced back at Pippa. "Don't worry, Lizzy," said Pippa gently. "They will take good care of you. And I shall be in to see you shortly."

"Thank you, miss," said Lizzy. Remembering Sir Henry's coat, she took it off of her shoulders and handed it to the baronet. Lizzy then went off meekly with the butler.

"Good lord, Pippa," said Bertie, who could no longer contain his curiosity, "what the deuce is this all about? Who is that girl?"

Pippa sighed. "You shall hear all about it, Bertie. But I think you should first assist Lord Allingham in finding some dry clothes."

The viscount shook his head. "That is not necessary, Miss Grey."

Pippa eyed him with a stern expression. "I insist you do so, my lord. You are thoroughly soaked. I would not want you to catch a chill."

He smiled down at her. "I am gratified to hear that, Miss Grey." Pippa smiled back at him.

Bertie turned to his lordship. "If you would follow me, my lord. I'm certain we shall be able to find something for you to wear." The viscount gave a slight nod and followed after him.

Pippa turned to the baronet who had put his coat back on. "Come, Sir Henry, let us go and wait in the drawing room."

Once inside the fashionable room, Sir Henry sat down on the sofa. "That was quite an adventure, was it not, Miss Grey?"

She nodded. "Indeed it was, sir."

The baronet smiled. "I must say my friend behaved most heroically, rushing into the pond after the girl as he did."

"Yes," said Pippa, "it was most remarkable. I should not have expected his lordship to do such a thing."

Sir Henry regarded her closely. "That it is only because you do not know Allingham very well, Miss Grey. Jack and I have been friends for ages and I can assure you, his behavior today was not at all unusual. He is an excellent fellow."

Pippa smiled and proceeded to ask the baronet about his friendship with the viscount. Sir Henry was most willing to provide the lady with information, launching into several anecdotes concerning incidents from their childhood. Finding herself suddenly rather eager to hear about his lordship, Pippa listened with great interest.

After they had been talking for a short time, the object of their discussion reentered the room. Attired in a pair of Bertie's cream-colored pantaloons and shiny black boots, Allingham made his way over toward his friend and Pippa. Bertie, a broad grin on his face, was following behind him.

"Well, Jack," said Sir Henry, "it appears young Grey was able to clothe you quite admirably."

Bertie appeared thrilled by this comment. "Oh, I fear the pantaloons are a bit too short for his lordship and the boots are frightfully tight," he said.

Allingham gave the young man a slightly impatient look. "They are fine, Grey. I am in your debt." He then took a chair next to Pippa. Bertie eagerly took another seat nearby and continued to beam proudly with the knowledge that the great Allingham was wearing his clothes.

"Well, Jack," said the baronet, smiling over at his friend, "while you were gone Miss Grey and I were having a most enjoyable chat."

"Were you?" asked Allingham regarding his friend a trifle warily.

"Yes, we were. I was telling Miss Grey all about you."

The viscount glanced over at Pippa and met that lady's amused gaze. "It was a most fascinating topic, my lord," she said mischievously.

Allingham frowned but did not reply. Sir Henry, noting his friend's expression, was rather enjoying himself. "You could hardly blame us for talking about you, Jack, after your heroic deed today."

"Heroic deed?" asked Bertie with considerable interest. "I do wish you would tell me what happened at the pond, Pippa. His lordship only said the young woman had an accident. He made it seem a small matter."

Pippa smiled. "It was not a small matter at all, Bertie. You see, the young woman was quite distraught and I fear she was trying to drown herself in the pond."

"The devil you say!" exclaimed her brother in astonishment.

Pippa nodded. "Lord Allingham went in after her. He rescued the poor girl."

Bertie regarded the viscount with a worshipful expression. "Good heavens! That was heroic of you, my lord!"

The viscount shook his head. "Do not be absurd, Grey."

"I do not think it at all absurd," said Pippa, gazing up at his lordship with a serious expression. "You *are* a hero, my lord, for saving Lizzy as you did."

The viscount experienced a shock when he found that the lady was regarding him with a look of admiration in her lovely blue eyes. At that moment Allingham had an almost overpowering urge to lean over and kiss her. Instead, he merely shrugged. "I assure you, Miss Grey, it took no great bravery. The water was not at all deep."

Pippa regarded him solemnly. "Well, perhaps." She paused and suddenly smiled impishly at him. "But, in any case, it was courageous of you to plunge into the pond like that when you knew it would doubtlessly ruin your boots, my lord."

Allingham smiled. "It was, indeed," he murmured. He turned to the baronet who had been watching their exchange with considerable interest. "I do think we should go, Harry, while Miss Grey holds such a charitable opinion of me."

Sir Henry laughed. "That is a good idea, Jack. I daresay, she cannot retain it for long."

After the gentlemen had taken their leave, Bertie shook his head. "By Jupiter, I am very sorry to have missed such excitement, Pippa. Lord Allingham rescuing the young woman from the pond! You must tell me everything!"

Pippa nodded and she proceeded to describe the incident to her brother at great length. Bertie listened to the tale with considerable relish, interrupting every so often with a "Good lord, Pippa!" Before Pippa had finished her account, her mother returned home from her afternoon calls. This forced Pippa to begin the story all over again.

Mrs. Grey was quite horrified by the tale. "Good heavens, you mean the girl was planning to do away with herself?" she asked.

"I fear so, Mama," said Pippa. "She seemed quite desperate."

Mrs. Grey shook her head. "Well, considering the predicament the girl got herself into, it is not so very surprising," she said.

Pippa frowned. "She hardly got into what you have called her 'predicament' by herself, Mama."

Mrs. Grey nodded. "That is very true, my dear. But, it was most fortunate that you happened upon the girl. And it appears that Lord Allingham acted quite splendidly."

"Yes, he did, Mama," said Pippa distractedly. She was somewhat puzzled by the viscount's apparently changed character. She had earlier formed an opinion of him that was decidedly unfavorable. Indeed, it was hard to forget the proud, imperious man who had handed them a list of persons they should avoid. Yet even then her feelings about Allingham had been rather confused. Now after his rescue of Lizzy, the viscount seemed somewhat of an enigma to her.

Pippa suddenly stood up. "If you will excuse me, I'm going to see how Lizzy is faring." She then left the room, giving her mother and brother ample opportunity to discuss the case of the unfortunate Lizzy Claypool.

Making her way to the kitchen, Pippa found Lizzy sitting at the table. She was now dressed in a dark blue dress and her dark hair was pulled up in a tidy knot on top of her head. As Pippa entered the room, Lizzy rose quickly to her feet.

"Do sit down, Lizzy," said Pippa.

"Thank you, miss," returned the girl, smiling gratefully at her.

Mrs. Collins, the Greys' cook, stood hovering behind the girl. A plump, good-natured woman, Mrs. Collins was quite concerned over Lizzy. She was eager to give Pippa a report on the young woman's progress. "The poor girl was quite famished, miss," she said, shaking her head. "I'll warrant she hasn't eaten proper in a month." The cook paused and smiled. "But we shall fatten her up in a short time, miss."

Pippa smiled in return. "I'm sure you will. Thank you, Mrs. Collins." She walked over to the table. "How are you, Lizzy?"

"Much better, miss. Mrs. Fox and Mrs. Collins have been ever so kind." Lizzy's voice suddenly trembled and a tear began to fall down her cheek. "Oh, miss, if you hadn't come along when you did . . ."

Pippa looked over at the cook. "Mrs. Collins, I need to talk to Lizzy alone for a moment."

"Yes, miss," she said, nodding and then hurrying out of the room.

Pippa put a hand on Lizzy's arm. "Don't be upset, Lizzy."

The girl shook her head. "I know it was wicked of me, miss, but I didn't know what else to do. I had no one to help me, you see. I thought perhaps it would be better for me and the baby to just . . ." She stopped and began to sob quietly.

"Now, now," said Pippa, "you have been through a dreadful time, Lizzy. But you will be all right now. You can stay here until your baby is born. You mustn't worry. We will think of something else later."

Lizzy wiped her eyes. "You are too good, miss."

Pippa smiled at her. She hesitated a moment. "I know you may not wish to speak of this, Lizzy, but what about the baby's father? Can he not help you?"

Lizzy shook her head. "No, miss."

"Does he know about the child?" asked Pippa.

Lizzy nodded. "Oh, yes, I told him. He said it was no concern of his. I got so angry I went and talked to his mother." She paused and then went on somewhat defiantly. "You see, miss, I was a maid in the young gentleman's house."

Pippa frowned. "And this gentleman took advantage of you?"

Lizzy sighed. "I have to confess, miss, that I did want him to. He was my mistress's son and had just come out of the army. He was ever so handsome and was very good to me. Well, miss, one thing led to another . . ." Lizzy blushed and then continued. "I figured I was going to have a baby, miss, and I was scared. I was too afraid to tell anyone. And then I knew the baby would be starting to show. So, I worked up my courage and told the gentleman." Lizzy faltered a moment. "He was very angry, Miss. He said it was all my fault."

"What a despicable man!" said Pippa disgustedly. "To take advantage of you, a young girl in his mother's employ, in such a disgraceful manner and then to blame you for what happened."

Lizzy shook her head sadly. "I realized he was just having his fun with me, miss. He didn't love me at all. As I said, I was so angry, I went and told my mistress. It was very stupid of me. She said I was lying and threw me out of her house."

"That is monstrous!" cried Pippa.

"I didn't have anywhere to go, miss," continued Lizzy. "I could not go back to my family. My mother would be furious. Oh, miss, I'm so ashamed."

Pippa hesitated. "But you are not to blame, Lizzy. You must not upset yourself. We will take care of you."

Lizzy looked at her gratefully. "You are the kindest lady, miss. But, I can work. Please, I should like to."

Pippa smiled. "We shall see." She stood up. "For now, Lizzy, you must get your strength back. Do you understand?"

The girl smiled up at her. "Yes, miss. Thank you, miss."

Pippa nodded and then left the kitchen. As she walked back to the drawing room, she reflected upon Lizzy's sad story and the perfidy of the male sex.

13

Pippa wasted no time in repeating Lizzy's sorry tale to her mother and brother. Mrs. Grey was quite shocked by the girl's story and Bertie agreed with his sister that Lizzy had been treated quite infamously by her former employer.

On returning home from his office, Mr. Grey was also informed of the day's surprising events. After hearing his daughter's impassioned account, Pippa's father declared that Lizzy could stay in their household as long as she wished. He also gave his opinion that the young gentleman responsible for Lizzy's condition should be horsewhipped.

The following afternoon, Pippa entered the drawing room to find her mother engaged in a serious conversation with their housekeeper, Mrs. Fox.

"Oh, do excuse me, Mama," said Pippa. "I did not know you were occupied."

Her mother looked over at her and smiled. "Do come in, Pippa. Mrs. Fox and I were finished with our business."

Taking the cue, the housekeeper rose from her chair and quickly departed. Pippa joined her mother on the sofa. "I hope I did not interrupt any serious discussion, Mama," she said. "You and Mrs. Fox appeared rather grave."

Mrs. Grey shook her head. "We were just discussing young Lizzy. It is all very distressing." She paused. "Mrs. Fox seems impressed with the girl. She said she is very pleasant and eager to earn her keep."

"She could hardly work in her condition, Mama," said Pippa.

"Oh, I don't mean that the poor girl would do any heavy work, but Mrs. Fox has discovered that Lizzy is rather handy with a needle. She will have her do some mending and perhaps some embroidery. Really, Pippa, I think the girl should prefer to do something."

"Yes, I'm sure you are right, Mama," said Pippa.

Mrs. Grey sighed and reluctantly took up her needlework. "Per-

haps I should have Lizzy finish this. I daresay, I am quite hopeless with a needle."

Pippa smiled. "Then why do you bother with it, Mama?"

Her mother looked up at her daughter in surprise. "Why, a lady
must do such things, Pippa, no matter how much she despises
them."

Pippa shook her head. "I cannot agree, Mama. A lady should
do what she wishes."

Mrs. Grey was silent for a moment as she considered her
daughter's peculiar notion. Fortunately, she did not have to ponder the matter for long since the butler suddenly appeared in the
drawing room. "Excuse me, Mrs. Grey," he said, "but Lord
Allingham is here to see you."

"Lord Allingham!" cried the lady excitedly. "Oh, do show him
in immediately, Hawkins," she said.

Pippa was somewhat surprised to hear of the viscount's visit.
She quickly put a hand up to her auburn hair, attempting to tuck
in a stray curl.

Mrs. Grey looked down and hastily straightened her lace collar.
"Oh, I do wish I had worn my yellow dress," she said mournfully.

"You look fine, Mama," said Pippa.

Mrs. Grey smiled at her daughter and glanced nervously toward the door, watching for Allingham's arrival. She did not have
to wait long for Hawkins returned shortly. "The Viscount Allingham," he announced.

That gentleman entered the room. As usual Allingham looked
handsome and fashionable in a well-cut coat of charcoal gray. He
directed a slight bow to Mrs. Grey. "Madam," he said. He then
turned toward Pippa. "Miss Grey."

Mrs. Grey appeared all in a flutter. "Oh, my lord, I am so
happy that you have called upon us. My daughter is very pleased
as well." At this remark, Allingham cast a curious glance toward
Pippa. While that lady was regarding him with a rather pleasant
smile, he could not detect any eagerness in her expression.

In truth, Pippa was not certain how she felt about the viscount
at that moment. She had so thoroughly disliked the gentleman that
she was now having some difficulty explaining the new feelings
she was experiencing toward him. As her eyes alighted on Allingham's familiar face and form, Pippa suddenly felt the rather disturbing stirring of an attraction for him.

Mrs. Grey smiled broadly at Allingham and motioned him to a
seat. "Do sit down in that chair, my lord. It is the most comfortable one in the room."

His lordship followed her instructions, sitting down in the designated chair. "I do hope I did not call at an inconvenient time, ma'am," he said, addressing Mrs. Grey.

"You could never do that, Lord Allingham!" insisted the lady. "We are delighted to have your lordship honor us so."

Pippa listened to this comment in some embarrassment. She wished her mother was not so effusive in her behavior toward the viscount.

Allingham, who was quite used to sycophancy, merely nodded benevolently. After casting another glance toward Pippa, he turned back to her mother. "I came to return the clothes that your son so graciously lent to me yesterday, Mrs. Grey. I gave them to your butler."

"Oh, you did not have to do so, my lord," said Mrs. Grey apologetically. "We could have sent someone to get them. In fact, we were going to return your clothes to you. It is only that the servants are having a bit of trouble with your boots." She paused and regarded him in some trepidation. "My butler tells me that some progress has been made on them, but I'm afraid, my lord, the boots are still in a rather sorry condition."

To her relief, this news did not seem to perturb his lordship. "It does not signify, ma'am. One could hardly expect it, after all. I shall take them back with me."

"Very well, my lord," said Mrs. Grey. Looking over at her daughter, the older woman smiled again. "Oh, Lord Allingham, Pippa has told me what happened yesterday at the park. My dear sir, you were most gallant! You behaved like one of the knights of the round table."

Raising an eyebrow slightly at this remark, Allingham looked over at Pippa and found she was regarding him in some amusement. "You are right, Mama," she said, smiling at the viscount, "his lordship did act very much like one of King Arthur's knights." She paused a moment and her smile grew wider. "It was fortunate, however, that you were not in armour, my lord. I daresay, wading through that pond in such an outfit would have been most difficult."

Allingham smiled over at her. "Yes, I daresay you are right, Miss Grey."

When Pippa smiled in return, Mrs. Grey was encouraged by what seemed to be a more amicable relationship between her daughter and the viscount. "I do hope you did not suffer any ill effects from your exertions yesterday, Lord Allingham," she said in a voice full of concern.

Allingham shook his head. "Not at all, Mrs. Grey." He turned again toward Pippa. "And how is the young woman, Lizzy was her name, was it not?"

Pippa smiled. "Yes, Lizzy. Lizzy Claypool. She is doing very well, my lord. The poor thing had scarcely eaten for weeks. But, we shall see that she is well taken care of here."

The viscount regarded her in some surprise. "You do not mean to say, Miss Grey, that you are having the girl stay with you?"

Pippa nodded. "She is sharing a room with my maid."

Allingham frowned. "I don't think that is wise, Miss Grey. After all, what do you know of the girl?"

Pippa, who had been so pleased at Allingham's affability, found herself now rather irked by this remark. "I know quite enough about her, my lord," she said.

"But one must be careful about taking such persons into one's home," said Allingham, his voice taking on the condescending tone that had always irritated her.

She frowned. "What would you have us do, my lord? Send her to an almshouse?"

"No, of course not," said his lordship hastily. Noting Pippa's expression, he regretted his words, for he realized that he wanted her good opinion.

Mrs. Grey, sensing trouble, was glad when a diversion arrived in the form of the butler carrying a silver salver. The servant gave a slight cough. "I do beg your pardon, ma'am, but there is a gentleman here to call upon Miss Grey."

Pippa's mother turned to the viscount. "It is probably the Marquess of Ravensly," she said with a knowing smile. "That gentleman has been showing considerable attention toward Pippa." Although this remark did not at all please Allingham, he merely responded with an expression of polite indifference.

"The gentleman is not Lord Ravensly, ma'am," said the servant. He advanced toward Pippa with the salver. That lady picked it up and smiled.

"Oh, it is Mr. Cartwright! Do show him in, Hawkins."

The viscount had a pang of jealousy when he saw Pippa's pleased reaction to the gentleman's calling card. Wondering just who this Cartwright was, he folded his arms in front of him and gazed grimly at the door.

Mrs. Grey was also trying to figure out who her daughter's caller was. "Mr. Cartwright," she said with a perplexed expression. "I do not remember the name, my dear."

"I did tell you about him, Mama," said Pippa. "Do you not remember? He is the gentleman I met at the bookstore."

"The gentleman at the bookstore," echoed Mrs. Grey, suddenly regarding her daughter in alarm. However, before she could protest further, the butler arrived with Cartwright in tow.

Pippa smiled brightly at the young man and extended her hand. "Mr. Cartwright," she said, "I'm so glad you have called."

He quickly approached her and took her hand in his own. Bowing slightly, he smiled charmingly at her. "Miss Grey, I am delighted to see you again. I would have come sooner but I fear some business matters prevented me from doing so."

The viscount was none too happy at seeing the handsome young Cartwright and Pippa together. It seemed obvious to him that the lady was very much delighted with the fellow's attentions.

"Mama," said Pippa, "this is Mr. William Cartwright. Mr. Cartwright, this is my mother."

Although Mrs. Grey was disturbed by the young man from the bookstore appearing in her drawing room, she managed to smile graciously at him. "Mr. Cartwright," she said.

He bowed. "I am charmed to meet you, ma'am," he said politely.

"And this is Lord Allingham," continued Pippa. His lordship gave the young gentleman a curt nod.

"Cartwright," he said coolly.

The publisher, who had heard of the famous arbiter of fashion, regarded him with interest. "Lord Allingham," he said.

"Do sit down, sir," said Pippa. The young gentleman was only too happy to do so. He smiled again and took a chair across from her. "I do hope your business is going well, Mr. Cartwright."

"Tolerably so, Miss Grey," he said.

"Oh dear, only tolerably so, Mr. Cartwright?" she asked.

He laughed. "I fear so, Miss Grey. Unfortunately, the nature of our books do not guarantee a wide audience."

Pippa shook her head. "Well, they certainly deserve much attention, sir." She turned to her mother. "You do recall, Mama, that Mr. Cartwright is a publisher?"

Mrs. Grey nodded. "Yes, my daughter told me of your business, Mr. Cartwright." She regarded him hopefully as she continued. "I daresay, it keeps you rather occupied."

"Yes, it does that, ma'am," he said with a grin. "My nose is most decidedly kept to the grindstone. Or perhaps, I should say, the printing press." He paused and looked at Pippa. "We have been working rather feverishly this past week putting out a new tract by Mr. Kent."

Pippa looked quite thrilled by this information. "I will be eager to read it, sir."

The viscount, who had been sitting in glum silence, suddenly entered the conversation. "Mr. Kent?" he asked, raising his dark eyebrows questioningly.

Cartwright looked over at him. "Yes, my lord. Mr. Josiah Kent."

"Good God," muttered Allingham, "you publish the rantings of that fellow?"

Pippa frowned at the viscount. "They are not rantings, Lord Allingham. Mr. Kent writes eloquently about the injustices in our society. I find him most admirable."

"Admirable?" repeated the viscount in disbelief. "The fellow is a radical. He wishes to be rid of the monarchy and the aristocracy. Your 'admirable' Mr. Kent will not be happy until we are all riding in tumbrels to the guillotine."

"That is preposterous, Lord Allingham!" cried Pippa. "You are being ridiculous!"

"Really, Pippa!" scolded Mrs. Grey. She looked over at the viscount. "You must forgive my daughter, my lord. She is sometimes too hasty in her speech." Allingham did not reply, but sat regarding Pippa with a frown. "Oh, dear," continued Mrs. Grey in great consternation, "I don't think we should speak about politics. It is much too unpleasant a subject."

Cartwright nodded. "Indeed, Mrs. Grey, politics can be decidedly unpleasant. 'Tis best to change the subject."

Mrs. Grey smiled gratefully at him. She was very impressed with the young gentleman, but she only wished that he was not in trade. "It does appear that it might rain today, do you not agree, Mr. Cartwright?" she asked, happy to turn to the safe topic of the weather.

He smiled and nodded. "I think it quite safe to concur with your prediction, ma'am." The publisher and Mrs. Grey proceeded to discuss the weather for a time. Mrs. Grey then ventured to tell the young man about the previous day's excitement. Cartwright listened to the story with considerable interest. Allingham remained stonily silent even as Mrs. Grey sang his praises for his part in Lizzy's rescue.

The publisher shook his head sadly after hearing the tale of the unfortunate girl. "It is terrible to think of the young woman's desperation," he said. "But, I fear it is not at all uncommon. There are far too many young women who find themselves in similar circumstances. In fact, a poor girl was just pulled out of the Thames this morning."

Pippa looked horrified. "Oh, no! How dreadful!"

"Really, Cartwright," said the viscount, "that is hardly a subject for ladies."

Cartwright shrugged. "Perhaps so. Forgive me, ladies."

"There is nothing to forgive, Mr. Cartwright," said Pippa. Directing a meaningful glance at Allingham, she continued. "I'm glad to find that some gentlemen believe that ladies can discuss serious topics."

"But it is so unpleasant," said Mrs. Grey.

"Yes, it is, ma'am," said Cartwright with a grave expression. "But sometimes it is necessary to face unpleasantness."

"Yes, that is very true," said Pippa.

Cartwright smiled at her. "You may be interested to know, Miss Grey, that I have an acquaintance who is doing something to alleviate this unfortunate problem. His name is Edward Bell and he has started a charitable house for such women."

"How very splendid of him," said Pippa. "I should be very happy to donate money to such an endeavor. Could you get me an address for Mr. Bell, sir?"

Cartwright smiled admiringly at her. "I would be delighted to do so. You have a very kind heart, Miss Grey."

A short time later, Cartwright announced that he must be going. Allingham could not fail to note Pippa's disappointment at this news. He scowled darkly as the gentleman departed.

As soon as Cartwright was gone, the viscount shook his head. "I fear I must be blunt." He looked over at Pippa. "Even though I risk displeasing you, Miss Grey. However, I have an obligation to advise your family."

"And we are only too happy to take your advice, Lord Allingham," said Mrs. Grey.

While the viscount might have replied that Pippa did not seem so inclined to take his advice, he wisely refrained from such a comment. "It is Cartwright. It is inadvisable to receive him. Indeed, there are few in society who could understand your welcoming such a man into your home. As a publisher of inflammatory literature, he is quite unacceptable. Why, I can scarcely imagine what the Prince Regent would think if he heard of it. No, you must never again admit Cartwright."

Pippa frowned ominously. She had begun to think Allingham very different from the snobbish haughty man she had first thought he was. She had even admitted to herself that she felt an attraction to him. But now he had returned to his old arrogant, insufferable ways. "I beg your pardon, Lord Allingham, but I do not think it is any business of yours whom we receive in our house."

"Pippa!" cried Mrs. Grey.

Allingham frowned in return at Pippa. "Since I was given the responsibility of assisting you in society, Miss Grey, I think I have every right to express such an opinion."

Pippa's blue eyes glinted dangerously. "Your opinions are not wanted, my lord. I find Mr. Cartwright a most charming gentleman, and I consider his publishing endeavors most praiseworthy."

Allingham abruptly got up from his chair. "I see we are in disagreement, Miss Grey," he said, regarding her with an icy stare. "I know that there is no point in trying to reason with you at this time. I will only say that society's good opinion, while hard to gain, is all too easily lost. Familiarity with such a man as Cartwright is a very serious mistake. I shall take my leave. Good day, Miss Grey." After nodding gravely to Pippa, he bowed to her mother. "Mrs. Grey. I shall show myself out." Without another word, the viscount strode out of the room.

When he had gone Mrs. Grey clutched her hands together in a despairing gesture. "Oh, Pippa!" she cried. "How could you have been so rude to Lord Allingham?"

"It is he who was rude," said Pippa. "How dare he speak so to us? You would think Mr. Cartwright was some sort of viper. Really, Mama, I find Allingham completely unreasonable." Mrs. Grey sighed and decided that controlling her wayward daughter was a totally hopeless task.

14

In the morning Pippa sat in the drawing room with her mother going through the mail. Patches slept peacefully at her feet.

While Mrs. Grey had been thoroughly put out with her daughter for her comments to Allingham the day before, she had by now put the matter behind her. Pippa, who did not enjoy having her mother angry with her, took care not to provoke any argument. She found it best to say nothing further about the viscount.

Mrs. Grey took up a letter. Breaking the seal, she unfolded it and read it eagerly. "It is from Lady Westborough. She is inviting us to dinner Tuesday next. She is Ravensly's aunt. I would not be surprised if Ravensly would be there."

"Now, Mama," said Pippa, "you know I think Lord Ravensly a very nice young man, but you will be disappointed if you imagine him as your son-in-law."

Mrs. Grey, who had been doing just that, frowned. "I only said that he may be there. I assure you I meant nothing by it, Pippa."

"I see, Mama," said Pippa, suppressing a smile. She opened another letter. "It is from Lady Granville. She says she will call today. She asks if we might ride with her in the park this afternoon."

"I don't know," said Mrs. Grey, taking Isabelle's note from her daughter's hand and scanning it. "I'm not sure if you should do so."

Pippa frowned. "Because Lord Allingham disapproves of her?"

"I do not wish to put you in a bad temper, Pippa, but I must remind you that Lord Allingham does not like Lady Granville. He said we must have nothing to do with her. I have never been altogether pleased above receiving her here, but going riding with her in the park is far worse. Everyone would see you. You know Lord Allingham will hear of it."

"Mama, why do you care so what he thinks? We are doing very well in society. I cannot imagine that riding in the park with Lady

Granville will doom us. I have yet to find what is so terrible about her save that she has aroused the great Allingham's displeasure."

Mrs. Grey frowned. "I was told that she is rather . . . wild."

"Oh, Mama," said Pippa. "She is received everywhere."

"That may be, but Allingham did say we should avoid her. I feel it wise to do as he says."

"Nonsense," said Pippa. "I intend to ride with Lady Granville in the park. I hope you will come as well."

While Mrs. Grey did not really wish to do so, she felt that she had little choice in the matter. After all, if Pippa was determined to ride about with Lady Granville, at least it would be better if her mother were beside her.

Soon after Isabelle arrived in the afternoon, Mrs. Grey and Pippa found themselves seated in Isabelle's new carriage, a commodious vehicle with two seats facing each other.

Isabelle and Mrs. Grey occupied the seat with its back to the driver while Pippa sat alone facing them. The weather was overcast, but pleasantly warm. As they rode along, Pippa was glad that her mother seemed to have forgotten her reluctance to go riding with Lady Granville. She seemed to be enjoying herself as she chatted with Isabelle.

Pippa was well aware that they were drawing a good deal of attention as they made their way to the park. A number of heads turned to see three elegantly dressed ladies riding in a fashionable carriage with the Granville coat of arms adorning its sides.

As the vehicle turned into the park, Isabelle espied a gentleman walking there. "Look, it's Seagrave! Do you know him?"

Pippa nodded. "We met at the Duchess of Northampton's soiree," she said. Remembering how Allingham had quarreled with the man, she regarded him with interest. He looked very handsome strolling along in his fine clothes. He carried a silver-tipped walking stick and wore a tall beaver hat.

Mrs. Grey eyed Seagrave disapprovingly, knowing that Allingham had placed him on his list of undesirables. She was not at all pleased when Isabelle commanded her driver to pull up alongside him.

Seagrave appeared very happy to see them. Hurrying up alongside the carriage, he tipped his hat. "Good afternoon, ladies."

"Seagrave," said Isabelle, smiling conspiratorially, "what a coincidence to find you here."

Pippa could not fail to notice how the two of them looked at each other. She suspected that the meeting was not a coincidence at all. Isabelle continued. "You do remember Mrs. Grey and her daughter, Miss Grey?"

"Of course," said Seagrave, bowing first to Mrs. Grey and then to Pippa. "How good it is to meet you again."

"You must come and ride with us, Seagrave," said Isabelle.

The baron needed no further encouragement. Opening the carriage door, he hoped agilely into the vehicle. Taking a seat beside Pippa, he smiled at the ladies. "I cannot believe my good fortune. I shall be the envy of everyone who sees me riding about with three beauties."

Mrs. Grey smiled at the compliment. "It is a fine day, is it not, Lord Seagrave?"

"It cannot be otherwise, ma'am, in such company as yours."

Pippa's mother blushed like a schoolgirl. Pippa, however, raised her eyebrows slightly and eyed Seagrave with faint disfavor. There was something about the man she did not like although she could not really know why. He seemed perfectly pleasant and affable. Still, there was something indefinable about him that put her off.

They continued on through the park with Isabelle's fine chestnut horses trotting smartly. Seagrave began to talk about his recent meeting with the Prince Regent, a topic of keen interest to the ladies.

Pippa listened and smiled as Seagrave told amusing anecdotes. As they rode along, she was aware that everyone in the park was looking at them. She received the nods and stares with aplomb until two horsemen appeared coming toward them.

Recognizing Allingham and Sir Henry Lonsdale, Pippa could not help but frown. "Look, my dear Isabelle," said Seagrave. "Allingham approaches with his friend Lonsdale."

Isabelle turned his head. "Why, yes." She turned back to smile at Seagrave and Pippa. "What a detestable man. Oh, I should not say so since I know he has been so kind to Miss Grey."

Pippa tried to appear indifferent as the carriage came upon the two riders. Seeing her sitting beside Seagrave, the viscount controlled himself admirably, his face registering no emotion whatsoever. Sir Henry, on the other hand, looked completely astonished.

As the carriage passed by the two gentlemen, Pippa's eyes met Allingham's. Seagrave tipped his hat in an ironical gesture. The viscount reacted by ignoring his old adversary. Taking his eyes away from Pippa, he did not respond in any way but rode on.

"I say," said Seagrave, "it appears that Allingham has given us the cut direct."

"Indeed he has," said Isabelle. "Not that we should care at all for his good opinion."

Mrs. Grey frowned at the viscount's retreating form. Unlike Isabelle, Pippa's mother cared very much for Allingham's good opinion. Knowing that he was doubtlessly very displeased to see them in a carriage with Lady Granville and Seagrave, she regarded her daughter with a worried look.

"I do think Allingham the most disagreeable man," said Isabelle. "Oh, I know he has been very civil to you ladies, but I have known him a good deal longer."

"And I have known him longest of all," said Seagrave. "That is probably why I dislike him the most."

"I should be interested in knowing why you so dislike him, Lord Seagrave," said Pippa.

"Oh, I shall be happy to tell you, Miss Grey. You see, I was at school with him. There was no more odious fellow. He was so very proud. Why, he considered everyone his inferior. Indeed, he would hardly deign to speak to anyone." Seagrave shook his head. "And he was one of the worst cricketers at school," he added as an afterthought.

"But he has been so kind to us," said Mrs. Grey, rising to Allingham's defense. "I think him quite likable."

"You do not know him very well, ma'am," said Isabelle. "But, indeed, why should we ruin our enjoyable ride discussing Allingham? Come, let us talk of something else."

"Yes, I do agree," said Seagrave. "Why don't you tell the ladies of your meeting with Princess Charlotte, Isabelle?"

Isabelle was only too happy to oblige and the conversation shifted to the royal princess. Although she tried to listen, Pippa found herself distracted by the idea of Allingham and his disapproval. Try as she would to convince herself she cared nothing for his opinion, she found that the incident disturbed her. As the carriage continued on, she looked thoughtful and then tried to concentrate on what Isabelle was saying.

15

When Pippa and her mother returned home, Mrs. Grey said that she had a headache and would retire to bed until dinner. Happy to have some time alone, Pippa went to her sitting room where she reflected about her outing with Isabelle. Since meeting Allingham in the park, she had not been able to think of anything but his look of disapproval. How shocked he must have been to have found her sitting with Seagrave in Lady Granville's carriage. Indeed, they were the two persons in society he had expressly advised her against.

Pippa frowned as she thought of Allingham. He was so certain that he could dictate whom she should see. She thought resentfully of his attitude toward Cartwright. His behavior toward that gentleman had been utterly contemptible.

Retrieving her new book on Greek mythology from the sitting-room table, Pippa decided to go to the drawing room. There she seated herself upon the sofa and opened her book. However, Pippa soon found she could not concentrate. She kept thinking of the viscount.

Thinking of his meeting with Cartwright, Pippa remembered how Allingham had been uncivil to the publisher from the moment he met him. She recalled the viscount's arrogant expression when Cartwright had been introduced to him. Allingham had made it very clear that he had considered Cartwright beneath him.

Angrily turning the page of her book, Pippa stared down at an illustration of the Greek god Zeus, a grim-bearded personage. The picture somehow reminded her of Allingham. After all he seemed to think himself some sort of god, ruling the Mount Olympus of London society.

Pippa frowned. How dare Allingham tell her that she should not see Mr. Cartwright or Lady Granville, she told herself. Deciding that the viscount was a totally insufferable man, she hoped that she never had to lay her eyes upon him again.

Sighing, Pippa set the book aside and got up from her chair.

Walking over toward the window, she looked outside. It had begun to rain, and the weather only added to Pippa's gloomy spirits.

Although she did not like to admit it to herself, Pippa was very disappointed in Allingham. His valiant exploit in rescuing Lizzy had made her think that she had misjudged him. And certainly, his friend Sir Henry Lonsdale had provided her with a very different portrait of the viscount.

Pippa frowned. Sir Henry was undoubtedly prejudiced where his friend was concerned. He apparently was able to overlook the viscount's arrogance and disregard for those persons he considered his inferiors, persons such as Mr. Cartwright.

Staring out of the window, Pippa's thoughts were distracted by an elegant carriage stopping on the street in front of their residence. A liveried footman quickly jumped off the vehicle and, opening an umbrella, proceeded to assist a lady from inside. Observing the lady as she walked up their front walk, Pippa recognized the Duchess of Northampton.

As she expected, Hawkins entered the drawing room to announce their august visitor. Pippa instructed him to usher Her Grace in. A short time later, the duchess appeared, wearing a stylish purple dress and matching hat that sported large pink feathers.

Rising from the sofa, Pippa curtsied gracefully. "Good afternoon, your grace. How kind of you to call."

The duchess smiled at her. "Thank you, Miss Grey. I'm very glad to see you again."

"I fear my mother is indisposed. She will be so frightfully disappointed at not seeing you."

"I do hope she is not ill," replied Her Grace with a concerned expression.

"It is not serious, ma'am. She has a headache and has retired to bed."

"That is a pity," said the duchess, who was actually quite pleased at the opportunity of having a private interview with Pippa. She glanced about her with approval. "What a charming room, my dear." Walking over to the picture of a child that Allingham had found overly sentimental, the duchess took out a gold quizzing glass and studied it carefully. "What a delightful painting. I quite adore it, Miss Grey." She scrutinized the corner of the canvas. "Ah, it is a Reynolds, I see."

Pippa regarded the duchess with an amused look. "Not *the* Reynolds, Your Grace. The artist of that painting was a Mr. Horace Reynolds. He was a renowned resident of Portsmouth."

The duchess lowered her quizzing glass and gazed at Pippa.

"Was he, indeed? Well, I must acquire some of the gentleman's works."

She walked back over toward Pippa who politely suggested that she sit down. The duchess was happy to comply, comfortably settling herself onto the sofa. Pippa sat down in a chair across from her.

"I'm sorry that your mother is feeling unwell, Miss Grey. Headaches are such a bother. I must send Mrs. Grey the headache remedy that Allingham told me about. It is really quite remarkable."

Pippa frowned at the mention of the gentleman's name. "I did not realize that his lordship was so knowledgeable about medicinal cures."

The duchess smiled. "Allingham knows about a good many things, my dear." She suddenly glanced down at the book that Pippa had left on the table. Picking it up, she peered at it approvingly. "What a handsome binding. Such a volume would look quite splendid on my bookshelf. I fear I am not a great reader, Miss Grey. However, I do consider books very useful for decorating a room. Of course, Allingham thinks me a great Philistine for such a notion."

Pippa regarded the duchess curiously. "I would not have suspected Lord Allingham as being a scholar, Your Grace."

She laughed. "I daresay, if his background had been different, he would have been a don at Oxford, Miss Grey. He is quite mad about books and learning."

Pippa raised her eyebrows at this surprising information. "Is he, Your Grace?"

"Oh, yes, my dear. You do not mean to say that you haven't seen his library? It is his pride and joy. You really must ask him to show it to you, Miss Grey."

Pippa shook her head. "I very much doubt I will be speaking with his lordship again to make such a request."

The duchess regarded her in surprise. "Why, whatever do you mean?"

Pippa hesitated. "I fear Lord Allingham and I are not on the best of terms."

"Indeed?" said Her Grace. "Well, you must not worry. All young couples will have their lovers' quarrels. Such things are inevitable. But I'm certain that all will soon be put right."

Pippa regarded her in astonishment. "I fear you are under some misconception, Your Grace."

"Misconception?" asked the duchess. "Whatever do you mean?"

"You cannot believe that there is some . . . romantic attachment between Lord Allingham and me."

"I can indeed," returned the duchess. "Do not attempt to deny it. It is only too clear that Allingham is in love with you."

The idea seemed so preposterous to Pippa that she was momentarily dumbstruck. It took her a few seconds to respond. "Your Grace, that is quite absurd," she said finally.

The duchess smiled knowingly. "Very well, my dear. If that is what you would have me believe, I shall say no more about it. Pray, tell me what your quarrel with Allingham was about."

Although quite discomfited by the conversation, Pippa managed to maintain her composure. "When Lord Allingham called upon us yesterday, he was barely civil to another gentleman who was a guest of ours."

The duchess smiled. "And was the other gentleman young and good looking, Miss Grey? And charming, perhaps? And a bachelor?"

"Mr. Cartwright is a very handsome, affable gentleman, Your Grace. But, I do not see . . ."

"There!" cried the elderly woman. "That is the explanation. Allingham was simply jealous, my dear."

Pippa regarded her incredulously for a moment and then burst into laughter. "I'm sorry, Your Grace, but it is ridiculous. Lord Allingham disapproves of me. The idea that he would be jealous is laughable. His lordship considers Mr. Cartwright a most unacceptable person.

"You see, Mr. Cartwright is a publisher, Your Grace, and Lord Allingham thinks the books he publishes are seditious. When he heard that Mr. Josiah Kent's books had been published by him . . ."

The duchess interrupted her. "Good heavens! Josiah Kent? You do not mean the fellow who was thrown into jail for his writings about the Prince Regent?"

Pippa nodded. "Yes, and I know you will probably disagree with me, Your Grace, but I think it was monstrous to arrest Mr. Kent for his political views."

The elderly woman smiled. "Oh, but I do agree with you, Miss Grey. I do not like to see a man arrested for his political views as misguided as they are. But the fellow did ridicule the Prince's . . . shall we say, corpulent figure." The duchess shook her head. "I find that most ill-mannered. For all his faults, HRH is a dear man. Indeed, Miss Grey, I do not like your Mr. Kent. A sensible man would not publish him. It is clear this Mr. Cartwright is not a sensible man. Now, you may become angry with me for saying so, my dear, but it appears to me that Allingham was right. It does seem most unwise for you to befriend this publisher."

"Then I choose to be unwise, Your Grace," said Pippa spiritedly.

"Do not tell me you have a *tendre* for this Cartwright?"

Pippa was about to say that whatever her feelings for the gentleman were, they were none of the duchess's business. However, for once, she restrained herself. "I don't know, Your Grace."

The duchess frowned. "My dear Miss Grey, I do hope you do not allow yourself to develop an affection for a man who appears to be quite unsuitable. I'm very fond of Allingham. While he may be overly proud and pigheaded at times, he is at heart the best of men.

"And I have known him for many years. I first met him when he was a student at Oxford. You see, my son George and Allingham were both at Balliol College."

"Oh, then his lordship was a friend of your son's?" asked Pippa.

The duchess laughed. "No, he most decidedly was not. George rather disliked Allingham. He thought him too dandified and bookish by half. And, of course, Allingham has never been a huntsman. My George lives and breathes for the sport."

Pippa regarded the duchess with considerable interest. She continued. "I first met Allingham when I went to Oxford to visit my son. George was engaged in a game of cricket. I watched for a time, but I do find cricket the most frightful bore so I decided to take a stroll.

"I walked down by the river and there was a young man sitting by himself on the bank. It was Allingham, of course. I began to speak to him and I must say, I liked him immediately. He was so very charming and well spoken.

"But he was not happy at Oxford. You see, Miss Grey, he had recently lost his parents. Both of them had come down with a fever and had died within a few days of each other."

"How very sad," said Pippa.

"Yes, it was tragic, my dear. Allingham had been devoted to them. He was an only child and very much doted upon. Losing both of them like that was a terrible shock to him."

Pippa looked reflective as she imagined the young viscount at Oxford. She could not help but feel sympathetic, imagining what such a loss would mean to her. "And you said Lord Allingham did not have any brothers or sisters, Your Grace?"

"No, although Sir Henry Lonsdale is very much like a brother to him."

"Sir Henry has told me how they have been friends since child-hood."

The duchess nodded. "Yes, he is fortunate in that. Allingham does not make friends easily. Oh, he has many acquaintances, but few people who are really close to him." The duchess shook her head. "I think he is reluctant to let anyone touch his heart. Indeed, I had quite despaired of him ever falling in love." She paused and smiled at Pippa. "Until now."

Pippa blushed and was about to protest, when the duchess continued. "Yes, I know you will say it is only an old woman's fantasy. But I am right in thinking he loves you. You must look into your heart and see how you truly feel about him."

Rather flustered by the duchess's words, Pippa did not know how to reply. Sensing her confusion, Her Grace rose to her feet. "I have taken too much of your time, Miss Grey. I shall leave you."

"But you have only just arrived, Your Grace," said Pippa.

"No, I cannot stay. Do think over what I have said, Miss Grey. No, do not reply now. Sometimes a young lady must have time to consider. You must call upon me very soon. Do tell Mrs. Grey that I shall expect you both. And bring that very charming and handsome brother of yours."

"Yes, that would be lovely. Thank you, Your Grace." Pippa, who had risen to her feet when the duchess had gotten up, rang for a servant to show her illustrious visitor out.

"Oh, Miss Grey," said the duchess, pausing at the doorway. "I should very much like it if you could bring your father. I'm very eager to meet him. I hear he is a very interesting gentleman."

"Indeed, I shall do so," said Pippa, surprised and delighted at the duchess's mention of her father. "Thank you, Your Grace."

After directing one more knowing smile at Pippa, the duchess walked regally from the drawing room. Going to the window, Pippa watched Her Grace as she got back into her carriage. She was a remarkable woman, thought Pippa.

Smiling, she shook her head. However had the duchess got the ridiculous notion that Allingham was in love with her? Pondering the matter, Pippa's smile vanished. It was simply an old lady's strange fancies. Or was it? She continued to reflect upon the duchess's words long after Her Grace's carriage had disappeared down the street.

16

The following morning, Pippa busied herself with correspondence and household affairs. Since the duchess's visit, she had been able to think of little but Her Grace's astonishing pronouncement that the viscount was in love with her. While she tried to dismiss the duchess's words as totally absurd, there was an odd nagging doubt. Could it possibly be true? And in the unlikely event that it was so, how did she feel about Allingham?

Since these thoughts had occupied Pippa all last evening and throughout much of the night, she had been determined to set them aside and deal with other matters. She had visited Lizzy and had been pleased to find that she was doing very well and appeared happy.

Later in the morning she had taken a walk with her mother and Patches. She took care not to mention what the duchess had said about Allingham, knowing well the effect such news would have on Mrs. Grey.

In the afternoon, Pippa and her mother received callers. After visiting with a number of persons eager to see them, Pippa began to grow rather weary. When what she hoped were the last of their guests left, Pippa was relieved.

However, a few minutes later, the butler arrived once more to announce another arrival. "Lord Allingham is here, madam."

"Lord Allingham?" said Mrs. Grey, clearly delighted. "Do show him in, Hawkins."

The butler bowed slightly and departed. When he returned a short time later with his lordship, Pippa found herself feeling strangely agitated. She looked up at Allingham questioningly, hoping that there would be something in his expression or demeanor that would show that he had feelings for her.

The viscount entered the room. As always he was impeccably dressed and looked very handsome. He approached in his regal fashion, bowing first to her mother and then to her. Their eyes met briefly, but she could glimpse no hint of emotion in them.

"Lord Allingham," cried Mrs. Grey, "how splendid of you to come. Do sit down, my lord."

"You are too kind, ma'am," returned the viscount, sitting down in an elegant French armchair that faced the ladies.

"We have had so many visitors today," said Mrs. Grey, "but you are certainly the most welcome of all of them, Lord Allingham. And you will never guess who called yesterday. The Duchess of Northampton!"

"How good of Her Grace to call," returned Allingham.

"Yes, was that not kind of her? But I was in bed with a headache! Pippa received her alone," said Mrs. Grey. "I was so desolated when Pippa told me at dinner. I do think the duchess the most charming woman."

"As do I," said the viscount. "She is an old and dear friend."

"Pippa scarcely told me anything about the visit," said Mrs. Grey, directing a disapproving look at her daughter.

"There was little to tell," said Pippa. "Her Grace did not stay long."

"But how wonderful that she called," said Mrs. Grey. "Truly, Lord Allingham, we owe all of our success to you. We are received everywhere and all of the finest people in society visit us."

"I'm glad of it," said his lordship. He looked closely at Pippa, who was trying very hard to appear indifferent.

"I do hope you will stay to tea, Lord Allingham."

"You are too kind, Mrs. Grey, but I cannot stay long. Indeed, I have only come to say some words of warning."

"Words of warning?" said Mrs. Grey, regarding him with surprise.

He nodded. "I am well aware that I shall further displease Miss Grey by what I shall say." He regarded Pippa with a serious look. "Indeed, Miss Grey, it is with some reluctance I come for I know full well how you will respond to my words. Yet the matter is of such grave consequence that I cannot ignore it.

"I fear you will damage your position in society should you persist in maintaining a relationship with Lady Granville. To ride with her in the park and with Seagrave was most unwise."

"Oh, dear," said Mrs. Grey. "I know that you disapprove of her. And Lord Seagrave as well. And I daresay you were quite vexed at seeing us with her in the park yesterday. I'm sure you are quite right. We will not do so again."

Pippa frowned at Allingham. She had been watching him carefully, hoping to see some sign that the Duchess of Northampton was not completely mistaken. Yet Allingham was not acting in the least like a man who had any feelings for her. His expression was only that of disapproval. "Indeed, Mama," said Pippa, "you are too hasty in saying we will not see Lady Granville. Do not forget that she invited us to dinner yesterday and we accepted."

"I must strongly advise you to send your regrets, Miss Grey," said Allingham, a severe expression on his face.

"I don't think I wish to do so, Lord Allingham," said Pippa, who was become increasingly irritated with her visitor.

The viscount looked at Mrs. Grey. "It is important that you ladies see nothing more of Lady Granville. Mrs. Grey, I assure you that associating with her will do nothing to advance your daughter in society."

Irritated that Allingham directed this remark to her mother, Pippa frowned at him. "I believe I have advanced sufficiently in society, my lord. You must not concern yourself about that any longer."

"You fail to understand, Miss Grey," said Allingham, frowning in return, "that imprudent actions on the part of young ladies can be very damaging."

"Imprudent? You mean riding with Lady Granville and Lord Seagrave?"

The viscount nodded gravely. "Indeed, that was most imprudent."

"And that is why you chose to snub us?" said Pippa indignantly. "To pass by without even a nod?"

"Did you think I would be happy to see you in their company?" said Allingham. "Seagrave is a notorious rakehell, Miss Grey. And Lady Granville . . . Well, I shall only say that she has not conducted herself in a way to gain admiration."

"I see," said Pippa. "Well, I don't care in the least what you say, Lord Allingham. If I care to converse with Lady Granville and to visit her at her home, I shall do so. I know that you dislike both Lady Granville and Lord Seagrave, but I find it ungentlemanly that you speak so ill of them to me. I have found Lady Granville charming and amusing. I enjoy her company. And I found nothing so terrible about Lord Seagrave. Indeed, he was very pleasant to me. There was nothing in his manner that could be faulted by any unprejudiced eye."

After speaking these words in a spirited way, Pippa regarded his lordship expectantly. She was not disappointed by his reaction. Rising abruptly from his chair, he shook his head. "I knew it was folly coming here. Do as you please, Miss Grey. From this moment I shall feel no further obligation to you and your family."

"And you should not," said Pippa. "You have fulfilled your duties. No more is expected of you."

"Pippa!" cried Mrs. Grey. "Do not forget yourself!" She looked imploringly at Allingham. "Do forgive Pippa. Indeed, my lord, we need your help."

"I shall assist you in any way, Mrs. Grey," said Allingham, "but since Miss Grey is so adamant about ignoring my advice, I bear no further responsibility. I pray you excuse me, Mrs. Grey." He frowned down at Pippa. "Good day, Miss Grey."

With these words he was gone, leaving Pippa's mother to once again lament that she had spoiled her daughter in a most shameful fashion.

Isabelle sat on the chaise longue in her sitting room, languidly reading a novel. After a time she set aside her book and picked up a fashion magazine. After paging listlessly through the periodical for a short while, Isabelle yawned. She was frightfully bored. The afternoon had stretched out forever even though she had not risen from bed until past noon.

Despite the fact that it was nearly teatime, the countess was still attired in her dressing gown. She had no appointments that day and had instructed her servants to turn away all her callers. When a maid entered the room, Isabelle arched one dark eyebrow at her disapprovingly.

"I beg your pardon, m'lady."

"What is it, Jane?" said her ladyship in a tone that implied very clearly that she did not wish to be disturbed by a servant.

"Lady Bellingham is here."

"Lady Bellingham? Do send her up, Jane."

The servant nodded and retreated. Isabelle tossed her magazine down and rose from the chaise longue. Since Lady Bellingham was her cousin and best friend, she was glad of her arrival.

The two ladies greeted each other with an embrace. "My dearest Kate, do sit down," said Isabelle, motioning her friend toward a chair."

Lady Bellingham sat down. A plump woman with a matronly figure and round face, Lady Bellingham prided herself as a lady of fashion. She was attired in a canary yellow pelisse and matching bonnet that was festooned with a good many ribbons and feathers. "Good heavens, Isabelle," she said, smiling at her cousin. "Did you just rise from bed?"

"I have been about for hours, my dear," said Isabelle, "but I was too bored to dress. Thank God that Seagrave is taking me to the opera tonight."

"And where is your husband?"

"Granville? Indeed, I have no idea. Now do tell me if you have heard any new gossip."

"Princess Charlotte has quarreled with her father."

"Oh, my dear Kate, that is very old news indeed."

"I expect it is," said her cousin amiably. "Indeed, it is you who always knows the gossip. Of course, I did hear an interesting story. It seems you were seen riding in the park yesterday with Seagrave and that girl, Miss Grey, and her mother."

"You hardly need to tell me that, Kate."

"I heard that Allingham snubbed you."

This remark succeeded in shaking Isabelle from her state of ennui. "Who told you that?"

"I heard it from Mrs. Paget who heard it from Arthur Worthington. He learned of it from Charles Fitzgibbon, who was there."

"Indeed?" said Isabelle.

"It was clever of you to make a friend of Miss Grey. She's such a success. They say her fortune is enormous."

"Yes, it explains her popularity."

Lady Bellingham nodded. "That is certainly true. Aside from her fortune there is nothing out of the ordinary about her. Allingham has certainly foisted her and her family upon society." She paused to smile at Isabelle. "I daresay you have taken her up to vex him."

"Exactly," replied Isabelle. "It amuses me to think how he must disapprove. I daresay he has warned the chit about me. But I am having my revenge. It was so funny to see his expression when he saw her with Seagrave."

"Do you think Allingham is fond of the girl?"

"Certainly not," said Isabelle. "You cannot believe he would be fond of her? Why, she is a provincial nobody with a father engaged in trade."

"Still, she is very wealthy," said Lady Bellingham. "And everyone is talking about her."

"Yes," said Isabelle thoughtfully.

"Miss Grey has much to offer a man like Allingham," Lady Bellingham persisted.

"Don't be ridiculous," said Isabelle, regarding her cousin in some irritation. She had a sudden thought. It would be most amusing to spread a rumor that Miss Grey was interested in Seagrave. "I believe she is fond of Seagrave. She seemed quite taken with him yesterday."

"Seagrave? Such audacity! I daresay you felt like boxing her ears."

"What a ninny you are, Kate." Isabelle laughed. "I'm growing rather tired of Seagrave. Miss Grey is welcome to him. Indeed, she told me she thought him the most handsome and charming man she has met in town."

"Did she? Why, that is very interesting. I shall have to tell that to Mrs. Fitzgibbon. She was certain that Miss Grey was in love with Ravensly."

"What nonsense! Miss Grey told me that she heartily disliked Ravensly. She thought him an empty-headed boy."

"Oh, dear," said Lady Bellingham. "I can scarcely wait to tell Mrs. Fitzgibbon how mistaken she is."

"Yes, you must do so," said Isabelle, smiling. A good many thoughts were now turning about in her devious brain. When her cousin began to chatter on, she nodded vaguely and smiled.

17

The next few days flew by quickly for Pippa, who had an unending number of social obligations to keep her busy. Although the viscount appeared at a few of the same society events that Pippa attended, Allingham had not deigned to speak to her. Instead, the viscount had confined his brief civilities to her mother and brother. His behavior toward her was decidedly frosty, making it clear to Pippa that he had no wish to make amends. Pippa was certain that the Duchess of Northampton had been very much mistaken, and that Allingham did not care one fig for her.

Despite her mother's objections, Pippa continued being friendly to Lady Granville. Isabelle called frequently, oftentimes inviting Pippa to ride with her in her carriage. Knowing how Allingham objected to her being seen with Isabelle, Pippa was determined to accompany her whenever possible.

The fact that Seagrave seemed to appear each time she was with Isabelle was not lost on Pippa, who did not grow to like the baron any better upon further acquaintance. When accompanying Isabelle and Seagrave in the park, Pippa rather hoped she might meet Allingham again so that he could see how little she cared for his advice. To her disappointment and her mother's relief, this did not occur.

Declaring that she was well rid of Allingham's meddling attentions, Pippa had tried not to think of the viscount. However, much to her annoyance, he continued to occupy her thoughts. And despite telling herself that she would not care if she ever saw Allingham again, she found herself glancing about the crowd at social gatherings, looking for him.

The night of the Huntingdons' ball, Pippa sat before her dressing room mirror as her maid put the finishing touches to her auburn tresses. "There, miss," said the servant proudly observing her handiwork, "I do think your hair looks quite lovely."

Pippa, who had been musing about whether Allingham would appear at the ball that evening, looked into the mirror and studied her reflection. "Yes, thank you, Betty. And I think I shall wear the necklace that Father gave me for my birthday."

Betty hastily went to her mistress's jewelry case and returned with a stunning ruby necklace. After she fastened it around Pippa's neck, the maid smiled. "You look beautiful, miss!"

Pippa smiled and looked at the glittering necklace in the mirror. She had to admit the jewels looked very well with Madame Dupre's magnificent crimson gown. Standing up, she took up her gloves and fan. She then went to join her family downstairs.

As she entered the drawing room, she found her parents and her brother waiting for her. Grey regarded her with fatherly pride. "Daughter, you look magnificent in that gown."

Mrs. Grey nodded a little uncertainly. "Yes, you look lovely, my dear. But do you not think you are wearing that color over-much?"

Bertie shook his head. "Mama, you cannot be serious. Pippa is quite the thing in her red gowns. Everyone admires her. My friend Percy has said that she is being called 'the Crimson Lady' in society."

"The Crimson Lady, eh?" said Pippa's father with amusement. He grinned at his daughter. "So you have become famous, Pippa."

"I do not think I like the idea of my daughter being called 'the Crimson Lady,' " said Mrs. Grey, frowning.

"Well, you mustn't worry about it, my dear," said Grey. "I'm sure it is very good for a lady to have such an appellation. One wants to be known in society. I daresay everyone knows our Pippa."

"Yes," said Mrs. Grey uncertainly. Fortunately, she was diverted by noticing the time on the mantel clock. "Oh, dear, it is getting late. I think we had best be going." She smiled at her children. "Is it not exciting, my dears, to be attending the Huntingdons' ball!"

Pippa sighed. "I would prefer staying home with Papa."

"What?" cried her mother in amazement. "Why, Pippa, this ball is one of the biggest events of the Season! You could not wish to miss it!"

"Indeed I could, Mama," she said. She looked over at her father.

"Oh, I do wish you were going, Papa. You would see the duchess. You seemed to like her when we called at Northampton House."

"My dear girl, I would be utterly miserable. No, indeed, I do not wish to go to this ball or any other. But you cannot disappoint all those young bucks at the ball. I don't doubt that they are eagerly awaiting the 'Crimson Lady.' "

Pippa smiled at him and then reluctantly followed her mother and brother to the awaiting carriage. A short time later, they were ushered into the Huntingdons' grand ballroom. There was a great crush of people and Pippa once again found herself glancing about to see if Allingham was in the crowd.

Her attention was quickly taken up by a string of gentlemen eagerly petitioning her for the evening's dances. The Marquess of Ravensly was the first among them, claiming the lady for several dances.

Pippa was flattered by the attention. A number of her admirers were charming, amusing young men and she enjoyed the dancing very much. Ravensly, who was obviously smitten with her, seemed to watch her every move. When he was not dancing with her, the marquess looked rather forlorn. His lack of interest in the other young ladies in attendance quite perturbed a good many matrons with marriageable daughters.

Arriving very late at the ball, Allingham glanced about the crowd with his usual look of ennui. He spotted the red-gowned Pippa immediately. She was dancing a spirited round dance with Ravensly.

Although his face bore no trace of emotion, the viscount was not at all pleased to find Pippa with the young marquess, whom he knew was totally enchanted by her. Indeed, Ravensly had been making a great cake of himself behaving like a silly mooncalf.

Allingham turned away from the dancers. He did not wish to appear as if he cared one whit what Miss Grey did. Spying his friend Sir Henry, he made his way to him. Sir Henry was engaged in conversation with his uncle, an elderly retired admiral, whom Allingham considered one of the greatest bores in society. While the viscount would normally have avoided the admiral at all costs, that evening he was content to join his friend and stand listening to the naval gentleman's account of the Battle of Trafalgar.

After some time, the admiral took his leave to move on. Sir Henry appeared very much relieved. "I could scarcely believe that you would join me when I was talking to Uncle Cornelius. I must say that you were admirably civil to him."

Allingham raised an eyebrow. "You seem surprised."

Sir Henry grinned. "I know you think him a great bore. I feared you would give him a set down and send him on his way."

"My dear Harry, he is your uncle." A slight smile appeared on his face. "But I must say I was very glad that he saw someone else to plague. But where is your charming wife?"

"Diana is dancing. It can be a trial to have such a pretty wife. She is too dashed popular with the young bucks."

Allingham's response to this was to stare over at the dancers. Seeing Pippa smiling at Ravensly, he frowned.

Noting the object of his friend's gaze, Sir Henry smiled. "She is beautiful, isn't she?"

"Lady Lonsdale is indeed beautiful," replied his lordship absently.

"I was not speaking of my wife. You know very well I meant Miss Grey. She is the sensation of the season."

"Yes," replied Allingham, adopting his usual pose of studied indifference.

"I don't understand why you don't dance with her, Jack. And don't say you do not dance. I know that is nonsense. You danced with Miss Grey before. Indeed, that is what caused her to be such a success."

"She is a success because she is a lady of charm and wit," replied the viscount. "And fortune," he added with a frown.

"Yes, of course, but you must admit your paying attention to her is what sparked her popularity. I daresay it is very odd that you have been avoiding her. I know you were angry about her going about with Seagrave."

"How else am I to feel? It is clear that Miss Grey cares nothing for my opinion or for me."

"I cannot believe that, Jack. But it appears odd that you are avoiding her. Everyone is saying that you have quarreled with her. It would be good if you talked with her. Just to cease the tongues from wagging, of course."

"I shall better serve Miss Grey by not speaking with her. She dislikes me so heartily that she would scarcely wish my company."

"That is utter bosh. Really, Jack, I do think you should ask her for a dance. Look, there's Seagrave. He is eyeing her like a fox studying a plump partridge. Lady Granville is not here so he is on the loose again."

Allingham fixed his gaze upon Seagrave. The disagreeable baron was smiling at Pippa. The sight of his old adversary watching her infuriated the viscount. "Excuse me, Harry," he said.

"Of course, old fellow," said Sir Henry, happy at his friend's reaction. He smiled as Allingham walked away.

After Ravensly reluctantly relinquished her to another eager gentleman, Pippa found herself dancing the mazurka with an inexpert partner. She was very glad when the music stopped and other gentlemen presented themselves. Pippa was surprised to note Allingham among them. While she had been looking for him all evening, she had not seen him until that moment.

Allingham stepped forward quickly, effectively blocking Seagrave. "Miss Grey, I should be grateful for the honor of the next dance."

"See here, Allingham," said Seagrave. "Miss Grey has promised me that honor."

"Indeed?" said Allingham, looking at Pippa for confirmation.

She hesitated. She had not actually promised Seagrave the dance, but she was not sure whether she wished to dance with Allingham. She saw how the other gentlemen were watching them, eager for her response.

"I'm sorry, Lord Seagrave," said Pippa. "I shall dance with Lord Allingham now. You may have the next dance if you wish."

"Very well," said Seagrave, clearly unhappy by this turn of events.

The viscount offered his arm to her, which she took. Looking up into his cool gray eyes, she felt a tremor of excitement. There was no denying the attraction she felt for him. As always he looked marvelously handsome attired in black evening clothes of excellent cut.

"I must say I am rather surprised that you allowed me this dance," said the viscount.

"Perhaps I surprised myself," replied Pippa.

Unsure of how to take this remark, Allingham ignored it. "You look lovely tonight, Miss Grey."

Pippa regarded him in some surprise. "Then you do not disapprove of my dress?"

"I should not dare disapprove of anything you wear, Miss Grey," replied Allingham in a voice tinged with irony. The orchestra started to play. "A waltz. How lucky for me, Miss Grey," said his lordship, reaching out to take her into his arms.

As they began to dance, Pippa looked up at him. His face betrayed little emotion. "I thought you were avoiding me, my lord. I thought we were no longer speaking."

Gazing down at her, the viscount felt a pang of deep longing.

She looked so beautiful in her crimson dress. He was suddenly very much aware of the enticing view provided by her low-cut bodice. "I didn't think you wished to speak with me. Our last meeting was less than congenial."

"You were quite dreadful when last I saw you," said Pippa. "I was right to be vexed with you."

"I do not wish to discuss that meeting," said Allingham. "I wish it had not occurred. I'm not in the habit of apologizing, Miss Grey. I shall not apologize for giving you what I consider to be good advice. But it was not my intention to upset you. That I sincerely regret."

This declaration surprised Pippa, who was rather disconcerted by the intense look Allingham was now directing at her. "I'm so glad that you have decided to speak to me. I shall not try to vex you."

He smiled for the first time. "Good. We will talk of other things. How is the girl, Lizzy?"

"Oh, very well, my lord," said Pippa, pleased that he had asked. "She seems very happy with our servants. She is exceedingly well-liked below stairs. She is now a cheerful, good-natured girl. She's very grateful to you."

"I'm glad she's doing well."

"Even if she is residing at our house?" said Pippa, smiling up at him. "Oh, dear, I said I would try not to vex you. I daresay that remark was calculated to do so. I fear changing old habits is hard."

Allingham smiled. "Yes, I confess I have always found that to be true. But I do appreciate your trying, Miss Grey."

Pippa returned his smile, delighted and surprised at his affability. Looking up into his handsome face, she wondered suddenly about what the Duchess of Northampton had said. Could he be in love with her? It seemed utterly fantastic, yet at that moment as she whirled about the room in his arms, the idea seemed decidedly less ridiculous.

"It is a wonderful ball, is it not, Lord Allingham?"

"As balls go, it is passable," returned the viscount.

Pippa smiled. "Faint praise indeed, my lord. But I have heard that you detest balls. I cannot imagine why."

"And you enjoy them?"

"Why, yes, I do, although I must say I did not believe I would."

"As I recollect, Miss Grey, when first we met, you had no interest in society. Now you enjoy balls and other affairs. I daresay it is because you are such a success and have so many admirers hanging about you."

This remark was accompanied by a look of disapproval that caused a slight smile to appear on Pippa's face. "The gentlemen have been very kind," she said. "One cannot help but be flattered by the attention even if so much of what is said is outrageous flummery. But do not fear, I'm quite sensible of the fact that it is my fortune that is attracting such a swarm of suitors."

"I don't think Ravensly cares about your fortune, Miss Grey," said Allingham with a frown. "The cub is obviously smitten with you. It will take very little encouragement for him to make you an offer. You could find yourself a duchess, Miss Grey."

"Indeed, Lord Allingham?" said Pippa, regarding him with interest. It was very clear that he did not like the idea very much. Was it jealousy? wondered Pippa, once again remembering her conversation with the Duchess of Northampton. She could not resist testing the theory. "I confess that I do like Lord Ravensly very much. He's a very charming gentleman. And certainly he is one of the most handsome men I have ever met."

Pippa noted that Allingham did not seem at all pleased at her remark. "He is an empty-headed puppy," returned the viscount. "You would be bored with him in a month."

Pippa raised her eyebrows. "It is exceedingly presumptuous of you to make such judgments, Lord Allingham." She paused and then a mischievous smile crossed her face. "Even though you are doubtlessly correct."

Allingham smiled in return. Looking down into her fine blue eyes, the viscount found himself wishing that the entire room of people could vanish and that he could be alone with her. He was not at all happy when the dance ended and he had to relinquish Pippa to Seagrave.

Knowing that tongues had already been set wagging by his attentions to Miss Grey that evening, he left the dancers, making his way across the ballroom to join Sir Henry once again. That gentleman was very glad that the viscount had danced with Pippa.

They stood talking for a long time until an unpleasantly familiar voice called the viscount's name. "Allingham." His lordship turned to find Seagrave standing beside him. When Allingham did not respond, the baron continued. "I hope you do not get the idea that because Miss Grey danced with you first that she prefers you over me."

"What an astonishing idea," said Allingham, eyeing the baron scornfully.

"She was very charming to me. I wanted you to know."

"Miss Grey is charming to everyone," replied the viscount icily.

"Yes, she is," said Sir Henry. "She's a very charming girl."

"And a fine-looking wench in the bargain," said Seagrave. "They say she will bring a tidy sum. Perhaps that explains your interest. Indeed, everyone is saying you have your eye on the girl's fortune."

"I suggest you leave, Seagrave," said Allingham.

"Oh, I shall be more than happy to leave the two of you," said Seagrave with a grin. "But don't think you will win the prize, Allingham. There are a good many others after her.

"Indeed, perhaps it is time for me to think of matrimony. I have been a widower for nearly two years."

"If you believe Miss Grey could possibly show such poor judgment as to consider you, you are very mistaken, Seagrave," replied Allingham, fixing his most withering look upon his adversary. "If you do not leave us, Seagrave, I promise you will regret it."

While the baron had no desire to allow Allingham to feel that he could intimidate him, there was something about the viscount's tone that made Seagrave feel it would be prudent to retreat. After directing a contemptuous smile at Allingham and Sir Henry, he took his leave.

Although she had hoped that his lordship would ask for another dance, Pippa did not have any further opportunity to speak with Allingham again that evening. She had caught a glimpse of him standing with a group of gentlemen, a look of ennui on his face, but he had not looked in her direction.

When it grew very late, Pippa found herself growing very tired. Protesting that she could not dance anymore, she extricated herself from her suitors to find her mother. Mrs. Grey was seated in a chair at one side of the ballroom, smiling and fanning herself. Bertie was standing beside her.

"Oh, Mama, I must say that I am exhausted. It is time we took our leave." She looked at Bertie. "Do say you wish to go home, Bertie."

"I should not object," returned her brother. "It does grow late. But it was a splendid ball. I had a bang-up time."

"Yes, it was lovely. I so enjoyed myself. Of course, I daresay I did not enjoy myself as much as you, my dear." Mrs. Grey smiled brightly at her daughter. "I scarcely spoke to you all evening,

Pippa. It seems the gentlemen have kept you well occupied." She paused and gave her daughter a sly look. "Especially Lord Ravensly. And you danced with Allingham! I was so glad to see it. Everyone took note of it, I daresay."

"Indeed," said Bertie, "it appeared that Allingham is not vexed with you in the least. I must say that you and he appeared on excellent terms. Allingham is such a good fellow. I spoke with him after you and he were dancing."

"You did?" said Pippa, very much interested. "What did you discuss?"

"Oh, various subjects," said Bertie. "We spoke of the opera for one thing. His lordship told me I might accompany him to the opera. Is that not splendid?"

Pippa regarded her younger brother in some surprise. "The opera, Bertie? I thought you said you detested it."

Bertie looked slightly sheepish. "Well, perhaps I did, but I shall give it another chance. I should be happy to tolerate the opera if I am in Allingham's company."

Mrs. Grey smiled. "Oh, that is wonderful, Bertie. Attending the opera with Lord Allingham. I should not doubt if you would sit in His Royal Highness's box. Would that not be wonderful? And certainly his lordship meant for Pippa to attend as well."

Her son appeared slightly perplexed. "He did not say anything about Pippa attending the opera, Mama. Indeed, he did not mention her at all"—Bertie paused to grin at his sister—"except to say he thought you were the most beautiful woman at the ball."

"He said that?" said Pippa, thinking that her brother was quizzing her.

"Indeed he did," said Bertie.

"Can you imagine, Pippa?" said Mrs. Grey. "He thinks you are beautiful even though you are always vexing him."

"I believe Allingham left the ball shortly afterward," said Bertie.

"I wish I had had more opportunity to speak with him," said Mrs. Grey. "I exchanged but a few words since that dreadful Mrs. Bingham was with me and she scarcely allowed me to speak. I do think she bored Allingham dreadfully. But it is late, my dears, and Pippa is right in believing it is time to go." Rising from her chair, Mrs. Grey took her son's arm. As Pippa followed her mother and brother from the ballroom, she found herself thinking only of Allingham and his changed behavior toward her.

18

Allingham sat in his library staring glumly at the fire. Pouring himself a glass of port, he frowned. Since the Huntingdons' ball three days ago, the viscount had spent most of his time squirreled away at his house like a hermit.

That the ball had made his lordship exceedingly unhappy would have surprised most who had witnessed him dancing with Pippa. His lordship's obvious partiality for the young lady had caused many a member of society to remark that the great Allingham's bachelor days were numbered.

As the viscount raised his glass to his lips, he appeared thoughtful. Since the ball, he had spent most of his time thinking about Pippa. He could no longer deny that he was in love with her and that he wished to marry her.

Remembering Pippa at the ball, surrounded by scores of eager suitors, Allingham muttered a curse. It was impossible. He could not ask her to marry him. He was still in financial difficulty and she was the daughter of one of the kingdom's richest men. Everyone would consider him a fortune hunter. Indeed, Seagrave had said as much to his face.

Allingham frowned again. In any case it was unlikely that Miss Grey would accept him. She was hardly in awe of his rank and title. Such things seemed to mean very little to her. And if she wanted a husband of rank, she would do far better marrying Ravensly.

Getting up from his chair, the viscount walked over to the window and peered out into the darkness. "Damn Ravensly," he muttered, heartily disliking the idea of Pippa marrying the young marquess. Indeed, he did not like the thought of her as any man's wife but his own.

He turned away from the window. Certainly Pippa had no shortage of suitors. Nearly every young buck in London was hopeful of capturing her attention. Even the odious Seagrave seemed to have hopes in that direction. And it was not only the

Grey fortune that was appealing. No, Pippa had captivated society with her beauty and charm.

Sitting back down, he poured another glass of port. Yes, Pippa could choose from any number of eligible men, many of whom had distinguished titles and substantial fortunes. Of course, she had not exhibited any real partiality to any of them. She appeared to be just as interested in the fellow Cartwright and he was probably as poor as a church mouse.

The viscount stared at the flickering flames in the fireplace. He thought of the Huntingdon ball and how he had held her in his arms, dancing about the ballroom. "Would that I had never laid eyes upon her," he said aloud.

Putting down his glass, he rose from his chair. There was no point sitting there, thinking about Pippa. He would go out and forget all about her. Calling for a servant to fetch his carriage, his lordship went to his room to change.

Some time later, Allingham was on his way to a gambling establishment on St. James Street that one wag had christened "the Pigeon Hole." The place was quite notorious for its high stakes card games. In fact, many fortunes had been lost and won at the gaming tables there.

Although the viscount had not ventured near a card game since coming so close to ruin, he was in a mood that evening to throw all caution to the wind. When he entered the room, several gentlemen noted his arrival with keen interest. It had been rumored that Allingham had sworn off games of chance. Happy to see that this tale was apparently false, the gentlemen called good-naturedly for the unlucky viscount to join them.

"Good God, it is you, Allingham," said Seagrave, looking up from the table of card players. "Come, sit down. I'm always eager to win money from you." An elderly baldheaded gentleman sitting next to Seagrave guffawed at this remark. The viscount gave the man an icy stare and he immediately stopped laughing.

At that moment, a young gentleman sitting at the table with his back to Allingham turned around. Staring up at his lordship with an inebriated grin, Bertie got unsteadily to his feet. "Lord Allingham," he said in a slurred voice. He turned to a young blond gentleman in the chair next to him. "Look, Percy it's Lord Allingham."

Lord Percy Whitworth, who appeared even more intoxicated than his friend, made an incoherent comment and then giggled. Bertie patted his friend on the shoulder and then turned back to face the viscount. "What good fortune to find you here, sir."

"Indeed it is," said Seagrave, with an amused wink at his companions.

The viscount regarded Bertie with disapproval. "What the devil do you think you're doing, Grey?" he asked in a stern tone. Bertie looked slightly crestfallen and then plopped back down into his chair.

"What do you think he's doing, Allingham?" said Seagrave with a contemptuous sneer. "Young Grey is in the game."

His lordship scowled. "And I would not be surprised to find that he is losing rather heavily."

Seagrave grinned again. "As a matter of fact, the young gentleman has not been overly lucky tonight. But the evening is still young, is it not, Grey?" Bertie nodded emphatically and then slouched down in his chair.

With some difficulty, Allingham managed to control his temper. "Come, Grey, it's time for you to go."

"Go?" said Bertie in some confusion. He suddenly grinned up at the viscount. "Are we going to the opera?" This provoked loud laughter from the gentlemen at the gaming table.

Allingham gave them a contemptuous look and then turned back to Bertie. "Come along now. Be a good lad."

"See here, Allingham," said Seagrave. "Grey cannot simply go off like this. The night is young."

"Yes, Lord Allingham," said Bertie, speaking in a slow, slurred voice. "I lost a bit, but my luck is changing."

"You must give the lad the chance to win back some of his blunt," said Seagrave.

"I do hate to disappoint you, Seagrave, but Grey is leaving with me."

"I am?" said Bertie with a befuddled expression.

"Indeed you are."

"Who are you, his wet nurse?" asked Seagrave.

The viscount replied by directing a look of unmistakable loathing at the baron. Grasping Bertie by the arm, he pulled him to his feet. Bertie stood unsteadily. "I'm sorry, gentlemen," he said. "I must be off. We are going to the opera."

This remark caused several of the gentlemen at the table to laugh uproariously. Allingham led Bertie forcefully toward the door. When he had finally propelled Bertie outside the gambling establishment, Allingham's driver hurried to assist him. "Help me get the young gentleman into the carriage. I'm taking him home."

"Aye, m'lord," returned the servant, very much surprised at his master's early departure.

Once Bertie was inside the carriage, he grinned at Allingham. "Will the prince be at the opera, Lord Allingham?" he asked in his stumbling speech.

The viscount crossed his arms impatiently. "He will not. And neither will you. I'm taking you home."

Bertie lurched forward and then leaned back against the wall. "But what about the op . . . er . . . a, sir?"

"You are drunk, man," said Allingham impatiently. "You must get to bed and sleep it off."

Bertie appeared perplexed by this news. "I had hoped to go to the opera," he said.

"Yes, yes," said his lordship. "We will go to the opera another time, Bertie. You are damned lucky I found you when I did. How much did you lose?"

Bertie looked at him with a befuddled expression. "Lose, sir?"

"Lose at cards?"

"Oh, that," said Bertie. "I can't remember."

"Good God. I suggest you stay away from the Pigeon Hole and from Seagrave. The man has the devil's own luck at cards. I know from experience."

Bertie nodded vaguely, but Allingham doubted he understood anything he was saying. As the carriage started off, Bertie slumped down in the vehicle's luxurious seat. Closing his eyes, he was asleep before the carriage had scarcely gone a block. Soon he was snoring lustily.

Allingham, who was sitting across from the inebriated young man, shook his head. It did not surprise him that Seagrave should take advantage of Grey in such a despicable manner. He only hoped that the young man had not wagered away a very large sum of money.

When the viscount's carriage pulled up at the Greys' residence, Allingham looked out the window. The house was dark and it appeared that the servants had all retired for the night.

"Wake up, Bertie," said Allingham, reaching over to shake the young man. "Wake up!"

"What?" said Bertie, eyeing his lordship with a startled look. "Lord Allingham?"

"Yes, it is Allingham. Now come along, get out. We are at your home. You must come to your senses."

Bertie's bewildered expression made it seem that coming to his senses was extremely unlikely. The carriage door opened and Allingham's servant peered inside. "Is the young gentleman all right, m'lord?"

"We'll have to help him, Rogers," said his lordship.

"Aye, m'lord," said the driver, climbing into the vehicle to assist Bertie out. As Allingham and his servant escorted the groggy Bertie up the front walk, the front door opened and the Greys' butler appeared before them.

The viscount glanced at the servant. "Hawkins, I have brought your young master home."

"Is he ill, my lord?" cried Hawkins rather alarmed at Bertie's state.

"He's drunk," said Allingham as he and his driver assisted Bertie inside. "There's no need to rouse anyone else. We will take him to bed if you would show us to his room."

The butler nodded. "Of course, my lord." Holding a candle to light the way, Hawkins led them toward the staircase. As Allingham and his servant struggled to drag him up the stairs, Bertie began to sing with drunken high spirits.

"Dammit, Bertie," growled the viscount quietly. "You will wake the entire household."

Although the young gentleman did not wake the entire household, he did wake one member of it. As they approached the top of the stairs, Allingham suddenly found Pippa standing with a candle, looking down at them. She was regarding them with a horrified expression. "Good heavens!" she cried in alarm. "Whatever has happened?" The viscount was struck temporarily dumb by the sight of Pippa standing there in her dressing gown, her auburn hair tumbling in charming disarray about her shoulders.

Bertie grinned up at his sister. "Pippa! I have had such a lark!" He turned to his lordship. "But I do wish we had gone to the opera."

Pippa regarded her brother in disgust. "You are foxed, Bertie." She turned to the viscount. "Lord Allingham, how could you have allowed my brother to get into such a condition?"

Allingham raised his eyebrows slightly. "I'm not the whelp's nursemaid, Miss Grey. And I assure you that he got into this condition by himself. I'm only bringing him home."

"His room is here, my lord," said Hawkins, gesturing down the hall.

"I can manage him, m'lord," said Allingham's driver.

"Very well, Rogers," said the viscount, relinquishing Bertie to his worthy servant. Hawkins and the driver proceeded to the room, escorting Bertie inside.

Pippa frowned at Allingham. "I do wish you would explain this, my lord."

"You must allow your brother to provide the explanations, Miss Grey. I only happened upon him at a certain . . . establishment. He was in a sorry condition. I decided it best to bring him home before he could get into further mischief."

Pippa regarded him with a questioning look. "A certain establishment, my lord?"

He hesitated a moment. "A gambling establishment, Miss Grey. Your brother was playing cards with a group of gentlemen. I fear they were doubtlessly taking advantage of his condition. I hope he did not lose a great deal of money."

Pippa's eyes had widened at hearing this account. "This is infamous! I daresay, I was afraid of this happening. My brother can be a great gull sometimes." Allingham did not immediately reply. He was finding the lady's close presence quite disturbing.

"There are many in this town who enjoy fleecing a greenhead like your brother," he said finally. "I know you have found my advice objectionable in the past, Miss Grey, but I do think your brother should choose his companions more wisely. He has been hanging about with young Lord Percy Whitworth and his friends. Whitworth is a wild, reckless young man, who is rapidly advancing toward a life of dissipation. I do not think he is an acceptable friend for your brother. And they were playing with Seagrave. There is nothing Seagrave enjoys better than getting a green lad into a card game."

Pippa frowned. "Seagrave?"

"Yes," said Allingham. "He can separate a man from his purse as effectively as a highwayman."

"You said he was someone to be avoided. It seems you were right." A slight smile appeared on the viscount's face. Pippa continued, "I do want to thank you for rescuing Bertie tonight. I truly am most grateful to you."

The viscount gazed into her blue eyes, wishing he could claim more than gratitude from the lady. "It is nothing, Miss Grey. I am only glad that I happened upon him when I did."

Pippa suddenly regarded him curiously. "What were you doing at that place, my lord? I do hope you were not gambling."

"That is what one generally does at such an establishment, Miss Grey," he said stiffly.

"But, do you not think . . ." she began. "Surely, in your circumstances you should not . . ." She stopped suddenly. "Oh, dear, I should not be meddling. I am sorry. What you do is your own business."

"No, you are right, of course. I should avoid such places. Indeed, I had done so until this evening. I daresay, your brother doubtlessly saved me from losing a good deal of money."

"Well, I'm happy that Bertie's drunken state served some useful purpose," said Pippa with an ironic smile. Allingham did not reply. He stood gazing down at her, thinking how lovely she looked in the flickering candlelight.

Returning his gaze, Pippa found herself somewhat discomfitted by the viscount's intent scrutiny. Looking up into his gray eyes, she had a sudden thrilling, if unsettling, sensation.

The viscount, also experiencing the spark between them, was about to take Pippa into his arms and fasten his lips upon hers. However, he was thwarted by the reappearance of Hawkins and his driver. Feeling greatly frustrated, the viscount frowned and took a step back from the lady.

Pippa, who was also strangely disappointed by the servants' interruption, managed to speak to the butler. "So, Hawkins, did you put my brother to bed?"

The butler nodded solemnly. "Yes, miss. Master Bertie is asleep now."

"Thank you, Hawkins," she said. She turned to the viscount's driver, "and . . ." Pippa eyed the servant questioningly.

"Rogers, Miss," said the driver, making a deferential nod.

"Thank you, Rogers," said Pippa, smiling at him.

Allingham, who had now recovered himself, glanced at the servants and then back at Pippa. "Well, I mustn't keep you up any longer, Miss Grey," said Allingham in a matter-of-fact tone.

She held out her hand to him. "I do thank you again, my lord," she said. "It was very good of you to help my brother as you did." Pippa suddenly smiled mischievously up at him. "It seems my mother is correct in comparing you to one of the knights of old. First, you rescue Lizzy and now you have gotten Bertie out of a muddle. I daresay, you will next be facing a dragon."

Smiling, he took her proferred hand. To Pippa's surprise, he raised it to his lips. Then gazing down into her eyes, Allingham made a slight bow. "Good night, Miss Grey."

Although rather disconcerted, Pippa maintained her composure. "Good night, Lord Allingham," she said. She stood watching the viscount's retreating form as he and his servant followed Hawkins down the stairs. When they were gone, she returned to her room. Taking off her dressing gown and tossing it upon the chaise longue, Pippa got back into bed and blew out her candle. Lying back in the bed, she thought about Allingham.

There was no mistaking her unsettling feelings for that gentleman. The memory of his lips on her hand made her tingle with excitement.

Pippa sighed. While she had thought Allingham to be so haughty and insufferable, she now thought of him in a very different light. Standing there before him in the hallway, she had had a most unladylike desire to throw her arms about his neck and lose herself in his embrace.

A slight smile appeared on her face. What if she had done so? Burying her head against her goose down pillow, Pippa sighed again. She was falling in love with Allingham! It was too absurd. Of course, she sensed that he was not altogether indifferent to her. Still, how could the great Allingham be interested in a tradesman's daughter? Surely that was impossible.

Pippa attempted to push the viscount from her thoughts and return to sleep. However, that seemed quite impossible and she remained awake for some time thinking of him.

19

The next morning the sound of servants in the corridor outside her door awakened Pippa just as she was in the midst of a dream involving Allingham. Slightly disoriented, she gazed up in some confusion at the canopy draping over her bed. Realizing that she had been dreaming, Pippa felt a keen sense of disappointment.

She lay in bed, remembering the dream. She had been at a ball amid a great crush of people. The Prince Regent had been there, dressed in a crimson coat. In fact, it had seemed that many of those in attendance at the ball were wearing red.

Pippa closed her eyes. In her dream, she had been waltzing with Seagrave and had wished it were Allingham. Then, as she had glanced back at her partner, she had been surprised to find that it was not Seagrave, but Allingham, who was dancing with her. He was smiling down at her, looking exceedingly handsome.

When the dance had ended, his lordship had taken her hand and kissed it. It was then that Pippa had suddenly become aware that they were no longer at the ball, but in the hallway outside her bedchamber. She had looked down to discover that she was wearing her dressing gown. Pippa remembered that she had looked back up to find Allingham still smiling at her. Taking her hand once more, he had silently begun to lead her to the door of her room. And then noise from the hallway had awakened her.

Imagining the direction that her fantasy was taking, Pippa blushed. She had found the dream very pleasant once Allingham had appeared in it. Indeed, she had been quite eager to follow the viscount into her room. Pippa sighed. Perhaps if she fell back asleep, she thought, she could reenter the dream where she had left it.

Pippa frowned. What was she thinking of to wish such a thing? It would not do at all. Casting aside the covers, she hastily got out of bed to get dressed.

Some time later, attired in a sea-green muslin dress with small puffed sleeves and a ruffled collar, Pippa joined her parents in the dining room for breakfast. Mrs. Grey appeared in an especially jovial mood that morning. They had agreed to go to the theater that night and sit with Lady Granville in her box. While Mrs. Grey was not altogether happy about the idea of sitting with Isabelle, she could not help but be excited at the idea of seeing the renowned actor Edmund Kean, who was to appear in a new production of *Richard III*.

Although her mother wondered out loud about what time Bertie would appear that morning, Pippa thought it best not to inform her parents of her brother's drunken return home the previous evening. Knowing that her father would not be at all pleased to hear about his son spending the evening in a gambling den, she decided to discuss the matter with Bertie herself.

Since she was certain that her brother would sleep late, Pippa spent the morning reading and writing letters. She then took Patches out for a long walk. Returning home shortly before noon, she decided that surely her brother must be awake by that time.

After ridding herself of her pelisse and bonnet, Pippa made her way to her brother's room. "Bertie," she called, knocking on the door. When there was no response, she opened the door and peered inside the dimly lit room. "Bertie?" she asked, looking over at the bed.

There was a sudden movement of the mound of bedclothes and a low groan. "Good lord, what is it, Pippa?" muttered her brother ill-temperedly.

Entering Bertie's room, Pippa walked over to the windows. She then began to briskly pull open the curtains, allowing the bright sunlight to come pouring into the room. Bertie groaned again and put a hand over his eyes. "Good morning," said Pippa as she went over to the side of his bed and smiled down at him.

Bertie took away his hand and glanced up at his sister with bleary eyes. "Good God, Pippa, did you have to wake me up and in that confounded cheerful manner?"

Pippa suddenly frowned and sat down on the edge of his bed. "It's very close to noon, Bertie," she said sternly. "You shouldn't be such a slugabed." She paused. "Of course, I realize you had a rather boisterous time last night."

Bertie met her disapproving gaze and reluctantly sat up in bed. Grimacing, he held one hand to his forehead. "Really, Pippa, I do hope that you do not intend to lecture me now. I already feel quite wretched enough without that."

His sister regarded him silently for a moment and then she shook her head. "I do not wish to be a scold, Bertie," she said.

"But, I cannot help but be concerned when you come home in such a state and then to hear that you were spending the evening drunkenly throwing away money at a gambling establishment. . . ."

Bertie looked over at her with a puzzled expression. "But how did you know . . . ?" He stopped and then regarded her in alarm. "Good lord, you don't mean to say that Lord Allingham . . . ?"

Pippa nodded. "Allingham found you in your drunken condition and brought you home."

"Oh, no," said Bertie, appearing quite upset. "I had a vague memory of Allingham in the place, but I thought I had been dreaming. Good lord, Allingham must consider me an idiot." He hesitated and then regarded his sister imploringly. "Did I make a complete and utter ass of myself, Pippa?"

She smiled. "I should say you did."

Bertie moaned and slumped down in the bed. "What must Allingham think of me?" he said, with a dramatic sigh.

"I should imagine that he thinks you a rather bad singer for one thing," said Pippa, still smiling.

"I was singing?" asked Bertie, regarding his sister with a horror-stricken expression.

She nodded. "As I recall, it was a song about a barmaid. I daresay, I should be glad that most of the lyrics were unintelligible."

For the first time, her brother smiled slightly. However, he quickly grew serious again. "Were Papa and Mama there when Allingham brought me home, Pippa?"

She shook her head. "No, they know nothing of it."

Bertie smiled gratefully at his sister. "It was good of you not to tell them, Pippa. I don't doubt that Papa would be very displeased with me. I fear the evening is not at all clear in my memory. It is all rather hazy, but I believe I lost a good deal of money."

"Good heavens, Bertie, I pray you try to remember. How much did you lose?"

"I think it was nearly three hundred," replied her brother.

"Three hundred pounds? Oh, Bertie! Thank heavens Lord Allingham found you before you lost more. You have fallen in with very bad company, Bertie. I do wish you would choose your friends more wisely. And in future, you must avoid Lord Seagrave."

"Seagrave?" said Bertie. "Yes, it was he who was winning. He had such deuced good luck. But if I had stayed in the game, perhaps my luck would have changed."

"It would have changed for the worse," said Pippa. "It was fortunate that Allingham arrived when he did."

"I cannot say I share your opinion," said Bertie miserably. "What he must think of me! They say he abhors drunkards."

"Then I hope you will do your best to regain his good opinion of you. It was very kind of him to bring you home."

Bertie appeared somewhat surprised by his sister's apparent change of heart concerning his lordship. "Well, at least it appears you are viewing Allingham in a more favorable light," he said. Despite his throbbing head, Bertie managed to smile at his sister. "Perhaps it was worth my getting drunk to have you do so."

"Do not be a goose, Bertie," said Pippa, quickly turning the subject away from his lordship. "It's lucky that you left the place when you did. You could have lost even more money. What will Papa say when he learns of it? Bertie, you have made a muddle of things."

"Yes, you are right, Pippa," said Bertie. "I swear I will never go to such a place again." He frowned. "Must I tell Papa, do you think?"

"I should advise it, Bertie. Make a clean breast of it. I don't know what else you might do. If you are serious about never doing this again, I know Papa will forgive you."

"But I feel like such an ass, Pippa."

"I know, but one must go on, Bertie. You must learn from this. Perhaps you will see less of those friends of yours such as Lord Percy. I've heard that he is not a very steady character."

To her surprise, her brother did not protest this remark. He looked at her for a moment and then he nodded. "Perhaps you are right, Pippa. I confess, that I have been thinking very much the same thing."

His sister smiled. "I'm glad that you are being so sensible." She stood up. "Then I shall cease plaguing you about the matter."

Bertie gave her a weak smile. "I should very much appreciate it," he said. "And Pippa . . ."

"Yes?" she said, fixing a questioning gaze on him.

"Could you please close those damnable curtains?" he asked pleadingly. She laughed and then proceeded to do as he wished.

Bertie was not the only one to sleep late that day. Seagrave, who had arrived home at dawn, had remained in bed well into the afternoon. Seagrave's servants were very familiar with the baron's habits and were not at all surprised by their master's late appearance. They were happy, however, to note that the baron was in an exceptionally good humor when he did finally arise from his bed.

Seagrave's jovial mood resulted from the profitable evening he had just spent at the card table. He had won a very tidy sum from a number of unfortunate gentlemen. In fact, he would have left the gaming establishment with even more money if it had not been for the appearance of Allingham.

The baron had not been at all pleased when the viscount had spirited away the Grey cub. Aware that the drunken young man was the son of a wealthy tradesman, Seagrave had considered Bertie a ripe pigeon for plucking. He had been very eager to have the drunken young man continue in the game.

Seagrave had also been disappointed that Allingham himself had not joined him at the card table. Having previously won a large amount of money from the viscount, the baron would have very much enjoyed seeing his lordship lose to him again.

Despite these two sources of frustration, Seagrave was still feeling quite jolly. Deciding that he was in the mood for some female company, the baron called to his servant to have his phaeton brought round.

Seagrave wasted no time in driving the vehicle to the lavish residence of the Earl of Granville. Boldly leaving his phaeton at the curb with a servant, the baron made his way to the front door of the house. He was soon admitted by the Granvilles' butler and ushered into a fashionable drawing room where he found the countess ensconced on a sofa.

"Seagrave," said Lady Granville, regarding him with a bored look, "Whatever are you doing here?"

Without answering her, the baron strode purposely over to the countess's side. Then, leaning down, Seagrave crushed his lips against hers. After a long and passionate kiss, he released her.

Lady Granville ran her fingers across her lips and then she frowned up at him. "Are you mad, Seagrave?" she asked. "What if someone should have come in just now?"

The baron grinned and took the seat next to her on the sofa. "Dammit, Isabelle, what do I care if your servants see us?"

The countess fixed her disapproving green eyes upon him. "And what if my husband should have come in to discover us in such a pose?"

Seagrave laughed. "Granville? No doubt the old fool would have apologized for disturbing us and gone tottering off. But do not fear, madam, I'm convinced your husband will not appear. I have been informed by your butler that the earl is at his club and will not return for several hours." The baron placed a familiar hand on the bodice of the countess's dress and gazed lasciviously at her. "I daresay, we shall have plenty of time for what I have in mind, my lovely Isabelle."

Lady Granville smiled seductively. "And just what do you have in mind, sir?"

The baron grinned again and leaning over, whispered in her ear. The countess listened and then gave a throaty laugh. "You are a dreadful man, Seagrave," she said.

"That I am," he replied and then, taking her roughly into his arms, he pinioned her against the back of the seat and hungrily kissed her again.

Lady Granville pushed the baron away. "Really, sir, do behave yourself. Remember where you are."

The baron grinned. "I'll be damned if I'll behave myself with you, Isabelle. Come, it's somewhat late to be acting the role of innocent wife." He leaned over and whispered into her ear once again. "Let us go to your bedchamber." He paused. "Unless you wish to stay here and truly shock your servants."

Isabelle smiled wickedly at him and stood up. "Very well," she said. As they walked out of the room, she said in a loud voice, "I must show you the painting that my husband just acquired, Lord Seagrave."

The baron grinned at this obvious ploy for the servants' benefit and leaned toward her. "I'll warrant the new painting is right over my lady's bed," he said in a low voice. After casting him a warning look, Lady Granville made her way upstairs, the eager baron right behind her.

Some time later, Seagrave and Lady Granville lay in the countess's large pink-canopied bed, the bedclothes tangled in wild disarray about them. The baron languidly reached over and fondled the lady's breast. "You are a tigress, Isabelle," he said with a satisfied smile.

In truth, Lady Granville did appear rather feline as she suddenly yawned and stretched out her bare arms. She turned toward the baron. "I do think you should go now. My husband may be returning from his club soon."

"You terrify me, madam," said Seagrave, laughing and then rolling over onto his back.

The countess did not appear amused. "I must say, you seem in a remarkably good humor today, Seagrave."

"And why should I not be, Isabelle, after our enjoyable sport here." He raised himself up in the bed and looked down at her. "Of course, my high spirits may also be due to the great good fortune I had last night."

"Oh?" asked the countess, raising a dark eyebrow. "And pray tell, what was the lady's name last night?"

Seagrave chortled. "My luck was not in the form of a female, my sweet. My success last evening was at the gaming table. I won a considerable sum." He paused. "The only thing that I would have enjoyed more would have been taking Allingham's money from him."

The countess was suddenly interested at hearing the mention of the viscount's name. "Allingham was gambling?" she asked in some surprise. Lady Granville had also been aware of the gossip that the viscount had sworn off such games.

The baron nodded. "Yes, he arrived at the Pigeon Hole, but unfortunately, he did not play. He was too busy acting the part of the solicitous elder brother to young Grey."

Lady Granville eyed the baron in astonishment. "Elder brother to young Grey? Miss Grey's brother?"

"Yes, of course, your dear friend's brother."

The countess smiled. "Yes, my dear friend, the esteemed Crimson Lady."

"You have certainly taken her up, Isabelle. Everyone thinks you are the dearest friends."

"Yes, is it not amusing? And Allingham is so vexed with me. But do tell me what happened with young Grey."

"Well, your dear friend's brother was at the gaming tables with me last night. He was drunk and losing quite a bit of his blunt to me. Then Allingham had to show his face and pull the cub out of the place. I do not doubt he was attempting to get the good opinion of his future father-in-law."

Lady Granville frowned. "You speak nonsense, Seagrave. His future father-in-law? That is absurd!"

The baron laughed. "Is it, my love? Why, I have a very good notion that Allingham is suddenly quite eager to taste the fruits of wedded bliss. Of course, I'll warrant the lady's fortune is his greatest inducement in wooing her. I would not be surprised if this Grey has promised Allingham a large dowry in exchange for some blue blood for his family line."

The countess attempted to appear indifferent, but in truth, the idea infuriated her. So Allingham thought he could make Miss Grey his wife?

The countess frowned as she thought of Allingham and Pippa. Although she did not want to admit it to herself, she had the galling notion that the viscount's interest in the girl might not just be mercenary. Vowing that she would do anything she could to ruin such a match, the countess's lovely face took on a rather sinister expression.

Seagrave, who was once again feeling in an amorous mood, was unaware of the lady's resolve concerning Allingham and Pippa. Reaching over, he eagerly pulled the countess toward him. "Seagrave!" she cried, pushing him away.

"What is the matter?"

"Do be serious for a time. There is much to discuss."

"Discuss? What do you mean?" said Seagrave, regarding her with a puzzled expression.

"I believe you should marry my dear friend Pippa Grey."

"I should marry her?" Seagrave eyed her in astonishment.

"Yes, why not?"

The baron shrugged. "So you wish to be rid of me?"

"Rid of you? No, my darling. I would not be rid of you simply because you marry her. We'd have many opportunities to amuse each other. If it's true that Allingham wants the girl, think how furious he will be if you steal her away."

Seagrave rubbed his chin thoughtfully. "That would be very funny, would it not?"

"And she is very rich."

"Yes," said Seagrave, nodding. "I suppose if I were to marry again, it may as well be to a rich wench."

"Yes, my dear. Yes, we will see that you win her."

"It would be a good idea, would it not?" said the baron, warming to the notion.

"Yes, it would. And I know she would not be able to resist you."

Seagrave seemed to share this opinion. Grinning, he pulled Isabelle roughly toward him and stifled any further conversation by covering her mouth with his own.

20

Some time after her interview with her brother, Pippa decided to see how Lizzy was doing. She found the young woman in the servants' hall, intently working a needle in and out of cloth.

"Hello, Lizzy," said Pippa, smiling at her. "How are you feeling today?"

The girl looked up from her sewing. "Oh, Miss Grey." She started to rise from her chair.

"Do not get up, Lizzy," said Pippa. "I daresay it is not an easy task for you."

Lizzy smiled. "Nay, miss, 'tis a bit difficult."

Pippa took a chair next to her. "I was wondering how you were."

"Oh, I'm fine, miss." She patted her large stomach. "Although the baby has been making a bit of a ruckus. I do think the little tyke is eager to be born."

Pippa smiled. "I'm glad you are looking so well, Lizzy. There's color in your cheeks."

Lizzy nodded. "I have Cook to thank for that, miss. Thanks to her I'm plump as a partridge. I'm ever so grateful, miss. I do thank you for all your kindness."

"You are most welcome, Lizzy," replied Pippa, noting with satisfaction the tremendous change that had been wrought in the young woman. In addition to putting on weight, Lizzy now appeared quite happy. With her rosy cheeks and bright smile, she seemed a different person from the one Allingham had rescued from the pond.

Pippa was also pleased that Lizzy seemed to be fitting into the household so well. Despite her scandalous condition, Lizzy had already won the affection of the other servants in the household. In fact, she had become something of a pet among them.

"And what are you working on now?" asked Pippa, glancing down at the cloth on Lizzy's lap.

The girl looked up and then she sighed. "Oh, miss, I was hop-

ing to surprise you. It is a handkerchief I was sewing for you."
Lizzy lifted up the white piece of cloth that was beautifully em-
broidered with red roses.

Pippa eyed it with admiration. "It is very lovely, Lizzy."

The young woman smiled again. "Betty has told me of how
you do like red, miss." She pointed to the center of the handkerchief. "I'm going to put your initials here."

"That will be very nice, indeed," said Pippa approvingly.

At that moment, they were interrupted by the appearance of
one of the Greys' footmen. A tall, gangly young man with dark
hair and blue eyes, the servant stopped in surprise at the sight of
his young mistress sitting there with Lizzy.

"Oh, I do beg your pardon, miss," he said, backing up toward
the door in some confusion.

Pippa eyed him curiously, noting that he was carrying a small
bunch of daisies in his hand. "That's all right, Robert," she said,
rising to her feet. "I had come down to see how Lizzy was doing.
I must be going."

Robert saw his mistress looking at the flowers. He blushed. "I
do hope you do not mind, miss. The daisies in the garden are all
blooming and I did think it might brighten things up a bit in
here."

Pippa smiled. "Of course, Robert, that is an excellent idea. Do
get a vase for them and put them on the table. I imagine Lizzy
will enjoy having them to look at."

Lizzy, who had remained quiet during Robert's appearance,
smiled shyly up at him. "Oh, yes, I would. I do thank you,
Robin."

The young man blushed even redder and then awkwardly hurried off to retrieve a container for the flowers. Pippa, who had
been quite interested in the flower-bearing footman and Lizzy's
reaction to him smiled at the girl. "Well, I shall be off. Do take
care of yourself, Lizzy. And I do thank you for making me the
beautiful handkerchief."

Lizzy smiled as Pippa left her to her work. Although she would
have liked to have seen Robert return with the flowers, Pippa was
quite certain that the young man would prefer to find Lizzy alone.

Making her way to the drawing room, Pippa reflected upon the
incident. It appeared that Lizzy had an admirer in Robert. And it
seemed that Lizzy liked the young footman as well.

Entering the drawing room, Pippa was greeted by Patches who
had been napping near the sofa. The big dog hurried to her mistress and wagged her tail enthusiastically. "Dear Patches," said

Pippa, reaching down to stroke the dog's neck. She then took a chair with Patches sitting at her feet.

Pippa stared thoughtfully out the window as she continued to ponder the matter of Lizzy and the young footman. However, she had little time to do so as her mother chose that moment to enter the room. Pippa could not fail to note that her usually cheerful mother had a worried look on her face.

"What is it, Mama?" asked Pippa. "Is something the matter?"

"Oh, no, of course not," said Mrs. Grey, taking a seat on the sofa.

"Now, Mama, I can see that something is wrong."

"Oh, very well, my dear. I have been thinking about our sitting with Lady Granville at the theater this evening. You know I never liked the idea overmuch. The more I think of it, the more I believe we should beg off."

"Good heavens, Mama, we have discussed this matter endlessly. You know very well I have no intention of ignoring Lady Granville simply because Allingham doesn't like her."

"Yes, I know that, my dear, but it is not only Allingham. Why, I had mentioned Lady Granville to Mrs. Mortimer and she disapproved of her."

"One cannot be so concerned with what others think, Mama," said Pippa. "And I will not give up my evening at the theater. We are to see Kean after all."

"Yes," said Mrs. Grey, "I did wish to see him. He is said to be the greatest actor to ever tread the stage."

"And Lady Granville assured me that her box at the theater is the very best. Now, Mama, I'm determined to go tonight. You will not persuade me otherwise. I hope you will accompany me."

Mrs. Grey hesitated. She really did not like to pass up an opportunity to see the great Kean. "Oh, very well."

"Good," said Pippa. "I'm very thrilled at the idea of finally seeing Kean. I know it will be very exciting."

Mrs. Grey agreed most emphatically and mother and daughter began a lively discussion of the famous thespian. They had not been talking long when the butler appeared in the drawing room. "Mr. Cartwright is here, ma'am."

"Cartwright," repeated Mrs. Grey, not looking at all pleased. "Really, I'm in no mood to see anyone."

"But, Mama," said Pippa, "it would be most inconsiderate to refuse to see Mr. Cartwright."

"Oh, very well. Hawkins, show the gentleman in."

"Very good, ma'am."

When the butler returned with Cartwright, Mrs. Grey smiled graciously at him. "How very kind of you to call, Mr. Cartwright," she said.

"Good afternoon, Mrs. Grey," said Cartwright, smiling at Pippa's mother. He then directed a smile at Pippa. "Miss Grey, how nice to see you again."

"Mr. Cartwright." Pippa nodded. The dog Patches eyed the visitor with an indifferent expression and then lay down on the floor and closed her eyes.

"Do sit down, Mr. Cartwright."

"Thank you, Mrs. Grey," returned Cartwright, taking a chair next to Pippa. He smiled at Pippa. "I saw Mr. Edward Bell yesterday. He told me that he had received a very generous donation from you, Miss Grey."

"I'm only too glad to help in such a worthy cause. I do hope other poor girls like Lizzy might be helped."

"And how is the young woman?" asked Cartwright.

"Oh, she is very well, sir," said Pippa.

"I'm certain that she is responding well to your kindness, Miss Grey. You ladies were very good to take the girl in. Such acts of charity are all too rare."

"Unfortunately, that is true," said Mrs. Grey.

"But Mr. Bell is doing admirable work." Cartwright launched into an enthusiastic description of Mr. Bell's charitable works.

While Cartwright talked, Pippa found herself studying the young publisher with a reflective expression. He was an admirable young man, intense, handsome, and idealistic, the very sort of person whom she had hoped to meet one day. Yet, while she listened to him, Pippa was aware of a distinct lack of romantic attraction.

It struck Pippa as ironical that she should find her passions directed toward Allingham rather than such a worthy object as Cartwright. It was clear by the way in which Cartwright looked at her that he was not indifferent. Yet Pippa felt no spark between them. Unfortunately, her heart had made its choice in a most illogical way. Why, Pippa wondered, did a person fall in love with someone who was so obviously unsuited to oneself?

Engaged with her own thoughts, Pippa did not contribute much to the conversation. Mrs. Grey, who did not like to encourage Cartwright, listened politely. She was relieved when the gentleman finally announced he must be going.

When he had gone, Mrs. Grey turned to her daughter. "Mr.

Cartwright is a nice young man. What a pity he publishes those books of his."

"Yes," said Pippa absently.

Mrs. Grey regarded her daughter in some surprise. She had expected Pippa to object to her last remark, but Pippa had not responded at all. Mrs. Grey felt optimistic. Perhaps her daughter was not so taken with the young man as she had feared.

"Well, I don't wish to see anyone else this afternoon. Shall we have tea, Pippa?"

"Yes, Mama," said Pippa, rising to her feet to ring for the servant. When she regained her seat the conversation returned quickly to the theater and Mrs. Grey felt very pleased that so little had been said of Mr. Cartwright.

21

Drury Lane Theater was ablaze with lights that evening as the-atergoers arrived for the eagerly awaited performance of Edmund Kean. There was an air of intense excitement in the place as people milled about, greeting acquaintances. Well-dressed ladies and gentlemen made their way to the exclusive boxes while more common folk flocked to the gallery or pit.

As Pippa entered Isabelle's well-situated box, she glanced down at the stage and the crush of people below her. She then turned her fascinated gaze to the other boxes where the fashionable members of the audience were gathering. Smiling, she once again turned her attention to the curtained stage.

The theater had always been a magical place to Pippa. She had loved it ever since her father had taken her to see her first play in Portsmouth when she was eight years old. She would never forget her great sense of wonder sitting there in the box, her eyes glued upon the costumed actors on the stage.

As she continued to look down at the brilliantly lit theater, Pippa was herself the object of considerable attention. Numerous ladies and gentlemen directed their opera glasses in her direction to get a better look at the 'Crimson Lady.'

Pippa did not disappoint for she looked quite magnificent in her vivid red gown. The dress had a low-cut bodice decorated with silver lace that was repeated on the hem of the skirt. Pippa's favorite ruby necklace was around her neck and a small tiara, also festooned with rubies, was fastened among her auburn tresses.

Lady Granville sat beside her attired in a gown of peacock blue satin. While it galled Isabelle to think that her companion was attracting more attention than she, she was pleased that Pippa was there beside her. Isabelle directed her opera glasses around the other boxes, hoping to see Allingham, but his box was empty.

Mrs. Grey had seemingly overcome her misgivings, She chattered excitedly to Pippa as the theater filled with people. Bertie had accompanied them and he was in an ebullient mood. Like most young men, he was not immune to Isabelle's charms. Sitting beside her, he laughed and talked, very pleased that the beautiful and desirable Lady Granville was hanging upon his every word.

After a short time, a gentleman entered the box. Looking back, Pippa recognized Seagrave. "Good evening to you," he said, smiling broadly at them. He bowed to the ladies and then nodded to Bertie.

Pippa's brother, remembering his unfortunate evening at the Pigeon Hole, was not very pleased to see Seagrave. He was reminded of the sum he had lost to the baron, an amount he had not as yet confessed to his father.

"Seagrave," said Isabelle, eyeing him with mock annoyance. "I did not know you would be here. Do not think you will join us."

"My dear Lady Granville, you could not be so cruel as to bar me from joining the three most beautiful ladies in the kingdom. Indeed, there is a chair." He motioned toward the empty chair next to Pippa, and then sat down in it. "Miss Grey, you look ravishing."

"Oh, dear," said Isabelle, rolling her eyes heavenward. "I don't know how we will rid ourselves of him. I fear we would create a scene if I ask Mr. Grey to toss him out."

Seagrave laughed heartily at this. "I can hardly be blamed for wishing to join you." Grinning at Pippa, he spoke in a low voice. "By God, you are the prettiest girl here, Miss Grey."

"You are too kind, Lord Seagrave," said Pippa, acknowledging the compliment with a polite nod. Thinking of his part in encouraging her brother to gamble, she regarded Seagrave coolly.

"You must not vex Miss Grey too much, Seagrave," said Isabelle. She smiled at Pippa's mother, who was seated next to her. "He will talk throughout the entire performance. The theater bores him."

"Indeed, it does," said Seagrave. "I care little for these actors prancing about on the stage. But I shall not disturb Miss Grey at all."

Glancing back at her daughter and Seagrave, Mrs. Grey found herself wishing that the play would start. Having not expected Seagrave to be there, she was not at all pleased to see him. Knowing that Allingham thought him most unsuitable, she did not like the idea of Pippa sitting with him in full view of everyone. She began to tap her fan impatiently against her hand. "I do wish they would begin."

Pippa found herself thinking the same thing. She looked out across the theater at the other boxes. She noted a number of members of society whom she had met at various functions. Her gaze suddenly alighted on the box directly across from them where a party of ladies and gentlemen were just now entering. A slight flush appeared on her face as she recognized the tall, somberly dressed figure of Allingham.

Seagrave looked in the direction of her gaze. "So the great Allingham has arrived," he said. "How odd that the entire company does not rise and make obeisance."

Pippa looked over at him. "You quite detest him, do you not, sir?"

"I confess I do," admitted Seagrave. "But I have known him for a long time. I know his true character. I have suffered too much at his hands, Miss Grey."

Pippa frowned slightly. She was certain Seagrave was talking nonsense.

Allingham was unaware of Pippa's presence. Having taken his seat, he looked down at the large crowd gathering below him. Sir Henry Lonsdale, his wife, and his mother-in-law were sitting in the box with him.

Lady Lonsdale looked very pretty that evening in a white gown. Her blond curls were elegantly coiffed and adorned with pink rosebuds. She was excitedly talking to her mother, an attractive older lady who wore a turbaned headdress.

Sir Henry, leaving the ladies to their conversation turned to his friend. "So, Jack, it appears to be a full house this evening. I wonder if His Royal Highness will attend."

Allingham glanced over toward the empty royal box. "I would expect that Prinny will put in an appearance. He's a great admirer of Kean."

Sir Henry smiled. "As is all of London, it would appear. Indeed, it looks as if the entire city is congregating here tonight." The baronet raised his opera glasses and began to survey the crowd. He stopped as Pippa came into his view. "Why, there is Miss Grey," he said. Catching sight of Seagrave sitting next to her, Sir Henry suddenly regretted his words. However, it was too late as Allingham had already directed his gaze toward the box where the lady and her party were sitting.

It was not difficult for the viscount to pick out Pippa in her red gown. Allingham had been somewhat amused by the lady's insistence on wearing the offending color, but as he observed the gentleman sitting next to her, his slight smile vanished. He watched Seagrave lean toward Pippa, say something, and then burst into laughter.

"I must say that Miss Grey looks very charming tonight," said Sir Henry, watching her with keep interest. "But, good God, what can she be thinking of to appear with Seagrave?"

Allingham adopted a look of practiced indifference. "Miss Grey doesn't concern me, Harry."

Sir Henry regarded his friend closely. He sensed that beneath the viscount's calm exterior, Allingham was very upset. Having decided that his friend was in love with Miss Grey, Sir Henry could well understand Allingham's feelings at seeing her sitting there with Seagrave.

Sir Henry lifted his glasses back toward Seagrave and Pippa. "I don't believe Miss Grey looks at all pleased to be with Seagrave, Jack."

The viscount cast a glance back at Lady Lonsdale and her mother. Seeing that those two ladies were still occupied in conversation, he turned back to Sir Henry. "Then, dammit, Harry, why is she with him?"

"You cannot think that she is fond of him? She has a good deal better judgment than that."

Allingham frowned. "As I have said, Harry, the matter is of no concern to me. I have told her what sort of man Seagrave is. I have told her she should not be friendly with Isabelle. Miss Grey delights in refusing to take my advice. I shall waste no more time on her or her family. I believe I have done my duty in that regard."

"Indeed you have," said Sir Henry. "But it is a pity. I did think you were rather fond of the girl, Jack." Allingham did not reply, but crossed his arms in front of him.

At that moment the curtain rose, signaling that the play was to begin. The viscount attempted to fix his attention on the actors appearing on stage, but he found himself glancing every so often toward Pippa's box. The sight of her with Seagrave only infuriated him, but he could not keep himself from looking across at them time and again.

Pippa, who had also been distracted by seeing Allingham that evening, tried hard to restrain herself from staring in his direction. She was glad when the play got underway so that her attention became focused on the stage below her.

As soon as the great Kean walked out into the footlights, Pippa was totally drawn into the drama of *Richard III*. Although short of stature, Kean had a commanding presence that overshadowed every other actor appearing with him. With his expressive eyes and forceful voice, he seemed to actually become the character of the hunchbacked king.

Sitting mesmerized, Pippa was disappointed when the play was suddenly interrupted. The actors stopped in the middle of their lines and bowed deeply. The crowd turned toward the royal box where the Prince Regent and his party had just appeared. The entire audience stood up in homage to His Royal Highness and there were some rowdy, good-natured shouts. The smiling prince put up a hand and then directed that the play continue.

Kean again stole the attention of the crowd as he made a passionate speech to the Lady Anne. Pippa put her chin in her hand and gazed down in rapt attention at the famous actor. She had never seen anyone so entirely convincing in a role before.

During Kean's final scene, every eye in the house was riveted to the stage. When the curtain went down for the last time, there was a thunderous burst of applause and loud shouts of approval. Appearing once more before the crowd, Kean bowed several times, a triumphant smile upon his lips.

Pippa clapped enthusiastically. "Was he not splendid?"

Seagrave shrugged. "I daresay I thought the fellow doing it a bit brown."

"I thought he was wonderful," said Pippa.

"Yes, perhaps so," said Seagrave, taking his silver snuffbox from his pocket and taking a pinch.

The crowd continued to clap and roar its approval for some time. Then, the people began to depart their seats. Now that the play was over, Pippa once again thought about Allingham. Casting a furtive glance over toward his box, she found that it was now empty.

"Shall we go?" said Isabelle, rising from her chair. Bertie was happy to escort his mother and Isabelle from the box, Seagrave offered his arm to Pippa, which she took with some reluctance.

There was a great crush of people in the hallway outside the boxes, causing Pippa and Seagrave to become separated from the others. The baron was not at all displeased with this development, especially since the crowd of people was nudging Pippa right up against him.

At that moment, there was a shout. "Make way for His Royal Highness!" The throng immediately parted to allow the prince Regent to pass by.

Pippa, who was standing out in front, saw the prince approaching, a large number of royal retainers following after him. She then noticed that Allingham was walking along right behind

Royal George. The viscount noticed Pippa at the same moment. Seeing her standing with Seagrave, Allingham frowned.

In contrast, the prince smiled broadly as he beheld Pippa standing among the crowd. He stopped in front of her and she managed to make a curtsy. "Ah, Miss Grey," said the prince, casting an admiring look at her, "you look lovely as ever."

Pippa smiled at him. "Thank you, Your Royal Highness." She glanced over at Allingham and found that he was regarding her with a disapproving look.

The prince nodded to Seagrave. "Seagrave, you are a lucky fellow to be in Miss Grey's company."

"I'm well aware of that, Your Royal Highness," replied the baron with a well-satisfied smile.

"Yes, you are a fortunate man, Seagrave, to be escorting such a fair lady."

The prince glanced about them and then he eyed Pippa with a stern expression. "And where is your mother, Miss Grey?"

"I fear we got separated in the crowd, sir," said Pippa.

"Separated, eh?" Royal George winked over at Seagrave. "Well done, sir." Allingham scowled at this remark. He was finding it very difficult standing there, watching Pippa and Seagrave together. His lordship looked impatiently at the prince, wishing he would continue out of the theater. However, that gentleman showed no inclination of doing so. His Royal Highness turned once again to Pippa. "And did you enjoy the play, Miss Grey?"

"Oh, yes," she said enthusiastically. "I thought Mr. Kean was wonderful."

"Wonderful, was he?" repeated the prince. He glanced at the gentlemen around him and smiled. "Kean does seem to thrill the ladies, does he not?"

"Not only the ladies, Your Royal Highness," chimed in a grinning gentleman in military dress who was standing near the Prince. "As I recall, Byron practically swooned once when he saw the fellow act."

The Prince Regent fixed a look of royal displeasure on the military gentleman. His Royal Highness did not like to hear mention of the scandalous poet, especially before a respectable female such as Miss Grey. He turned once again to that lady. "I must not keep you any longer, madam." Pippa curtsied again and Royal George smiled graciously at her. He nodded at Seagrave and then continued on his way.

Pippa glanced up at Allingham, who had hesitated momentarily

before her. Meeting his solemn gaze, she smiled. "Lord Allingham," she said.

He bowed stiffly. "Miss Grey." Then, ignoring Seagrave, he
strode off after the prince.

Seagrave was so pleased that he had irritated his enemy so effectively that he only grinned. "It appears Allingham was not very
happy to see me."

Pippa, who was not at all pleased at this meeting with the viscount, frowned. "Let us find the others, Lord Seagrave," she said.
Seagrave nodded and then, grinning happily, escorted Pippa out
of the theater.

22

After his departure from the theater, Allingham accompanied the Prince Regent and his party to Carleton House where he spent the rest of the evening playing cards. Not in the best of moods and distracted by thoughts of Pippa, the viscount departed at first opportunity. Returning home he retired to bed, but spent a restless night thinking about Pippa.

Unable to rid himself of the picture of Pippa sitting beside Seagrave in the theater box, Allingham had a fitful night's slumber. He arose from his bed at an uncharacteristically early hour the next morning, and, feeling restless, he called for his horse.

In a short time, Allingham was mounted on his favorite dappled gray and was making his way through the streets of London. There were few people about as yet. As the viscount turned his horse down a usually bustling avenue, only a lone wagon rumbled past him.

As he rode along the quiet streets, Allingham was scarcely aware of the sights around him. His thoughts were still centered on Pippa. That he had fallen in love with her could not be denied, a fact that still surprised him. He had always thought himself immune to Cupid's darts, but now he knew he had lost his heart.

The viscount continued riding until he found himself in the proximity of the residential neighborhood where the Greys lived. Pulling up his horse, he hesitated for a moment and then he proceeded on toward Pippa's house. He knew that it was hardly the thing to hang about the area at such an hour. It was the sort of thing a besotted schoolboy might do, go to the home of his lady love to hope for a glimpse of her.

Recognizing that he was acting in a most uncharacteristic fashion, Allingham nevertheless proceeded toward Pippa's home. Arriving at the Greys' elegant brick town house, he stopped his horse once more. Gazing up at the windows along the street, he wondered which room was Pippa's. Frustrated with longing for her, the viscount stared up at the house for some time.

Suddenly his attention was distracted by a dog's loud barking. Glancing back down at the street, Allingham was astonished to see Patches bounding along the sidewalk with Pippa at her side. He was dismayed to see her. He had never imagined that she would rise so early after an evening at the theater. Whatever would she think to find him there staring at her house like a mooncalf?

Pippa was quite astonished to find the viscount on horseback in front of her house. She could not help but experience the now familiar excitement at seeing him. Why had he come at such an early hour? Surely he could not think to pay a call at such a time.

Patches appeared thrilled at seeing the horse and rider. She strained at her leash, pulling her mistress hastily along until they arrived before him. "Lord Allingham," said Pippa, regarding him in surprise. "Whatever are you doing here?"

Dismounting from his horse, the viscount tipped his tall beaver hat and attempted to appear nonchalant. "I was out riding and just happened by your neighborhood, Miss Grey," he said somewhat lamely.

Pippa regarded him curiously. "You are out early, my lord."

He smiled at her, noting the fashionable lavender pelisse and fetching bonnet she was wearing. She looked beautiful, her face flushed with exertion and strands of her auburn hair peeking out from beneath her bonnet. "As are you, Miss Grey. You have been out walking?" he asked.

Pippa nodded. "Yes, we have already been to the park. It was quite lovely."

"I don't think it wise for a young lady to walk about alone, Miss Grey. I should feel much better if you allowed a servant to accompany you. There may be footpads about at this hour."

Pippa regarded him in surprise. As always he was disapproving. "Footpads? I daresay, none would be so foolhardy as to approach me with Patches as my companion." She leaned down and fondly patted the huge black-and-white dog. "Although she is a gentle giant, my lord, I assure you she can be quite fierce if the necessity arises."

Allingham smiled slightly. "I'm glad to hear it, ma'am. I do not doubt that Patches would do her duty admirably." Patches wagged her tail furiously at the compliment. His lordship obligingly reached down to scratch the canine behind her ears. Patches appeared overjoyed by this attention, staring up at the viscount with an ecstatic grin.

Pippa smiled. "At least *you* have little to fear from my ferocious beast, my lord."

Allingham stood up. "It would seem so," he said, fixing his intent gaze upon Pippa.

Feeling somewhat flustered by his scrutiny, Pippa spoke. "I did not think that you would wish to speak to me. I know you were displeased at seeing me with Lord Seagrave and Lady Granville."

"I have said enough on that subject, Miss Grey. I can see no point in discussing it further. With whom you wish to spend your time is no business of mine."

Pippa's blue eyes met his gray ones. She found herself strangely disappointed that he appeared to have no intention of chiding her for appearing with unacceptable company. His expression of indifference was disheartening. "Did you enjoy the play, my lord?"

"One cannot help but enjoy Kean," said the viscount. "And you?"

"Oh, it was wonderful," Pippa managed to say even though she was finding it exceedingly awkward standing there with him.

"Yes," said the viscount with a slight frown.

Pippa felt at a loss for what to say. "I expect it is exciting accompanying the prince."

"You are mistaken, Miss Grey. It's not in the least exciting."

"Oh," said Pippa.

"I'm pleased to see that you have abandoned crimson for a time, Miss Grey."

Smiling, she replied in a mischievous tone, "I should certainly not have done so if I had known that I would see you, my lord. I know how fond of the color you are."

To her surprise, Allingham responded seriously. "I confess that I have come to like the color very much, Miss Grey. I realize how mistaken I was to have thought it unbecoming. It is very becoming on you."

Pippa was rather disconcerted by his words. "Come, my lord, there's no need to spout such fustian to me."

"I have never spouted fustian to anyone in my life, Miss Grey. I assure you, I'm in total earnest."

Pippa regarded him with a questioning look. At that moment one of the Greys' maids appeared at the front door preparing to shake out a rug. Observing her mistress with the viscount, the servant made a hasty bob and then disappeared back inside the house.

Pippa glanced at the retreating maid and then looked back at

Allingham. "I should be going in, Lord Allingham," she said. "Perhaps you might join us for breakfast."

"That is very kind of you," replied the viscount, "but I could not impose upon you in such a manner. And I must be returning home. Good day, Miss Grey."

Pippa, who was unhappy at ending their meeting, nodded and watched him as he climbed up into the saddle.

"Good day, Lord Allingham."

The viscount smiled slightly and then rode off. Pippa stood watching him until he disappeared. She then made her way into the house with Patches at her side.

Once inside, Pippa went to the drawing room where she sat down upon the sofa to reflect about her unexpected meeting with the viscount. Could he be in love with her? Pippa smiled. What other explanation could there be? "Oh, Patches, what do you think?" said Pippa addressing the dog.

Patches cocked her head and regarded her mistress seriously, causing Pippa to burst into laughter. "Whatever is so amusing, my dear?"

Pippa looked up to see her father enter the drawing room. She rose up and met him, greeting him with a kiss. "Good morning, Papa. Oh, it's nothing. I was only having a conversation with Patches. We had a lovely walk. We went to the park and Patches was quite thrilled to see several squirrels and a rabbit there."

"How lucky for you, old girl," said Grey, patting the dog. "I must say I'm very surprised to see you about at such an hour. You arrived home so late after your excursion to the theater."

"I couldn't sleep," said Pippa.

"Well, you must have a rest this afternoon, my girl. I'll not have you overly tired."

"Do not worry about me, Papa, I assure you I feel fine." She hesitated for a moment before continuing. "Papa, the most curious thing just happened. You will not guess whom I met upon my return from my walk."

"I daresay I cannot guess," replied her father. "Whom would one meet at such an early hour?"

"It was Allingham," said Pippa.

"Allingham here?"

Pippa nodded. She noted that her father did not look very pleased. "He was out riding and just happened by."

"Just happened by? I think that unlikely." Grey frowned. "I do not very much like Allingham prowling about our doorstep."

Pippa shook her head. "Prowling about? Really, Papa, you act as if the man was planning to rob us."

Grey nodded. "Perhaps he is. And I daresay, he has his eye on something considerably more valuable than the silver. It is you he wants. What a blockhead I've been. I might have known this might happen. Has he made an offer for you?"

Pippa regarded her father in surprise. "No, of course not."

"It's only a matter of time. I confess I was happy that you seemed to dislike him so much. Now it seems you have developed a more favorable opinion of Allingham."

Pippa nodded. "I confess that I do not think he is so bad as I once thought. You do not approve of him?"

"Indeed, I do not," said Grey forcefully. "He's not the sort of man I might wish for you. Oh, I know very well that your mother would think him a wonderful son-in-law. She hangs upon his every word. But he is an idle fellow, a spendthrift who would squander whatever money came his way. I do not believe he would make you happy."

"Well, you mustn't worry, Papa. Lord Allingham is quite displeased with me. If you had seen how he looked at me last night at the theater, you wouldn't worry about his making an offer of marriage. Besides, he is said to be a confirmed bachelor."

Grey appeared unconvinced. "Many a confirmed bachelor has changed his mind when he has decided that he must find a rich wife." The minute he had spoken, Grey regretted his words. "Oh, I do not mean to say that is his only motivation, Pippa."

Pippa regarded her father with a hurt expression. "But it's his primary motivation? So you think Allingham is a fortune hunter, out to ensnare me?"

Grey shrugged. "I know enough of the world to know that the high and mighty Lord Allingham would hardly want to marry a tradesman's daughter if it were not for the money she would bring him. Oh, I know I'm harsh. Any man would be a fool not to wish to marry a girl like you, but one must be a realist. The man is nearly penniless due to his extravagance. I know his sort."

Pippa frowned. Patches, sensing her mistress's distress hurried to place her enormous head upon Pippa's knee. "Allingham has not attempted to woo me. He has said nothing to make me think he wishes to marry me."

Grey considered this for a moment. "It's true that he has scarcely played the role of an ardent suitor. Well, perhaps I am wrong about the fellow. I do hope you haven't lost your heart to him." When Pippa made no reply, Grey frowned again. "You *have* lost your heart to him!"

"Oh, I don't know, Papa," said Pippa. "Perhaps I have."

"Oh, my dear Pippa," said Grey, placing his arm protectively around her shoulders.

"I beg you, let us not speak any further of it. And please, do not mention any of this to Mama."

"I'm not so addlepated to do such a thing, my girl. But come, let us go to breakfast." Although very much disheartened, Pippa nodded and accompanied her father to the dining room.

23

The next several days went by slowly for Pippa. There was the usual amount of activity with callers and visits, but a sense of gloom had settled over her. Since seeing Allingham outside her door, he had never been far from her thoughts.

Pippa was certain that he must have some feelings for her, but if he did, why did he not call on her? As the days went by and he did not appear, Pippa felt confused and depressed for she could only conclude that he cared nothing for her. It seemed that the great Allingham could have no feelings for a tradesman's daughter. He was far too proud and toplofty for that, she reasoned.

The weather seemed to echo Pippa's mood. After what had been a period of exceptionally fine weather, rain set in. It now seemed that virtually every day was gray with cold rain falling.

Mrs. Grey, however, was in an exceedingly good humor. She was very pleased that their new social position seemed more and more assured with each passing day. What especially pleased Pippa's mother was that the Marquess of Ravensly was becoming a most ardent suitor, calling each day and regarding Pippa with such an earnest expression that it was clear he was close to proposing.

The only bright spot for Pippa during this time was Lizzy's announcement that the footman, Robert, had asked for her hand in marriage. While Mrs. Grey would have normally been opposed to junior servants marrying, the special circumstances made the idea of Lizzy entering the state of matrimony quite acceptable.

After hearing the news from Hawkins, Pippa went to the servants' hall to see Lizzy. She found her seated in a chair, intent upon her sewing.

"Lizzy," said Pippa, coming to sit beside her before Lizzy could even attempt to get up from her chair, since her advanced pregnancy made rising exceedingly awkward. "Hawkins has told us the news. I'm very glad for you."

"Oh, miss," said Lizzy, "Robin is a dear man. I do love him."

"How wonderful for you," said Pippa. "You are feeling well?"

"Oh, quite well, miss, although I'll be happy when my time comes and the baby is here. 'Tis not much longer, miss."

"Well, we will take good care of you, Lizzy. You are not to worry."

"Truly, miss, you have been so kind. Everyone has been so good to me. I shall never forget your kindness."

"We were all very glad to have helped, Lizzy," said Pippa, smiling brightly at her.

"Well, I did not think there was that sort of kindness anywhere, miss." She paused and sighed. "And when I remember how miserable I was, miss, how I wished to do away with myself. 'Tis very hard to believe now. I sometimes think about that, miss. About what if you had not come by. And if his lordship had not pulled me from the water."

"You must not dwell on that, Lizzy. We were there."

"Aye, miss, you were. And to think it was the great Lord Allingham to have saved me! He must be a very good gentleman, miss."

Pippa was unsure how to respond to this comment. "I daresay he is, Lizzy."

"Oh, yes, I'm certain he is. You will tell him how grateful I am when you see his lordship."

"Certainly, Lizzy," replied Pippa, although she found herself wondering whether she would have that opportunity. "Well, I must go." She rose from her chair. "But do rest and if you need anything, you must call me."

Lizzy once again expressed her gratitude and Pippa made her way upstairs. She was very pleased that the girl appeared so well and happy. As she entered the drawing room, Pippa resolved to do all she could to help the young couple.

Allingham stood in his drawing room gazing out at the rain falling on the street outside his fashionable town house. He did not notice when the butler entered the room. "My lord?"

Turning, the viscount frowned at his servant. "Yes, Morris?"

"The Duchess of Northampton is here, my lord, and Sir Henry and Lady Lonsdale."

"Then show them in, Morris," replied Allingham, his face grave.

The servant bowed and retreated, returning a short time later with the callers. While his lordship was not in the mood to receive anyone, he was not displeased at seeing his good friends.

The duchess entered the room followed by Sir Henry and his wife. "My dear Allingham! There you are!"

"Indeed, here I am, Duchess," returned the viscount, greeting Her Grace with a formal bow.

When everyone had been seated, the duchess smiled at his lordship. "Sir Henry and Lady Lonsdale were paying a call at Northampton House. We were talking about you, Allingham."

"Indeed?" said the viscount, smiling slightly.

"Yes, we were," said the duchess. "Then I said that I must call on you and Sir Henry said that we must all do so. So we came here at once."

"I'm pleased that you would do me that honor," said Allingham.

"I had hoped to see you at Almack's last evening," said Her Grace reprovingly.

"Good God, Duchess, you know I detest Almack's."

"That's hardly enough reason for not going," replied Her Grace.

"Indeed not," said Lady Lonsdale. "Everyone was looking for you. You know how the young men are when you're not there to show them how their cravats should be tied." Allingham smiled at his friend's wife. "We were concerned that you were unwell," continued Lady Lonsdale.

"I'm very well," replied Allingham.

"Well, you look rather pale," said Her Grace.

"I assure you I have never felt better, Duchess."

"Well, you are attending my soiree Saturday evening, are you not, Allingham? I shall not take it kindly if you say you are not coming."

"Then I shall say I am coming, Duchess."

"Good," returned Her Grace. "Now do tell us why you are acting like some sort of hermit."

"I am doing no such thing," said the viscount. "It's only that I have been very busy. There were many business matters I had to see to. But do tell me what news you have. I daresay, you found Almack's as exciting as always."

"It was certainly not dull," said Lady Lonsdale. "Miss Grey was there." Lady Lonsdale regarded Allingham expectantly, but he exhibited no reaction to this information. "She looked very lovely, did she not, Harry?"

"Oh, she did," said Sir Henry. "And you would have been amazed to see her. She was wearing a blue dress."

"Yes, she looked quite lovely," said the duchess. "I do like

Miss Grey. Of course, I do believe that she is seeing far too much of Lady Granville."

"Yes," said Lady Lonsdale. "And Seagrave." Her ladyship had hoped that the mention of his enemy's name would elicit a reaction from Allingham, but he maintained his pose of complete indifference.

"You know that there is talk that Seagrave wishes to marry her," said the duchess with a frown.

"Yes, and that horrid Lady Granville is spreading it about that Miss Grey has a *tendre* for him," said Sir Henry.

"You cannot believe it could be true?" said Lady Lonsdale, directing her remark to Allingham. "You could not think that Miss Grey might accept Seagrave?"

"That is hardly likely," said the viscount, still betraying little emotion.

"I do hope so," said Lady Lonsdale. "She did dance with him at Almack's last evening. She was very civil to him. They say he is very eager to have her fortune. And you know, my dear Allingham, a good many ladies find him very appealing although I cannot understand why."

"Well, I cannot abide him," said the duchess. "But there are a good many gentlemen in pursuit of Miss Grey, Allingham. I do not understand why you are dillydallying. Don't you wish to marry her?"

"My dear Duchess, you know I'm a committed bachelor."

"Stuff and nonsense," said the duchess. "You had best come to your senses quickly before someone else steals her away. They say Ravensly is very interested. His father is not happy at the idea, but he will not object due to the lady's fortune."

"Indeed, I should like to discuss something other than Miss Grey," said Allingham as if the subject bored him.

The duchess regarded him in some frustration. "I'm convinced that you are in love with her, Allingham, so do not act as if you care nothing for the girl."

"My dear Duchess, you are unfortunately prone to romantic fancies," said his lordship.

"Well, perhaps I am," returned Her Grace. "But I cannot understand why you are acting in such a cork-brained fashion." She rose from her chair and the others followed suit. "Come, Sir Henry and Lady Lonsdale. Allingham is in a vexatious mood. There is no point in staying any further."

Sir Henry could only regard his friend with some amusement

as the duchess took her leave. "I shall call on you later," said the baronet before following the duchess and his wife from the room.

When they had gone, Allingham went back to the window where he stared sullenly out at the rain. Although he had feigned indifference, he was not at all pleased to think of Pippa and other men. So she had danced with Seagrave at Almack's? The idea was especially distasteful. Of course, he had no concern that she would be impressed by Seagrave. She had far too much sense for that.

Still, as the viscount mulled over the matter, he was not at all happy. Leaving the drawing room, he went to the library. There he sat at his desk staring thoughtfully into space. Why had he ever agreed to accept Peter Grey's proposal? To sell his influence was entirely dishonorable.

Having thus established himself as a mercenary blackguard, he could never make an offer for Pippa's hand. He would seem an odious fortune hunter.

Allingham frowned at the thought. He resolved to pay Peter Grey back the entire sum the man had given him. At least he could do that. Folding his arms across his chest, the viscount started to mull over just how he might raise the needed money.

24

Isabelle opened her eyes to see the early morning sunlight streaming in through the crack between the draperies. Yawning, she turned toward the recumbent figure beside her in the bed. Seagrave was fast asleep, snoring peacefully.

A smile came to Isabelle's face as she looked at her lover. She had had a wonderful night. With her husband gone to the country, it had been easy for Seagrave to appear at her door very late and come to her. Now that it was morning, however, he had better leave discreetly. She reached over and touched his shoulder. "Seagrave," she said. When there was no response, she shook him. "Seagrave. Do wake up!"

"What?" came the groggy response. "Dammit, Isabelle, I was sleeping."

"You cannot stay here all day. You must leave here before anyone sees you."

Seagrave smiled and pulled her toward him. "I have no intention of leaving just yet."

Isabelle pulled away. "No, it's time you were going." Eluding his grasp, she rose from the bed and put on her dressing gown. "I don't want anyone to see you. If Miss Grey should hear that you were here, she would not want to marry you."

"Is that it?" said Seagrave, sitting up in bed. "By God, I don't think she will wish to marry me in any case. Indeed, she seems damned cool to me."

"She did not look so cool to you when she danced with you at Almack's. Everyone noted how she looked at you. I believe she is succumbing to your charm, my darling."

"Is she?" said Seagrave in some surprise. "It didn't seem so to me."

"It did to me," returned the countess, eager to encourage him. "And I was there at Almack's. I saw the two of you. I suspect Miss Grey to be one of those ladies who prefers to hide her feelings."

Seagrave rubbed the stubble on his chin thoughtfully. "Perhaps you are right. I did think I saw her smile once. But there are so many others who want her. It's not surprising if her fortune is as enormous as everyone says. I daresay I don't know how I might win her short of carrying her off."

"That's an interesting idea," said Isabelle, sitting down at her dressing table and looking into the mirror. She turned back to Seagrave. "Perhaps that is the answer."

"What?" said the baron, regarding her with a puzzled look.

"Carrying her off. Yes, you might elope with her."

"Elope with her?" said Seagrave.

"Yes, of course. Why, what girl has not dreamed of some handsome man carrying her off. I shall consider this. Truly, I believe you have had a splendid idea."

"You are quite daft, my girl," said Seagrave. "Now come back to bed."

"No, I will not. You must get up and leave at once. Come, come, my lord."

"Oh, very well, dammit," muttered Seagrave, tossing aside the bedclothes.

Isabelle smiled. Turning back to the mirror, she picked up her hairbrush and began brushing her dark tresses.

When the clerk saw Allingham's tall figure approach, he jumped to his feet. He had not forgotten the viscount's last visit to the offices of Grey Shipping, Ltd. No, indeed, the young man's last encounter with the great Allingham was vivid in his recollection.

"My lord," he said as he hurried toward the viscount. "Do you wish to see Mr. Grey?"

Allingham directed an imperious look at the clerk. "Yes," he said.

"If you would wait but a moment, my lord. I shall see if Mr. Grey is available. Do excuse me, my lord."

Allingham nodded as the clerk scurried off. He returned shortly to escort the viscount to Grey's office. "Lord Allingham," said Peter Grey, rising to his feet. "This is a surprise. Do sit down."

His lordship took a seat across from Grey's desk. Pippa's father sat down at the desk and regarded the viscount with keen interest. He had an unwelcome thought that Allingham was about to ask for Pippa's hand in marriage. He began to mull over what he would say in response.

"Mr. Grey, I have wanted to speak to you of this for some time."

Grey frowned at Allingham's words. "I feared this would happen. No, my lord, there is no need for you to continue. I will only refuse you."

"Refuse me?" said the viscount, regarding the older man in some surprise.

"Yes, for I do not think you are the man who would ensure my daughter's happiness."

Allingham regarded him in surprise. "I fear you are under some misconception, sir."

"Misconception? I think not, my lord. I shall be blunt. I believe you to be a fortune hunter, and I don't doubt that you would make my daughter very unhappy. I have given you twenty-five thousand pounds. I will not give you my daughter and her fortune as well."

The viscount listened to these words with astonishment. He angrily rose to his feet.

Extracting a piece of paper from the breast pocket of his coat, he tossed it onto the desk. "I did not come here to ask for your daughter's hand, Mr. Grey. This is why I have come." Grey regarded the outraged viscount for a moment before picking up the paper. It was a check for five thousand pounds.

"What is the meaning of this?" asked Grey.

"I have not been pleased at taking money from you, Mr. Grey," said Allingham. "This is partial repayment. I fully intend to repay the entire sum."

"There is no need for that," said Grey, very much embarrassed. "We had an agreement. You fulfilled your obligation admirably. My wife is very pleased. Indeed, I'm very pleased. My family is accepted anywhere in society. Without your assistance, this would not have happened."

"Regardless if that is true," said Allingham, "I shall repay you. I did little enough for the money. Taking it in the first place was not the act of a gentleman."

"I'm so sorry that I misconstrued the nature of your visit, Lord Allingham."

The viscount directed an icy look at Pippa's father. "It may take me some time to repay the rest, but I assure you I shall do so."

"Really, Lord Allingham, there is no need."

"There is need, sir," said the viscount firmly. "It is clear you think me a blackguard."

"I am sorry, my lord. I didn't mean to offend you. But Pippa is very dear to me. I would not have her hurt for all the world."

The viscount frowned ominously. "I have profited from this experience, Mr. Grey. I shall never allow my extravagance to once again bring me to the brink of ruin. I will not be in anyone's debt ever again. Now do excuse me, sir."

Allingham stalked off. So Grey thought him a fortune hunter! He might have known. Pippa's father viewed him with contempt. His lordship considered this incredulously. The Viscount Allingham viewed with contempt by a tradesman!

As he climbed into his awaiting carriage, his lordship shook his head. Such humiliation was hard to bear. As his carriage started off, Allingham scowled. Why had he ever met these wretched Greys? he asked himself. He continued to think these black thoughts as the vehicle made its way down the street.

While Allingham sat in his carriage glumly contemplating his meeting with her father, Pippa returned home from her morning walk with Patches. She found her brother in the dining room eating breakfast. "Good morning, Bertie."

Bertie looked up from his food. "Good morning, Pippa. And Patches, my girl." The big dog hurried to Bertie. She stood beside his chair, wagging her tail furiously and regarding him with an expectant look. "None of this begging, Patches," said Bertie with mock severity. "It is undignified. I shall not be browbeaten into giving you any food."

After taking some food from the sideboard, Pippa sat down beside her brother. "Where are Mama and Papa?"

"Papa has gone off to his office. Mama has not yet risen."

"Well, you are up early, Bertie."

"Yes, I'm turning over a new leaf. Early to bed and early to rise."

"Indeed?" said Pippa, regarding him skeptically.

He grinned. "At least I'm rising early today. I am going with Geoffrey St. James to have a look at a horse."

"You cannot be thinking of buying another horse, Bertie."

"Of course not. It is St. James who will do the buying. I shall simply be a spectator. And what will you do today?"

Pippa shrugged. "I shall go to the dressmaker with Mama and then we will make calls. And we are to dine with Lady Throckmorton tonight."

"Dash it all, I had forgotten," said Bertie. "Must I go?"

"Indeed, you must."

"It will be so very tedious," said Bertie. "No one of any interest would ever have dinner with Lady Throckmorton. Allingham said

Lady Throckmorton surrounded herself with the dullest people so that she would be thought brilliant in comparison."

"So that is why she has invited us, Bertie."

He grinned. "I expect she decided to make an exception inviting a few charming and witty guests. But I don't know why Mama accepted this dinner invitation. I know that Allingham would not have done so."

"Bertie, I really do not care what Allingham would do. I grow tired of hearing his opinions."

"But I thought you did not dislike him."

"I do not dislike him, but I am weary of your spouting his pronouncements as if he were the oracle of Delphi."

Bertie directed an inquiring look at his sister, surprised that she seemed vexed at the mention of the viscount. "I have not seen Allingham in some days. I had hoped he would be at Almack's when we were there, but he was not." Bertie glanced over at the mantel clock. "Oh, dear, it's time I was going." He rose from his chair. "St. James will be waiting for me. Do tell Mama I shall return in the afternoon."

When Bertie had gone, Pippa and Patches retired to the library where the morning post had been put. Sitting down at her father's desk, she began looking through the letters. She picked up one of them that was addressed to her and was soaked with strong perfume.

Opening the missive, Pippa saw that it was from Isabelle. She read it curiously. It was an invitation to go with Lady Granville to her country home for a few days. She was insistent that Pippa must go or the countess "would be utterly devastated with disappointment."

. Putting down the letter, Pippa considered it. Perhaps it would be good to go to the country for a time. Of course, her mother would not be happy at the idea of her accompanying Isabelle. Mrs. Grey still thought Lady Granville an unacceptable companion for her daughter.

Setting the letter aside, Pippa took up a pen and paper. She had meant to write to her old friend Agnes for some days now, but had not done so. Dipping her pen in the ink, she began to write. She had barely completed this task when the butler entered the room.

"Miss Grey, the Duchess of Northampton is here. She wishes to see you."

"The duchess here?" said Pippa, very much surprised that Her Grace would have come at such an unorthodox time.

Hawkins nodded gravely. "She is waiting in the drawing room, miss. I have sent Millie to inform the mistress."

"I shall go to the duchess at once," said Pippa, rising to her feet. Patches rose eagerly as well, but was commanded to stay in the library.

Entering the drawing room, Pippa found the duchess studying the painting that had interested her during her last visit. She was dressed in a splendid pelisse of pea-green silk and a bonnet adorned with huge ostrich plumes. "Miss Grey," she said, acknowledging Pippa's entrance with a smile. "I do like this painting."

Pippa made a polite curtsy. "Your Grace. How good of you to call."

"Nonsense, my dear. It is quite rude of me to appear at such an hour. But I did wish to speak to you."

"Do sit down, Your Grace," said Pippa. "I'm sure that my mother will be down shortly."

The duchess took a seat on the sofa. "It is you I have come to see, Miss Grey."

"Indeed, ma'am?" said Pippa, regarding her curiously as she seated herself in an armchair across from the elderly duchess.

"I have not been happy to hear that you have been seen about with Lady Granville. She is a most unacceptable person."

"Really, Your Grace, I cannot imagine that whom I see should interest you."

"Of course it interests me," returned the duchess. "Isabelle Granville is an odious woman. No good will come of any association with her. And the horrid woman is putting it about that you are fond of Seagrave and will marry him."

"That is absurd," said Pippa, very much surprised. "I cannot imagine that Lady Granville has said such a thing."

"She has indeed. Lord Thomas Spencer told me that, according to Lady Granville, you have lost your heart to Seagrave."

"It is certainly not true," said Pippa.

"I'm relieved," said the duchess. "If it were true, it would kill Allingham. He and Seagrave detest each other. And you know he loves you."

"In truth, Your Grace, I know nothing of the kind. If Lord Allingham has any feelings for me, he has taken great pains to hide them. I have not seen his lordship for many days."

"Miss Grey, you seem to be a perceptive young woman. I daresay you must have imagined why Allingham would pay such attention to you and your family. I assure you he is not in the habit of escorting unknown persons into society. It was clear to me that he fell in love with you from the first."

Pippa shook her head. "I fear you are very much mistaken, Your Grace. Lord Allingham assisted my family only because my father agreed to pay his debts if he would do so."

"What!" cried the duchess, her eyes widening in astonishment.

"I should not have told you," said Pippa, rather regretting her words, "but I wanted you to see that you are wrong. Now that Allingham has done his duty in establishing us in society, it appears that he wants nothing more to do with me. It is not surprising. After all, his lordship does not consider my father to be a gentleman."

The duchess, who had been taken aback by Pippa's words, seemed dumbfounded. She found herself wondering if she had been mistaken. Perhaps Allingham did not care for the girl. She felt like a foolish, meddling old woman. She scarcely knew what she would say to Allingham when she saw him at her soiree the next evening.

At that moment Mrs. Grey entered the drawing room, "Your Grace, what a great honor. I'm so glad you have condescended to visit us."

The duchess rose from the sofa. "Good morning, Mrs. Grey. You are kind to receive me at such an inconvenient hour. I cannot stay."

Mrs. Grey, who had hurried to dress and make herself presentable enough to receive such an illustrious visitor regarded Her Grace in dismay. "But you have only just arrived, Your Grace."

But the duchess could not be persuaded to remain there any longer. Much to Mrs. Grey's disappointment, she took her leave. To make matters worse, Pippa was maddeningly uncommunicative about the duchess's visit, leaving Mrs. Grey to unhappily conclude that her wayward daughter had somehow displeased their guest.

25

The following morning Pippa surprised her mother by announcing that she intended to go to the country with Lady Granville that afternoon. Mrs. Grey, who was astonished by the news, was very much opposed to the idea.

The two ladies were seated in Mrs. Grey's sitting room after breakfast. Mrs. Grey regarded her daughter in some astonishment. "Pippa, you cannot think to go off with Lady Granville today! That is utterly impossible. The Duchess of Northampton's soiree is this evening. You must attend."

"I do not wish to attend, Mama. You will have to tell the duchess that I went to the country."

"I can hardly do that," said Mrs. Grey. "Indeed, if you are not going, I cannot go to the duchess's soiree. And I have so been looking forward to it."

"I'm sorry, Mama, but I sent a note to Lady Granville yesterdays saying I would accompany her."

"Pippa, you are well aware that I do not approve of your association with Lady Granville. And now you say you are going to the country with her. And you did not even mention it last evening. What will your father say if he returns home from the city and finds that you have gone off with that woman?"

"Oh, Mama," said Pippa. "Papa will not mind in the least. It is only a short visit to the country. I shall return in a few days. I pray you do not make a fuss, Mama. I'm eager to leave the city for a few days."

"But I do not like it. It is far too slapdash going off with hardly a moment's notice. And what will you do in the country? Here there are parties and balls and Almack's."

"I should like some time away from the parties and balls. It would be nice to have some quiet. We are so busy here. One seldom has time to think."

"I don't know why one needs time to think," said Mrs. Grey.

"No, indeed, I find it very odd that you would wish to leave at such a time."

"At such a time, Mama?"

"Yes, I daresay Lord Ravensly intends to ask for your hand at any moment."

"Oh, Mama."

"There you will be in the country with that woman with the Marquess of Ravensly calling upon you here. And he is not the only gentleman who might call. Truly, Pippa, I suggest you write to Lady Granville and tell her you cannot go with her."

"But I have already told her that I will go. You are making far too much of this, Mama. I promise I will return in three days or four at most."

"I cannot imagine going to the trouble of going away if one is only to return in three or four days," said Mrs. Grey. She frowned again and returned to her embroidery.

Pippa suppressed a sigh. While she had not been at first eager to accompany Isabelle to the country, the meeting with the Duchess of Northampton had changed her mind. It would be good to leave London for a short time. And even though her mother despaired of Lady Granville, Pippa considered her an interesting companion who was always cheerful and full of amusing stories.

As she sat there near her mother, Pippa found herself glad that she was going. Despite her mother's displeasure, it would be good to be away from society. She looked forward to respite from the endless social affairs that had lost their luster without Allingham.

Rising from her chair, Pippa announced that she must prepare for her trip. Mrs. Grey could only frown again as her daughter left the sitting room and proceeded to her room.

That afternoon rain pelted the carriage roof as Isabelle's carriage made its way north of London. "My dear Miss Grey, you are a saint to come with me," said Isabelle, smiling across at Pippa. Seated next to her was her maid, a somber-looking middle-aged woman whom her ladyship addressed as Sanders.

Pippa sat in the seat opposite the other two women. Since Isabelle had assured her that there was no need to bring her own lady's maid, Pippa had left Betty behind. "It is good to leave the city," said Pippa.

"It is indeed," said Isabelle, "but still, it was kind of you to come. I know that you are so occupied with the season in town. I know it's such a nuisance to go to Oakwood Lodge at this time of year, but my dear old aunt so looks forward to my visits."

Pippa nodded. Isabelle had informed her that the object of the hurried trip to the country was to visit an aged great-aunt who lived in the nearby village. Lady Granville had said that she dutifully visited this aunt throughout the year. Pippa had found it very commendable that Isabelle seemed so concerned about her elderly relative. As she sat there in the carriage, she decided that many people were wrong about Isabelle Granville. Of course, reflected Pippa, people were often eager to judge members of the female sex very harshly.

"I think it so good of you to visit your aunt, Lady Granville."

"Oh, I enjoy doing so," said Isabelle. "I do hope you will not find Oakwood Lodge too uncomfortable. I have never been able to persuade my husband to make any improvements to it. He so seldom goes there. I fear it is really rather grim. But there are some very fine walks thereabouts."

"I shall enjoy that," said Pippa. "That is, if it ever ceases raining."

"Yes, the weather has been simply dreadful," said Isabelle. "Rain and more rain. I wonder if the sun will ever shine again. Oh, I'm sure that it will."

Pippa smiled in reply, but she was not feeling particularly optimistic. Since her meeting with the duchess, she had been thinking about Allingham. Why had she fallen in love with him? It was terribly ironic that she should lose her heart to a man who now seemed so indifferent to her. How much better it might have been to have fastened her affections on one of the eager suitors who were courting her in town. Of course, thought Pippa glumly, those ardent gentlemen were in all probability more interested in her fortune.

The carriage continued on its way. Fortunately, their destination was not so very far from London, and after scarcely four hours on the road, the vehicle pulled into a narrow lane.

"Why, we are here already," said Isabelle, peering out the window. The rain had by now nearly stopped and only a light drizzle was now falling. "How short a journey can seem when one has a companion such as yourself, Miss Grey. We will be at Oakwood Lodge in a trice."

Pippa looked out the window, noting that the lane wound its way through dense woods. Although it was early afternoon, the gloomy weather and the thick trees made it seem very dark.

When the carriage stopped, a servant opened the door and assisted Pippa down from the vehicle. "Yes, here we are," said Isabelle. "This is Oakwood Lodge."

Noting the grim edifice before her, Pippa found herself thinking that the lodge was a most unprepossessing residence. Accustomed to far more luxurious accommodations, Pippa was rather surprised at the forlorn, ill-kempt appearance of the place. She noted in particular that the shrubbery was in dire need of trimming and that the stone walk leading to the house was overgrown with weeds.

The interior of the lodge was even less inviting. As she entered the residence, Pippa was aware of a damp, musty smell. She looked around the entry hall, noting with distaste the moth-eaten boar's head that adorned the wall.

"It is quite appalling," said Isabelle cheerfully. "And the rest is little better. But there is an excellent cook and we will have a splendid dinner."

Pippa found this remark somewhat encouraging since she was very hungry. Following a servant to her room, she found that her bedchamber was only slightly more appealing than the entry hall. It was cold and drafty with stone floors. The furniture was dark and heavy and looked as if it dated from the Restoration. The only cheery note was the fire burning in the fireplace.

When the servant had left her, Pippa took off her bonnet and cloak and placed them on the tall, canopied bed. "You are too accustomed to luxury, Pippa Grey," she said aloud. "Where is your spirit of adventure?" Then with a smile, she left the room to rejoin her hostess.

As Isabelle had promised, dinner that evening was excellent. The two ladies were seated in the lodge's dining room at an enormous oak table that would easily seat twenty. The room was filled with hunting trophies much the worse for wear after many years of decorating the walls. Pippa did not much appreciate the shopworn stags' heads and antlers. She tried not to look at them as she ate her meal.

When they had finished eating, Isabelle and Pippa went to the drawing room where a fire blazed in the enormous stone fireplace. "It is odd just the two of us, is it not, Miss Grey?" said Isabelle, taking a seat in a leather chair near the fire. "And no gentlemen drinking port in the dining room."

"It is a change," said Pippa, sitting down in another chair.

"Well, it is a good opportunity for us to become far better acquainted."

"Yes, it is, Lady Granville."

"Do call me Isabelle, my dear. It seems we are too well acquainted to be so formal. And might I call you Pippa? That is such a delightful name."

"Yes, of course," said Pippa."

"Now what shall we talk about? I know, let us speak of all your suitors in town. You must tell me which of them you like best."

"Really, Isabelle, I should prefer another topic."

The countess laughed. "But I shouldn't. Come, come, my dear, you must tell me. I do envy you having so many admirers. I can see that you will have a very difficult task choosing among them. There is Ravensly, of course. He will be a duke one day. But he is rather insipid and a bit of a fool. No, I don't believe you will choose Ravensly."

"Do tell me whom you think I will choose," said Pippa.

"Oh, I should not dare to do so," said Isabelle, smiling at her.

Pippa regarded her thoughtfully. "Perhaps you believe it is Lord Seagrave."

"Seagrave? Why, I confess I did think it might be he. When I saw you dancing with him at Almack's, I could not help thinking that you seemed well-suited. Seagrave is a dear friend of my husband, of course. I had not thought he would remarry. He was so devoted to his late wife. My dear Pippa, he was so desolated by her untimely passing! But life must go on. You are the first young lady who has touched his heart since that terrible tragedy.

"I'm betraying his confidence, but I feel I must tell you that Seagrave is very fond of you. You could do far worse than Seagrave, my dear."

Pippa frowned at her. "Then it's true that you have been telling people that I am fond of Lord Seagrave and that I wish to marry him."

"My dear girl, I only have mentioned once or twice that you seemed to be favoring him."

"I must ask you to cease saying anything of the kind. It is not true in the least."

"It isn't? Oh, you must forgive me. I was mistaken. Oh, I hope you are not vexed with me? Oh dear, you are."

"It is only that I do not like hearing that you are talking about me and saying things that are not true."

"Oh, I am sorry," said Isabelle, looking very contrite. "It must have been dreadful hearing that from someone."

"It was. Indeed, the Duchess of Northampton was very upset about it."

"The Duchess of Northampton?" Isabelle frowned. "That horrible woman. You must know that she detests me. She goes about slandering me to everyone. It is because she is Allingham's friend, of course." The countess leaned forward in her chair. "My dear Pippa, I believe it is time I tell you about Allingham and me."

Pippa's eyebrows arched slightly. "About Allingham and you?"

Isabelle nodded gravely. "I know that Allingham has been kind to you. I have never before told you the truth, because I did not wish to poison you against him. But I shall now tell you.

"You see, I once fancied myself in love with Allingham. Of course, as I now am well aware, a woman is a fool to be in love with him. I shall confess to you, my dear, that I have in my time committed one or two very great follies. A woman will commit such follies in her time. I fear it is the nature of things. But it was utterly bird-witted of me to fall in love with Allingham.

"In my defense I will say that he pursued me so shamelessly. Indeed, he could hardly keep away from me. In time he overcame my defenses by saying he loved me. How could I have believed him?"

Isabelle paused to adopt a melodramatic pose. "Once I had dishonored myself for him, he was only too eager to cast me off. Yes, he used me quite shamefully, my dear Pippa. I know you will understand why I have come to hate him."

Pippa stared at Isabelle. While she knew that the viscount had his faults, she could not believe that he could have behaved in such a fashion. "I can scarcely imagine Lord Allingham acting in this way," she said.

"Oh, I know. I realize that no one will take my part over the great Allingham. That is why I remain silent. You must promise you will never tell a soul what I have told you."

"Indeed, I will not," replied Pippa.

"Good," said the countess, smiling at her guest. "But why don't we have a game of cards? I do not want to discuss unpleasant subjects any further."

Pippa nodded as the countess rose to get a deck of cards. Sitting there in the dreary room, she wished she had never come. Still, there was nothing to do, but smile pleasantly and act as if she were enjoying herself. This she managed to do as Isabelle returned and began to deal the cards.

26

While Pippa dined with Isabelle at Oakwood Lodge, Allingham sat in his library drinking sherry and thumbing through some of his beloved books. The viscount had been in a somber, reflective mood all day. Although he had told the Duchess of Northampton that he would attend her soiree that evening, he decided that he would not go.

Indeed, he was not very eager to find himself at a party that might include Pippa. The viscount had resolved that the best course of action for him was to keep his distance from her.

As he sipped his sherry, Allingham's reflections grew gloomier. He had devoted his life to fashion and society. Indeed, he told himself, he could hardly have committed his efforts to anything more worthless.

In the past his lordship had always enjoyed making pronouncements on what one should wear and how ladies and gentlemen should comport themselves in society. Indeed, it had been amusing that so many were eager to do as he decreed. Now everything seemed so absurd.

Allingham sat for a long time before finally retiring to bed. In the morning he returned to his library where he tried to busy himself with correspondence and business matters. Yet try as he would, it seemed impossible to keep Pippa Grey far from his thoughts.

At eleven o'clock his butler entered the library. "My Lord, Her Grace, the Duchess of Northampton, is here."

"The duchess here now?" said his lordship, looking up from a pile of papers on his desk. "Damn and blast," he muttered. He had no desire to see his old friend that morning. "Tell Her Grace that I am indisposed."

"Very good, my lord," said Morris, bowing slightly and then retreating from the room.

In a few minutes the duchess strode into the library followed by a harried-looking servant. "Indisposed are you?" she demanded. "I told Morris that was stuff and nonsense."

Rising to his feet, the viscount frowned at his unwelcome guest. "Duchess," he said.

"Do not fix that disapproving look at me, Allingham. While it may terrify those young bucks hoping to curry your favor, it has no effect on me."

Allingham could not help but smile. "Do be seated, ma'am."

"Indeed, I shall," said Her Grace, sitting down on a leather sofa.

Allingham left his desk to join her there. "I did not expect the honor of your visit."

"I must tell you, Allingham, that I am very vexed with you. You said that you would come to my soiree last evening. You were not in attendance. I was most eager to speak with you."

"I am sorry, Duchess, but I was not in the mood for company."

"So you mean to hide yourself away here?"

Allingham shrugged. "And why not? Society has begun to bore me."

"Has it indeed? I daresay it is more likely that you had no desire to see Miss Grey, but she was not at my soiree, Allingham. No, indeed, and I shall not soon forgive you for not coming." She paused to direct a disapproving look at him. "I so wished to speak with you last night. You see, Allingham, while I did not see the young lady last evening, I had called upon Miss Grey Friday morning. I had a most disturbing conversation with her."

"Disturbing?" said the viscount.

The duchess nodded. "I told Miss Grey that you were in love with her."

"You did what?" cried Allingham.

"Yes, I did. Do you deny that you are in love with the girl?"

The viscount regarded the duchess in some frustration. "Very well, I am in love with her. I daresay you will plague me until I admit it."

"Then why don't you tell her? Indeed you are a great blockhead, Allingham. Miss Grey thought I was quite addlepated. And then she told me that you only showed an interest in her because her father paid your debts. Is this true, sir?"

"It is true that her father paid my debts," replied Allingham. Agitated, he rose from the sofa. "I was sorely in debt. Grey offered to give me money if I would introduce his family into society. I accepted."

"That is infamous!" said the duchess.

"Yes, it is," said the viscount. "But my interest in Miss Grey has nothing to do with my obligation to her family. And I have informed Grey that I shall repay him. I have already begun to do so. But he thinks me an unscrupulous fortune hunter. He has told me that he will not consent to my marrying his daughter."

"You asked for her hand?"

"No. Grey suspected I wished to do so and informed me that I was very much mistaken to think that he would consent to the match."

"And so you have given up? You admit defeat and decide you will never see Miss Grey again? By my faith, Allingham, I expected better from you."

"What can I do?" said his lordship. "Grey has made it very clear what he thinks of me."

"My dear boy, it does not signify what Grey thinks of you. It is what Miss Grey thinks that matters. And I suspect that she is in love with you.

"I have met Mr. Grey and I believe him to be a sensible man. He would be a fool to object to you if he knows your true feelings about his daughter. You must go to Miss Grey at once. Declare your feelings to her."

Allingham looked thoughtful. "Perhaps you are right, Duchess."

"Of course, I'm right. I'm right most of the time. Now go. I shall never speak to you again if you don't go at once."

The viscount leaned down to kiss Her Grace on the cheek. "I shall do as you say. Thank you, Duchess."

"Then go! I shall see myself out. Go along and when you return you must come to Northampton House. I shall wait for you."

Allingham nodded and took his leave of his guest. A short time later he was in his carriage on his way to the Greys' residence. He sat looking out the carriage window, thinking about the duchess's words. She was right, he decided. He must know what Pippa thought. Perhaps she did love him. In any case, he must tell her how he felt.

Arriving at the Greys' residence, he strode purposefully up to the door and knocked sharply on it using the brass door knocker. In moments the butler answered the summons. "My lord," he said, ushering the viscount inside.

"I should like to see Miss Grey, Hawkins."

"I am sorry, my lord, but Miss Grey is not at home. But Mr. Grey is here. Do follow me, my lord. I shall inform the master you have arrived."

Allingham frowned, clearly disappointed that Pippa was not

there. Yet he welcomed another opportunity to speak with her father. "Thank you, Hawkins," he said.

The butler nodded and then escorted the viscount to the drawing room. Finding his master in the morning room, Hawkins announced that Lord Allingham had called.

Grey, who had been sitting in a comfortable chair reading the paper, did not try to hide his surprise. "Allingham here, Hawkins?"

"Indeed, sir. He is in the drawing room. He asked to see Miss Grey. I informed him that miss was not at home."

Grey frowned at this communication. So Allingham was there to see Pippa despite their previous meeting? "I shall see him," said Grey, placing his newspaper down on the table beside the chair.

Pippa's father had given a great deal of thought to his last conversation with the viscount. He remembered how affronted Allingham had been. Rising from his chair, a rather curious Grey made his way to the drawing room.

"Lord Allingham."

"Mr. Grey." The two men eyed each other warily. Allingham stood very tall, a somber expression on his handsome face. "Thank you for receiving me."

"Mrs. Grey will be sorry to have missed your visit, my lord," said Grey. "Do be seated."

Allingham nodded and sat down. "Thank you."

Grey seated himself in a chair across from the viscount. "I must say, Lord Allingham, I did not expect you."

"I came to see your daughter, Mr. Grey," said Allingham.

"You wished to see Pippa?" said Grey, frowning. "I believe that I made my feelings very clear on the subject of you and my daughter."

"And I feel that I did not make my feelings clear to you or to Miss Grey," said Allingham. "I must tell you that I do wish to marry your daughter."

"See here, my lord, I have already told you that I do not approve."

"You have said so, Mr. Grey. You thought I cared only for your daughter's fortune. I will tell you, sir, that that is not in the least true. You see, I'm in love with Pippa, Mr. Grey. I don't know if she loves me, but I must find out.

"As to Miss Grey's fortune, I don't care one fig for that. I cannot blame you for thinking me a mercenary creature since I have taken that accursed money from you. I deeply regret it and, as I have told you, I shall pay you back.

"But I am not entirely without the means to support a wife, Mr. Grey. I have my estates. With prudent management I shall have a respectable income. Indeed, my income has always been respectable. It has been my excessive expenditures that have been the problem.

"And while I have not lived prudently in the past, I swear to you, I shall do so now. You have my word as a gentleman, Mr. Grey. If your daughter honors me with her love, I shall be a good husband to her."

Grey listened to this speech in some surprise. "I believe you are serious."

"I am indeed," said Allingham.

"Why did you not tell me this before?" asked Pippa's father. "And you say you love my daughter?"

"With all my heart."

"Perhaps I have misjudged you," said Grey. "You see, my lord, I assumed that a gentleman such as yourself would not be interested in Pippa save for her fortune."

"You assumed wrongly, sir," said the viscount. "Your daughter is an extraordinary lady."

"That she is," said Grey. He smiled. "If Pippa wishes to marry you, I shall not object, my lord."

"I'm very grateful to you, Mr. Grey," said his lordship smiling at the man he hoped would be his future father-in-law. "If you will permit me, Mr. Grey, I should like to wait until Miss Grey returns home."

"I fear, Lord Allingham, that Pippa will not be home for some time. She has gone to the country with Lady Granville."

"With Lady Granville?"

"Yes, she left yesterday afternoon to go to a residence called Oakwood Lodge. It was all very abrupt. Indeed, I knew nothing of it until I returned home and found her gone. I must say I was none too pleased. It's not like Pippa to act so impulsively. But she will be gone but a few days. She will return soon and you will see her then."

Allingham nodded, but he was disturbed at hearing Pippa had gone off with Isabelle. By the time he took his leave of Grey, he had decided to go to Oakwood Lodge.

27

In the afternoon, the rain abated long enough for Pippa to take a long walk. Isabelle could not be persuaded to accompany her since the countess claimed she detested exercise.

As she walked along a wooded path that led away from Oakwood Lodge, Pippa was glad that her hostess had not joined her. Since arriving there the day before, Pippa had begun to reassess her opinion of Lady Granville.

While she had never imagined Isabelle to be the sort of person who would be an intimate friend, Pippa now concluded that she didn't even like the countess. Their close association at the lodge had made Isabelle's faults very clear. Indeed, Pippa admitted to herself, she had only associated with Isabelle because she had been irritated with Allingham.

Pippa continued walking for a long time. It felt good to be out in the fresh air and the woods were beautiful. And despite her dissatisfaction with her hostess, it was rather a relief to be away from London for a time. The endless whirl of social life had become rather tiresome now that she no longer saw Allingham.

"I do not wish to think of him," said Pippa aloud to herself. Yet that was easier said than done and the viscount occupied her thoughts for some time as she walked along the path.

It was late in the afternoon when Pippa returned to the house. Entering the gloomy lodge, she asked a servant where Lady Granville would be found.

"Her ladyship has gone out, miss," came the servant's reply.

"Did she say when she will return?"

The servant, a lanky young man with close-cropped red hair, shrugged. "Nay, miss. She has gone to visit her aunt. She said naught about returning."

Pippa went to her room where Isabelle's lady's maid took her bonnet and cloak. Taking up the novel she had brought with her, she made her way to the drawing room. There she sat down in a chair and tried to read.

After a time she glanced up at a boar's head that decorated the wall of the drawing room. Frowning at the grisly trophy, Pippa found herself thinking that Oakwood Lodge was a horrible place. Thoughts of her family's comfortable residence came to her and she suddenly wished she were back home with her family and Patches at her feet.

"Excuse me, Miss Grey." Pippa looked over to see the red-haired servant enter the room. " 'Tis a gentleman here. Shall I send him in, miss?"

"A gentleman? Who is he?"

"I don't know, miss," said the young man, looking rather perplexed. "I didn't dare ask his name. He gave me such a look, you see. But he is a true gentleman, a nob by the look of him. And he had very fine horses."

For a brief moment Pippa thought it must be Allingham. Then she told herself that she must not be ridiculous. Why would she expect the viscount to appear at Oakwood Lodge? "Show the gentleman in," said Pippa. "I shall see him."

The servant nodded and left. When he returned with the visitor, Pippa regarded the newcomer in surprise and disapproval. It was Seagrave. "Miss Grey," said the baron, entering the room and coming to stand before her.

Pippa extended her hand and Seagrave bowed over it. "Lord Seagrave." There was a distinct coolness in her voice as Pippa spoke his name. "I had not expected you to come here."

"Well, town was a dead bore with you and Lady Granville away. I thought I should surprise you both. But where is your hostess?"

"She is out visiting her aunt."

Seagrave sat down in a chair without waiting for an invitation. "I must say that I'm glad for this opportunity to speak with you alone."

Pippa frowned slightly. She did not like being alone with Seagrave and she regretted admitting him. Knowing his reputation, she was well aware that many would consider it most improper for her to be there with him. She had the sudden suspicion that Lady Granville had conspired to bring her there so that she would meet Seagrave like this. Isabelle had been very eager to thrust the baron upon her. While they had played cards the night before, she had chattered on and on about what a handsome and amusing man he was.

"I expect Lady Granville will return shortly."

"I hope she will not return too quickly," said Seagrave, leaning forward in his chair and smiling. "It is you I came to see. What good fortune to have the opportunity to speak with you alone.

"What I mean to say, Miss Grey, is that I have grown very fond of you. You are a deuced pretty woman."

Pippa did not like the direction the conversation was taking. "In truth, Lord Seagrave, I prefer that our conversation be conducted in the presence of Lady Granville. I pray you excuse me." Pippa rose from her chair. "I expect that Lady Granville will return soon."

Seagrave hurried to his feet. "Wait, Miss Grey, you must hear what I wish to say. I believe you are aware that I am a widower?"

"Yes, but really, my lord, you must excuse me."

Reaching out he grasped her arm. "Miss Grey, I want to marry you."

Pippa pulled her arm away. "That is very flattering, Lord Seagrave, but I must refuse you."

The baron appeared genuinely surprised. "Refuse me? You haven't had time to think on the matter."

"I do not need any time to think, sir. I do not wish to marry you."

"Perhaps this will change your mind, my dear," said Seagrave with a smile. To Pippa's amazement, the baron reached out and, grasping her roughly by the arms, pulled her to him.

"What is the meaning of this!" cried Pippa.

The baron stifled her protest by crushing her in his embrace and kissing her roughly on the lips. When he finally pulled his face away, she regarded him in horror. "How dare you!"

Seagrave laughed as Pippa tried to extricate herself from his grip. Holding her fast, he shook his head. "Come, now, you cannot say you didn't enjoy that kiss?"

"I most certainly did not!" cried Pippa indignantly. "And I warn you, Lord Seagrave, if you do not release me at once, I shall scream."

This remark only seemed to amuse the baron. "You may scream all you want. No one will come to your aid."

"What do you mean!" cried Pippa. "Let me go." She began to struggle again.

Pulling one of her arms behind her, Seagrave pinned it in his viselike grip. "Stop, you fool, or I'll break your arm."

The pain made her cease struggling. "You must be insane!" she said, regarding him incredulously.

"I am perfectly sane. I had hoped you would be more agreeable, but, willing or not, you will marry me."

"You cannot believe you can force me to marry you!"

"I can indeed."

"My father will . . ."

"Your father is not here," said Seagrave, cutting her off. "And by the time he discovers what has happened there will be nothing he can do. After this night, you'll have no choice but to marry me."

It took a moment for the meaning of his words to sink in. Pippa regarded him in horror. "Even you could not be so despicable!"

He smiled unpleasantly. "Can't I? By God, I've had a good many women in my time. Most of them willing and a few not so willing. That will be your choice. But I'll have you in any case. You'll be eager to marry me. Indeed, what else can you do? No other man will want you."

"If you believe that my father will settle a fortune on you . . ."

He pulled on her arm and she gasped in pain. "He'll give me money, all right. I'm taking you to France where we'll be wed. You'll write your father saying that you love me and that we eloped. By the time we return to England, you'll be an obedient wife." Seagrave suddenly released her arm and she sprang away from him. "We are leaving here at once."

Pippa stared at him for a brief moment and then ran for the door. "Help me!" she cried.

Lunging forward, Seagrave caught her before she had gone more than ten feet. Holding her wrist tightly, he pulled her toward him and then slapped her hard across her face. She reeled from the blow and then regarded him like a terrified animal. "You'll have another in a moment!" he said, raising his hand threateningly. "A man has got a right to bring his wife to heel. Now, come, we're going." Grasping her roughly, he started to drag her to the door.

Pippa tried to resist, but another blow from Seagrave's hand brought tears to her face. As he pulled her along, she looked desperately around for some assistance. Surely the servants would help her. But the house appeared empty. The red-haired servant had vanished and no one came to her aid.

Forcing her outside, Seagrave shouted to a servant, who hurried to open the door to his carriage. The baron picked up Pippa and threw her inside. Climbing up behind her, he ordered the servant to make haste and within moments the carriage was on its way.

Allingham pulled up his horse in front of the gray stone building. His lordship eyed the house with disfavor as he dismounted. As his critical gaze surveyed the residence, Allingham decided that Oakwood Lodge had little to recommend it.

The viscount was weary after his long ride from London. Yet despite that he was very eager to see Pippa again. He had had much time to think of what he would say to her. He only hoped that Pippa might have some feeling for him.

There was no one about to see to his horse so his lordship tied the animal and proceeded to the door. It was some time before there was a response to his repeated knocking. A young man with red hair finally opened the door and stood staring at him.

"I am Lord Allingham," said the viscount, directing his most imperious look at the servant. "I'm here to see Miss Grey."

"Miss Grey?" The young man looked decidedly uncomfortable. "Why, she is not here . . . m'lord."

"Is Lady Granville here?"

"I . . ." the servant hesitated. "I cannot say. That is, I am not certain."

Thinking the young man a most unsatisfactory servant, Allingham pushed him aside and stepped inside. "Where is Lady Granville?"

The young man's only response was to cast a rather nervous glance toward a corridor that went out from the entry hall. "I shall find her myself," said Allingham, impatiently walking in toward the corridor.

Locating the drawing room, he stepped inside. Isabelle, who was the soul occupant of the room, was seated upon the sofa paging through a magazine. She did not look up as Allingham entered.

"Lady Granville," he said.

"What?" Isabelle appeared startled. Her eyes grew wide at the sight of the viscount. "Allingham!"

"Yes, it is I, Isabelle," he said, coming in to stand before her.

"What are you doing here?" demanded Isabelle. "Who admitted you?"

"I admitted myself," said his lordship. "Your addlepated servant seemed incapable of it. Where is Miss Grey?"

"You have come so far to see Miss Grey?" said Isabelle. Although she had been very much startled to see the viscount appear, she regained her composure quickly. "Then perhaps it is true what they are saying. Are you in love with her?"

Allingham ignored the question. "Where is she?"

"She is not here, Allingham. She has gone."

"Gone?"

Isabelle nodded. "Yes, she left this afternoon. I must say I was very surprised that she did so. I fear she did not like Oakwood Lodge overmuch. Perhaps she was bored. I'm told she went to the village to hire a chaise. She found one and left immediately for town. I must say I found it rather ill-mannered of her, but it is what one might expect from one of her breeding."

"I don't believe you," said Allingham. "Where is she?"

"You may search the house if you wish. I assure you I'm telling you the truth. Miss Grey is no longer here. I must say I am rather glad. She is very dull company, Allingham."

The viscount stared at Isabelle. He knew her to be a deceitful, unscrupulous female. He could not believe anything she said.

"I'm so sorry to disappoint you, my lord," continued Isabelle. "You have come such a long way for nothing. And you will find the inn at the village most unsatisfactory. A gentleman of your tastes will doubtless think it intolerable." She fixed an ironical smile on him. "If you would prefer to stay here, I should be very happy to furnish you a bed, Allingham."

"How very good of you," said his lordship, "but I should prefer the inn. If you will excuse me, I shall leave you." He started to go, but turned back to face her. "And before I go, I shall look for Miss Grey. Perhaps she has returned without your knowledge."

"By all means search for her everywhere. You will see I'm telling the truth."

Allingham frowned at her once more and then departed. He walked around the dreary house, checking each of the bedchambers. There was no sign of Pippa. Rather disheartened, Allingham made his way out of the house. Mounting his horse once again, he set off toward the village.

28

Although Allingham was inclined to doubt anything Isabelle said, he discovered that she had been telling the truth about the village inn. The sole place of lodging for some miles around, the Red Lion Inn was a dirty, foul-smelling place.

His lordship did not look forward to spending the night in the cramped room that the landlord had shown him. Since the bed looked as though it was infested with bedbugs, Allingham had little desire to take his rest there. Therefore, he positioned himself in the inn's public room and ordered food and ale.

The Red Lion was not noted for its cuisine and the viscount found himself dining on an unpalatable plate of cold mutton and badly cooked potatoes. Since his lordship's culinary sense was well developed indeed, he found such fare difficult to tolerate.

As he sat at a rough-hewn table attempting to eat his meal, he found himself thinking about Pippa. He had been very disappointed to find that she was not there. He did not like the thought of her traveling back to town alone. Allingham took a drink of his ale and glanced about the room. There was not much activity. Only two other tables were occupied.

At that moment the door of the inn opened and a young man entered. The viscount recognized him as the red-haired servant at Oakwood Lodge.

Allingham watched him look around the room. When he caught sight of his lordship, the young man headed toward him. The viscount frowned, thinking the servant had come from Isabelle.

"What do you want?" he asked gruffly as the young man came along side his table.

The red-haired young man appeared nervous. "I must talk with you, m'lord. 'Tis about Miss Grey."

Noting his expression, Allingham motioned for him to be seated. "What is it?"

The servant sat down across from the viscount. "I did not know what to do, m'lord. When you came looking for her, I thought I might tell you. I would have come sooner, but I was only now able to leave the house without her ladyship seeing me. You see, m'lord, Miss Grey is in danger. You must help her."

"What the devil do you mean?" demanded Allingham.

"A gentleman came to Oakwood Lodge while Miss Grey was on a walk. I heard him and her ladyship talking. They said something about the gentleman marrying Miss Grey."

"What the devil!" cried Allingham.

"Then Miss Grey returned. I took the gentleman in to see Miss Grey." The servant looked down at his hands. "It was terrible, m'lord. He was a beast to her. He said she must marry him. She said she would not, but he would hear none of it. And he struck her, m'lord. I should have gone to help Miss Grey, but I was afraid. Her ladyship had said I was to pay no attention to whatever happened. He kidnapped her, m'lord, taking her off in his carriage. The poor young lady!"

"Good God!" said Allingham, very much agitated by this extraordinary news. "When did this occur?"

"More than two hours ago, m'lord. But I thought someone might still catch them. I heard the plan what he told my mistress. He was taking her to Huddlesea. 'Tis a tiny village on the coast. There they would find a ship. He would take the young lady to France where they would be married. I have never seen such a villainous man, be he gentleman or no, m'lord."

"Do you know his name?"

"The mistress called him Seagrave, m'lord."

"Seagrave!" Allingham looked solemn. He found the story incredible. Seagrave had kidnapped Pippa and was taking her to France!

"How do I get to this Huddlesea?"

" 'Tis the road to the west, m'lord. It's not very far. Perhaps seven miles from here."

Allingham rose from his chair. "I have not a minute to spare. If you are telling me the truth, you will be amply rewarded." The viscount then hurried out to fetch his horse.

Pippa sat in the tiny cabin on the ship, tears of frustration streaming down her face. The door was locked and there was no escape. She had spent a good deal of time searching every inch of the enclosure for a way out. Finally she had given up.

Pippa could hear the voices of the ship's crewmen, laughing and talking loudly. Every so often there was also the sound of footsteps in the narrow corridor outside the cabin. Each time the footsteps seemed to stop outside her door, she cringed, thinking that Seagrave had returned.

Folding her arms closely in front of her, Pippa tried to be brave. The past few hours had been a nightmare. Even now as she sat in the miserable cabin, she could scarcely believe the fact that Seagrave had taken her captive. He had struck her and threatened her, and at any moment he would come back.

Pippa wiped away the tears from her cheek. Seagrave had made it very clear what would happen that night. It was only a matter of time before he would come to have his way with her.

Horrified at the thought, Pippa rose from her chair. Pacing nervously across the tiny room, she prayed that somehow she might be delivered from this horrible situation.

29

Since Allingham's horse was not fully rested from the long trip from town, he had to find another mount to take him to Huddlesea. After paying an exorbitant sum to an unsavory-looking stableman, the viscount obtained the use of a respectable-looking bay gelding and he made the trip to Huddlesea in good time.

It was dark when the viscount arrived at the tiny fishing village. There were only a few houses to be found there. There was no one about so the viscount pounded on the door of the closest cottage.

A middle-aged man smoking a clay pipe answered the door. Unaccustomed to finding gentlemen of quality in the vicinity, he stared at Allingham. "Aye, sir?"

"I'm looking for a man who was taking a lady to a ship. Did you see them or perhaps you saw the carriage?"

"I did hear of a carriage coming to the village. My wife told me of it when I had my supper. Come here, woman, there's a gentleman asking about the carriage."

A stout woman wrapped in a gray shawl joined her husband at the door. She regarded Allingham with interest. "You are asking about the carriage, sir?"

"Yes."

"Oh, I did see it. A right fine carriage it was, sir. Never had I seen a finer one. There was a crest upon it. 'Twas some sort of lord, sir. A proper nobleman. And he was a fine, handsome gentleman."

"Was there a lady?"

"Aye, I heard there was, but I did not see her. They were taken to the ship." She pointed toward the sea, which was shrouded in darkness. "They'll sail at dawn. She'll stay the night here."

"The ship is still here?" said Allingham, very much relieved at this information.

"Aye, sir," said the man, taking the pipe from his mouth.

"I must get to that ship. Do you have a boat? I shall pay you anything you like."

"I do have a boat," said the man, "but 'tis very late, sir."

"It is a matter of great urgency," said Allingham. "The welfare of a lady is at stake."

"Do help the gentleman, Mr. Potter," said the woman.

"Very well, sir, I shall take you in my boat. Fetch me my coat and hat, woman." His wife hurried to do so and the man led Allingham to his boat.

Seagrave was not without misgivings about his dastardly plot to kidnap Pippa and make her his wife. Although Isabelle had assured him that all would go well, he had been somewhat doubtful.

Now that he had Pippa aboard the ship, he was beginning to feel more confident. It was not very difficult to control a woman if a man was willing to take his hand to her. And once he had his way with her, there would be little she could do but marry him. In time it would work out very nicely and he would have a tidy fortune to spend as he pleased.

After locking Pippa in the cabin, he had joined the captain of the ship for a drink. That gentleman, an unprincipled rogue whose chief occupation was smuggling, had been in a jovial mood. He was very much addicted to Spanish rum and he was only too happy to have a drinking partner.

Seagrave sat in the captain's quarters drinking glass after glass of rum. By the time he took his leave, he felt that the captain was one of the dearest friends he had ever had.

Arriving back at the cabin, he pulled the key from his pocket and a bit unsteadily put it into the lock. He turned the key and pushed open the door. "Here I am, my dear. Your husband has returned to claim his bride."

Pippa cowered in the corner of the tiny room. A lantern hung from the ceiling, swinging to and fro with the motion of the ship. "Keep away from me," said Pippa. "I shall scream."

"Will you now?" said Seagrave. "Scream and you will feel the back of my hand, my girl. Now you will only make it hard on yourself. It will go far easier on you if you do not resist."

"I should rather die than allow you to touch me," said Pippa.

"Is that any way for a wife to speak?" asked Seagrave. "A husband has certain rights."

"You are not my husband!" cried Pippa.

"I shall be, my dear," he said with a smile. He closed the door behind him and walked toward her. "We will be wed very soon. Now there is no point in fighting me."

"Keep away from me!" said Pippa.

Seagrave made no reply, but kept coming toward her, a lecherous look on his face. Pippa tried to elude him, but he quickly grabbed her. She screamed and struggled valiantly as he pulled her to the small bed.

At that moment the door to the cabin flew open. "Get away from her, you bloody bastard!"

Seagrave turned toward the door in astonishment. "Allingham?"

The viscount was upon him in a flash. Grabbing him by the shoulders, he pulled him from Pippa. Then spinning him around, Allingham planted a blow to his chin. Pippa screamed again as Seagrave went sprawling and landed with a thud on the wooden floor. The baron staggered to his feet, an expression of rage on his face. "Allingham, I'll kill you."

Seagrave ran toward the viscount, who deftly stepped aside and tripped the heavier man as he lunged toward him. The baron went flying through the open doorway, falling to the floor of the corridor just outside the cabin. Allingham pulled him to his feet and hit him hard in the stomach.

When Seagrave doubled over in pain, the viscount grasped him roughly by the shoulders and shoved him down the corridor. When the baron stumbled, Allingham got him to his feet and forced him up the stairs to the deck of the ship. "You will pay for this, Seagrave. By God, you will pay."

The baron staggered away from his furious opponent. "Help!" he cried. "Captain Evans!"

The commotion had brought some of the ship's crew to the site of the altercation. They stood by watching the gentlemen, unsure how to react. "You goddamned blackguard, Seagrave," cried Allingham, shaking his fist menacingly at the baron.

Seagrave scowled. He had taken the worst of it so far and blood streamed from his nose. He could not bear to think his oldest enemy had bested him. He looked at the crewmen, hoping someone would come to his aid, but they just stood there watching them. Then letting out a loud yell, Seagrave ran toward Allingham.

The viscount moved sideways, dodging his opponent once again, causing Seagrave to land against the ship's railing with a thud. Allingham was beside him at once. With another punch, the baron fell backward, careening over the railing and into the sea.

"Man overboard!" shouted one of the sailors.

Allingham watched Seagrave land with a splash and come bob-bing to the surface. He then turned to face the ship's crew. They were a ragged-looking lot of old salts, sea-toughened sailors who had seen more than their share of fights. "That man was a black-guard who had abducted a lady," said the viscount.

The sailors only stared at Allingham, impressed that a man who was so obviously a gentleman could handle his fists so well. They had no intention of taking Seagrave's part. Indeed, the two crew-men who went to pull Seagrave from the water seemed to do so reluctantly.

"Oh, Allingham!" Pippa had come up on deck where she had witnessed the viscount's vanquishing of Seagrave.

"Pippa!" His lordship opened his arms as Pippa ran to him. He enfolded her into a tight embrace. "My darling!"

This touching display caused the sailors to applaud. Allingham scarcely noticed them. "Did he hurt you? I should have killed him."

"Oh, Allingham, if you hadn't come," said Pippa, burying her face against his chest.

"But I did come. You will be fine, my dearest Pippa. Come, let us leave here."

With his arm around her shoulder, Allingham escorted a very shaken Pippa from the ship and into the boat where Mr. Potter was waiting.

In the morning Pippa awakened to find the sun streaming into the small bedroom where she had been sleeping. She looked about the room, rather disoriented for a time. The Potters had taken them into their home. Mrs. Potter had been most solicitous, offer-ing Pippa a clean nightgown and the bed she normally shared with her husband.

Pippa had been too exhausted to protest. She had allowed Mrs. Potter to help her to bed where she had lain awake for a time, try-ing to convince herself that her ordeal was over and that Alling-ham had rescued her. Finally she had fallen into an exhausted slumber.

Rising from the bed, Pippa looked out the window. The sun was rising over the sea. The seagulls were flying about, calling noisily. Pippa listened to the waves for a time before turning from the window and dressing.

When she had finished she came out into the cottage's only other room. Mrs. Potter was standing by the fireplace stirring a pot that hung there. "Ah, there you are, miss. Did you sleep well?"

"Oh, very well, Mrs. Potter. But I'm so sorry to have taken your bed."

"What nonsense, my dear. After what you had gone through, you were in need of a bed."

"I do thank you with all my heart," said Pippa.

" 'Tis very little I did," said Mrs. Potter. "From what my man tells me, 'tis his lordship who was the hero."

"Yes," said Pippa, smiling at her. "Where is Lord Allingham?"

"He's out walking along the beach, miss. Go see him. But take my shawl." She wrapped a knitted wrap around Pippa's shoulders. "Tell his lordship breakfast will be ready soon."

"Yes," said Pippa, fastening a grateful smile on the other woman before leaving the cottage.

The early morning air felt cool. Pippa pulled the shawl tightly around her as she walked along the beach. She saw Allingham's tall form ahead. He was standing there staring out into the ocean.

As she neared him, he turned and saw her. A smile appeared on his face as he started toward her. "Miss Grey."

"Lord Allingham." When they met Pippa smiled up at him. "It seems I owe you an enormous debt." She extended her hand, which he took in his own. "I do thank you, my lord."

The viscount did not release her hand. "I only thank God that I arrived in time."

"Yes," said Pippa, her blue eyes meeting his gray ones.

"But are you all right?"

Pippa nodded. "Yes, I believe I am. It's strange, but it all seems like a terrible dream. But it did happen for here we are." She smiled. "However did you happen to be there?"

He smiled in return. "I came to see you at Oakwood Lodge. One of Isabelle's servants told me what had happened. He will be richly rewarded."

"You came to see me?" said Pippa. "I didn't expect that. Indeed, we had seen so little of each other, my lord. I owe you so much. If you had not come . . ."

"No, don't think of that. I did come. And you are fine."

"What happened to Seagrave?" asked Pippa, looking out at the sea.

Allingham tightened his grip of her hand. "You mustn't worry about him. The ship sailed. He must have been on it. I daresay he will he afraid to return to England for a good long time."

"I still cannot believe it," said Pippa. "That anyone would think to do such a thing! And Lady Granville. She must have known about it. Indeed, she must have been part of this plot."

"I'm certain of it," said Allingham. "After all, she was his mistress."

"His mistress?" said Pippa.

"Surely you knew? It was common knowledge."

Pippa shook her head. "She said he was a friend of her husband's. Oh, I knew that he seemed to always appear when I was with Lady Granville, but I thought that was only because she wished to throw us together. What a goose I've been."

A thoughtful expression appeared on Pippa's face as she continued. "How right you were about her, Allingham." She frowned. "There is something I must ask you. Lady Granville said she was in love with you and that you and she were . . ."

"Were lovers?"

Pippa looked down in some embarrassment.

"By God, that is a lie. Indeed, the woman detested me because I would have no part of her."

"I knew there was no truth in it," said Pippa, looking up at him. "What a horrid woman."

"Yes, even I did not suspect she would act in such a manner, conspiring with Seagrave in this damnable scheme."

"Yes, indeed. But let us speak no more of her." He reached down and took her other hand. "My dear Pippa, I have been such a fool. If the Duchess of Northampton had not talked sense to me, I would still be in London behaving like an idiot. You see, Pippa, I'm in love with you. I have been so since I first saw you. I did not feel I could tell you because I thought you and everyone else would think me a fortune hunter."

"Oh, my dear Allingham," said Pippa. "How utterly ridiculous of you." She gazed up at him. "I do love you."

This admission appeared to delight his lordship who smiled. "You do?"

"Of course. I thought you could never care for me because of my family, that is, my father being in trade."

"My darling simpleton," said the viscount, smiling down at her, "you were very much mistaken." To reinforce his words, Allingham pulled her close, and, leaning down, kissed her gently at first and then with increasing passion.

Pippa responded to Allingham's kiss with a fervor that matched his own. When their lips parted, Pippa looked up at him adoringly. "My dear Allingham. I love you so much."

"Then you will marry me?"

Pippa smiled in reply and answered him by throwing her arms around his neck and kissing him once again.

30

While Allingham was of the opinion that they should go directly back to town from Huddlesea, Pippa surprised him by announcing that she wished to return to Oakwood Lodge. The viscount, worried that Pippa was still rather shaken from her ordeal, was unsure that this was a good idea. Pippa, however, was adamant so as soon as a carriage could be arranged, she and Allingham set off from the tiny village.

The weather had finally improved. The sky was clear and bright with billowy clouds overhead. Pippa sat beside her future husband in the carriage, her arm enfolded in his. She felt blissfully happy sitting there beside him.

"I was such a simpleton to go with Lady Granville," she said, looking up at him. "If only I had followed your advice."

Allingham smiled. "I daresay you have learned your lesson, my dearest Pippa. From this day forth you will follow your husband's advice to the letter."

"Indeed, I shall, my lord," said Pippa. Then directing a mischievous smile at him, she continued, "when it suits me."

Laughing, he reacted to this pronouncement by kissing her soundly. They continued on and the ride passed so agreeably that it hardly seemed very long at all before the carriage pulled up in front of Oakwood Lodge.

Allingham got out of the vehicle and then assisted Pippa down. When they reached the door, the viscount pounded vigorously upon it. The door was finally opened by the same red-haired servant who had told Allingham of Pippa's abduction.

"My lord! Miss!" The man appeared very pleased to see them both.

"All is well thanks to you," said his lordship, reaching into his pocket to produce a handful of coins. "This is for you . . . I daresay I don't know your name."

"Tom Rigby, my lord," said the young man, taking the money.

"You are very generous, my lord. I am very happy to see that the young lady was not harmed."

"I, too, am grateful to you, Rigby," said Pippa, smiling at the servant. "Now you must take us to Lady Granville."

Rigby appeared quite reluctant to do so. "Truly, miss, it might be best if you would go."

"I shall not go before I retrieve my things and see your mistress," said Pippa, stepping inside. "Is she at home?"

Rigby nodded. "We will find her then," said Allingham.

Pippa and the viscount went to the drawing room. Finding it empty, they proceeded to the library. There they found Isabelle seated at a desk writing.

"Lady Granville!" Pippa's voice caused Isabelle to look up in astonishment.

"Miss Grey! Pippa!"

"You are surprised, are you not?" cried Pippa, striding into the room. "You thought I was in France by now with Seagrave!"

"I assure you I do not know what you are talking about," said Isabelle. "When I returned yesterday I was informed that you had gone. That is what I told Allingham. It appears he has found you. I don't know anything about Seagrave."

"Do not pretend you are innocent," said Allingham. "We know very well that you planned this with Seagrave. Your plot did not succeed."

"Plot?" Isabelle regarded them coolly. "I cannot imagine what you mean, Allingham."

While his lordship could have cheerfully strangled Isabelle at that moment, he only frowned. "Miss Grey will get her things and we will go. I suggest that you do not return to London. If you do, I shall see that you are ruined in society. You will not be received anywhere."

"You do not have the power," said Isabelle.

"Oh, don't I?" said his lordship, directing his most scornful look at her. "You will see what power I have if you return to town. Come, Pippa, I shall help you fetch your clothes."

"I hope we will never meet again, Lady Granville," said Pippa. With these words, she turned and she and Allingham exited the room, leaving Isabelle to stare after them, a worried look on her face.

At the sound of the bell, Hawkins hurried to the door. Opening it wide, he found Pippa standing with Lord Allingham. An observant man, he did not fail to note that his young mistress's arm was tucked inside his lordship's and that the two of them were standing very close together. "Miss Grey! My lord!"

"Good day, Hawkins," said Pippa, a bright smile on her face. She and the viscount entered the house. "Is my mother at home? I daresay my father is at his office."

"Indeed, no, miss. The master and Mrs. Grey are both at home. As is Master Albert. They will be very glad to see you."

At that moment Patches came running into the entry hall. Having heard her mistress's voice, the huge canine was eager to see her. "Patches!" cried Pippa, bending down to hug the dog. Patches's tail wagged furiously. When Pippa finally released her, she hurried to the viscount.

"Good girl, Patches," said Allingham. These words caused the dog to regard his lordship with an adoring gaze. He smiled as he patted her enormous head.

"Where is everyone, Hawkins?"

The butler did not have opportunity to reply to this query for Bertie suddenly appeared. "Pippa! You're back! And Lord Allingham!"

"Good day, Bertie," said the viscount.

"Well, I'm dashed glad you are here," said Pippa's brother. "We have had a lot of excitement about the place. Lizzy had her baby last night."

"What?" exclaimed Pippa.

"Oh, yes, indeed," said Bertie with a grin. "And the tyke chose a dashed inconvenient time to decide to be born. The household was in an uproar. But all is well. Lizzy is well as is the baby."

"Oh, I'm so glad," cried Pippa.

"It was a boy and a fine lusty fellow he is. They are in the small blue bedroom if you would wish to see them."

"Oh, I should like that," said Pippa, looking over at his lordship. "Do let us go to them, Allingham."

Smiling, the viscount took Pippa's hand and the two of them proceeded up the stairs. Bertie exchanged a glance with the butler and then followed his sister.

They met Mr. and Mrs. Grey at the entrance to the bedchamber. "Pippa!" cried her mother, rushing to embrace her. "I did not expect you for some time."

"Oh, Mama," said Pippa. "I should never have gone there. It was quite horrid. I shall tell you all about it later. But Lord Allingham came to my rescue. I came back to town with him."

"With Lord Allingham?" said Mrs. Grey, eyeing them in considerable astonishment.

"Good day, Mrs. Grey," said his lordship. "Mr. Grey."

Pippa's father directed a questioning look at the viscount. "Good day to you, Lord Allingham," said Mr. Grey.

"We have heard the wonderful news about Lizzy. May we see her?"

"Why, yes, my dear," said Mrs. Grey, "but only for a short time. She is very weary. I know that she would wish to see you. Do go in."

"We will only be a moment," said Pippa. Taking Allingham's hand once again, she led him inside.

Lizzy was lying in bed. Sitting beside her in a chair was Robert, the footman. Beside him was a crib.

Robert hurried to his feet. "Lizzy, 'tis Miss Grey and Lord Allingham."

Lizzy looked tired but very happy. "Oh, miss, I'm so glad you're here."

"Lizzy, I have heard your splendid news," said Pippa, coming to her bedside and taking her hand. "I'm so glad." She turned to the crib where the baby was sleeping so peacefully. "Oh, Lizzy, what a darling baby."

"He is a handsome lad," said Robert.

"What is his name?" said Pippa.

"We had not quite decided," said Lizzy. She looked up at Allingham. "Had it been a girl, I was going to call her after you, miss."

"I'm touched, Lizzy," said Pippa.

"But now that he is a boy, Robin and I thought that we should like to call him after his lordship. If you would not mind, my lord."

The viscount smiled. "I should be honored."

"But we did not know what your Christian name might be, my lord," said Lizzy.

"It is John," said Allingham.

"John," said Lizzy. "Then John he will be."

"Well, we must not keep you from your rest, Lizzy," said Pippa. "Come . . . John, let us go."

Allingham smiled at this use of his given name. Taking her arm, he escorted her out. Mr. and Mrs. Grey and Bertie had gone to the drawing room. Pippa and Allingham joined them there.

"He's an adorable baby," said Mrs. Grey. "He's very like Bertie. What an angel he was."

"Oh, Mama," said Bertie, reddening in embarrassment.

Everyone laughed. "Let us all sit down," said Mr. Grey, motioning them to the seats. "We wish to hear all about Pippa's stay with Lady Granville."

Pippa and the viscount exchanged a glance before seating themselves on the sofa. "I shall tell you all about that later," said Pippa. "Indeed, I have something else to tell you."

"Yes?" said Mr. Grey, regarding Allingham and his daughter expectantly.

The viscount took Pippa's hand. "I have asked Pippa to marry me and she has accepted."

"The devil you say!" cried Bertie.

Patches, who had been sitting quietly at Pippa's feet now erupted into barks.

Mrs. Grey placed her hand on her bosom and stared at them in utter bewilderment. "Pippa!"

Pippa burst into laughter. "I'm sorry to surprise you so, Mama. It was rather sudden."

"You're going to marry Lord Allingham!" cried her mother.

Pippa nodded. "I hope you don't mind."

"Mind?" said Mrs. Grey. "My dear girl, I'm beside myself with joy."

There was a good deal of laughter and excited talk. It was a long time before Pippa and Allingham were able to have a minute alone. Ducking into the library, the viscount pulled his prospective bride to him and kissed her.

"My dearest Pippa, you have made me the happiest man in the kingdom. But I have only one request."

"One request, John?"

He smiled. "That you do not wear a crimson wedding dress."

Laughing in reply, Pippa threw her arms around his neck and kissed him once again.